A bitter end . . .

I went back to the kitchen and picked up my cell phone. And an extra-large copper ladle. Just in case.

The light came from a small reading lamp we'd placed on a side table. I flicked on the overhead lights, which were the superefficient kind that came on slowly as they warmed up. I paused, ready to pounce or run away if anything moved.

The perfume was even stronger in here, mixed with something kind of almond-tinged that I'd never smelled before, medicinal on the surface but dank and dark underneath. When I moved closer, I saw very long legs sticking out from a high-backed chair facing the bookstore. Denise was the only person I knew with legs that long.

"Denise?"

Nothing.

I walked over and saw that she was leaning her head against the right side wing and holding on to her stomach as if she'd fallen asleep in pain. A box of my chocolates sat in front of her on the coffee table and I couldn't help but notice they were all Denise's favorites, Amaretto Palle Darks, and that three were missing. "Denise?" I touched her shoulder.

Still nothing. My heart started to pound.

I shook her shoulder this time and her head dropped forward, chocolate froth falling from her mouth.

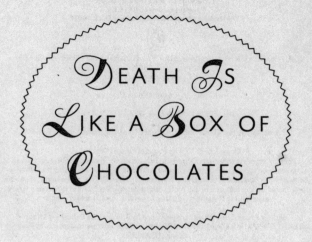

Death Is Like a Box of Chocolates

KATHY AARONS

BERKLEY PRIME CRIME, NEW YORK

THE BERKLEY PUBLISHING GROUP
Published by the Penguin Group
Penguin Group (USA) LLC
375 Hudson Street, New York, New York 10014

USA • Canada • UK • Ireland • Australia • New Zealand • India • South Africa • China

penguin.com

A Penguin Random House Company

DEATH IS LIKE A BOX OF CHOCOLATES

A Berkley Prime Crime Book / published by arrangement with the author

PUBLISHING HISTORY
Berkley Prime Crime mass-market edition / September 2014

PRINTED IN THE UNITED STATES OF AMERICA

10 9 8 7 6 5 4 3 2 1

Cover illustration by Mary Ann Lasher.
Cover design by George Long.
Interior text design by Laura K. Corless.

To my mom, Pat Sultzbach,
for instilling a love of reading and writing in me,
and to my dad and stepmother, Jim and Lee Hegarty,
for their steadfast love and support.

ACKNOWLEDGMENTS

I'd like to thank Jessica Faust, who waved her magic agent wand and made my writing dreams come true, and my wonderful editor, Robin Barletta, who said "Yes" and then proceeded to make this book so much better.

This book wouldn't exist without my incredible critique group, the Denny's Chicks, Kelly Hayes and Barrie Summy.

I would not be writing today if it wasn't for the gentle editing of my first critique group, Betsy, Sandy Levin and the late Elizabeth Skrezyna. Special thanks to the members of RWA-San Diego, for their years of workshops, enthusiasm and unwavering support.

Love and thanks to my best friends, Lynne Bath and Lori Maloney, who always support me and make me laugh! Thanks to my Artist's Way group: Amy Bellefeuille, Sue Britt, Hilda Majewski and Cathie Wier, for their creative inspiration every day. A "Ya-Ya" shout-out to the ladies of Ssusan's Salon, especially our leader (and plot twist guru), Ssusan Forte O'Neill.

Thank you to my book club for their love of the written word, and to my Moms' Night Out group for fourteen years of fun and great company! Thanks to Cindy Aaron for her support of this project.

ACKNOWLEDGMENTS

Special gratitude to Michael Hegarty, a talented artist and wonderful human being.

Thanks to Jeremy, Joclyn, Madhavi, and Matthew Krevat for their ongoing support and enthusiasm for my writing.

Special thanks to those who provided technical assistance:

Patty DiSandro and Kristen Koster for their Maryland knowledge.

Elizabeth Gompf, RN, BSN, CCRN, and Dr. Susan Levy for their medical expertise.

Jim Hegarty for website and technical assistance and his delightful humor, some of which found its way into this book.

Isabella Knack, owner of Dallmann Fine Chocolates, the best chocolates in the world.

Manny and Sandra Krevat for their photography expertise.

Brian Lowenthal, of Brian Lowenthal Photography, for his photography expertise.

Donna Lowenthal for her project-planning expertise.

Annette Palmer, co-owner of Earth Song Books and Gifts.

St. Michael's Chief of Police Anthony T. Smith for his help with police procedure.

Judy Twigg, for help with the Russian language.

Nick, for technical assistance.

Any mistakes are my own.

And most important, mountains of gratitude and love to my brilliant, beautiful and creative daughters, Shaina and Devyn Krevat, and the love of my life, my husband, Lee Krevat. I'm definitely the lucky one!

1

"I don't do cupcakes," I told Erica, who obviously hadn't been listening to me in the two years we'd been best friends.

"I know, I know." She waved her hand around as if dissipating my nonsense and reached over the counter to grab a Fleur de Sel Caramel from one of the trays I was about to parade around in front of the store. While I'd enjoyed a huge rush in the week leading up to Mother's Day, maybe I could entice a few more customers into buying chocolate for their moms before the special day was over.

"Have you ever seen me bake even one cupcake?" I asked her. Erica and I shared a store on Main Street in the town of West Riverdale, Maryland. She and her sister, Colleen, managed the family-owned bookstore in one half of our space while I ran my chocolate shop in the other half. I should have known she wanted something when she crossed over to my side during such a busy Sunday afternoon.

"I get it," Erica said, nibbling the caramel. "You're a chocolate snob, I mean *chocolatier,* and you don't bake. Oh wait. What did that DC reporter call you? 'Michelle Serrano, Chocolate Artisan.'"

"Glad we got that straight," I said. "I suggest Summer Berry Milks. Grown-ups love them, yet they have that element of whimsy that even rug rats appreciate." I dumped newly ground coffee into the machine and turned it on. The fragrance of the coffee mixing with the ever-present chocolate scent made my mouth water even though I'd been experiencing it all day. Owning Chocolates and Chapters never got old.

Erica rolled her eyes. "Someday your distaste for anyone under the age of eighteen is going to bite you on the butt." She pushed her librarian glasses up on her nose and gave me The Look. The one that somehow combined puppylike begging with steely-eyed command, and inevitably made everyone do her bidding. Maybe that's why she'd won the Future Leader award so long ago at our high school graduation. "Cupcakes decorated with softball icing are even more whimsical than chocolates."

I crossed my arms.

"It's for the good of the Boys and Girls Club!" she said.

"I'm not baking cupcakes," I said.

Erica seemed astounded at my stubbornness. "Really? Remember that beautiful field where you showed Sammy Duncan that girls are better hitters than boys?" She threw her hand out as if pointing to it. "You know, the field that needs to be reseeded every single year?"

She was pulling out the big guns. Before she could remind me that playing sports at the Boys and Girls Club was the main reason for my annual success in the West Riverdale Softball Tournament, I gave in. "Fine. But I'm not making them. I'll ask Kona."

"Awesome!" Erica was enough of a master manipulator not to show anything except gratitude, but I was sure she'd gloat later.

" 'Awesome'? Is that an official Fulbright scholar expression?" I said to pay her back.

Erica had come home two years before, just as I was opening my shop. My whole life, I'd heard of Erica Russell, girl genius, who went to Stanford on a full scholarship, got a master's in writing, and then became a Fulbright scholar. I still wasn't clear what that was.

I totally expected her to stick her nose up at me, the community college dropout, but we'd become best friends, and now business partners and housemates.

She made a note on her spreadsheet. "My next victim, I mean prospective donor, is Denise."

"Do not harass the committee," I said. "We're lucky they haven't run for the hills with the way this thing has exploded."

Back in February, when Erica had suggested a Great Fudge Cook-off to celebrate the one-year anniversary of our renovation, I'd jumped at it. Our normally mild Maryland winter had been brutal, and after what seemed like the thirtieth nasty ice storm of the season, anything that made me think of spring was welcome.

I'd imagined a group of fifty or so neighbors gathered in our store, tasting all the entries, and buying *real* chocolate from me to wipe the taste of fudge from their palates. Erica would send out photos and a press release to the local papers, and the resulting articles would remind everyone that they needed more candy and books in their lives.

But taking the suggestion from the mayor to schedule our contest during West Riverdale's Memorial Day weekend celebrations had been a big mistake. Somehow our little fudge contest had mushroomed into the opening event of the first ever West Riverdale Arts Festival in the park. And our book signing the Sunday night before Memorial Day now included a silent auction fundraiser for the Boys and Girls Club. We counted our blessings that the actual parade on Monday hadn't been added to our plate. The parade committee was an exclusive group of old-timers who wouldn't think of letting anyone under the age of sixty interfere.

I delivered steaming cups of coffee and a small plate of assorted chocolates to the table of grandmothers showing off photos of grandchildren on their phones, and discreetly left the bill on the table.

Erica continued when I returned to the counter. "I'm donating the I So Don't Do Mysteries series and some Michael Connelly first editions for the silent auction." Erica also ran a thriving used and rare book business out of the storage room in the back. "And you'll be really happy about the big surprise I have for today's meeting."

"What is it?"

"If I told you, it wouldn't be a surprise." She gave me a mysterious smile and headed back to her side.

I picked up my tray and opened the front door as Erica's sister, Colleen, struggled through with one blond-haired two-year-old boy on her hip and the other twin rebelliously dragging behind her.

"Erica," Colleen called after her sister with a rush of relief. "Can I leave the twins in the play section while I take Prudence to her dance recital?"

The two sisters worked well together, but lately Colleen had been busier than usual with kid duty, and Erica had taken up the slack. I sometimes wondered if Colleen would even be working in the bookstore if she hadn't become pregnant with her first child during her freshman year of college. She didn't have Erica's love of books, though she enjoyed the business side of the store. But back when she was eighteen and pregnant, working in her parents' bookstore was a good option while her husband, Mark, finished up his business degree.

While Colleen made an effort to appear somewhat professional when she worked in the store, today she had on a stretched-out orange cardigan that had seen better days, and her hair was falling out of her wilted scrunchie.

"Sure, but where's Mark?" Erica seemed confused as the twins ran toward the wall of brightly colored bricks that separated the small play area—what I called the first circle of hell—from the rest of the store.

Colleen scowled. "He says he has the flu. He just got back from yet another trip and he's too sick to do anything. And the nanny is out of town." She sounded mad at both of them.

If I had twins like Gabe and Graham, I'd have the flu pretty often too, I thought, as they expertly opened the child-proof gate and double-teamed a boy twice their size, wrenching a firefighter's hat away from him.

"I guess," Erica said. She ran to comfort the howling victim as Colleen gave a helpless flutter of her hands and escaped. Through the front window, I could see her daughter, Prudence, wearing a lime-colored leotard and fancy headpiece and waiting in their ancient Volvo station wagon. That girl had the patience of a saint, or even better, the patience of an older sibling of twin boys.

I took a step to help Erica, but instantly the wailing stopped and the twins were soon sitting in Erica's lap waving around the latest cardboard books. I watched for a moment and, sure enough, one of them whacked Erica in the jaw with a book before settling down.

The Pampered Pet Store across the street was holding their monthly adoption event and when I went outside with the sample-sized caramels, the local animal lovers emptied my tray in a few minutes. Kona called these petite caramels my "gateway drug." Once people ate this perfect bite of caramel wrapped in creamy chocolate, with the tiniest sprinkle of sea salt on top, they always came back for more.

After serving the burst of customers who'd followed me back into the store, I did a spot-check of our dining area, which was perfect. It had been Erica's idea to remove the wall between the two stores to increase our usable space. We'd all survived the renovation, but Colleen and I had grumbled a lot more than Erica, maybe because she could visualize what it would look like today.

A homey, welcoming room with books lining the walls, tempting customers to pick one up and read in an overstuffed chair, and the smell of chocolate enticing them to choose from my selection of sinful sweets. Chocolates and Chapters had become an unofficial community center for our little town. Our smattering of mismatched couches and coffee tables now hosted various committee meetings, knitting circles, book clubs and, my least favorite, birthday parties.

I straightened a painting from a local artist who was new to our rotation wall. Erica had told me ahead of time that he interpreted famous paintings using the opposite on the color wheel, so the paintings appeared familiar and strange at the same time.

My assistant and right hand, Kona, walked in from the back kitchen with a tray of assorted tortes, her specialty. I was lucky to have her. Although I still didn't understand why, sometimes customers wanted pastries instead of chocolates. And while I could whip up a thousand truffles in a few hours, I couldn't bake to save my life.

"I just volunteered you for a couple dozen softball-decorated cupcakes for the book launch," I told her.

"No problem," she said, her almond eyes laughing at me. She knew how I felt about cupcakes. "By the way, I opened the latest shipment from the supply company." She paused. "Did you order a lot of the new jeweled cocoa butter? They charged us extra to rush it."

"Oh, yeah." I tried to appear nonchalant. "That's okay."

"What are you going to use it for?" she asked.

I avoided answering her. "Just thinking about a few new ideas."

"Want me to cover the front so you can try it out?" Kona knew how much I loved to play with anything new, but I had plans for that gold cocoa butter that no one could know about. "I put it in the kitchen."

"Um," I said. "I'm going to try it out at home, but I want to look at it for a minute."

She started placing the tortes in the one measly glass display case I allowed for pastries. "No problem. I'll handle the counter."

"Thanks." I headed to the back kitchen to see if my new gold cocoa butter would do the trick. We had a small kitchen out front where customers watched us dip fruit in chocolate or put finishing touches on the truffles, but we did most of our work in the larger back kitchen.

I didn't want our customers to see the messy part of my magic, like when we mixed ganache by hand to achieve the ideal consistency; or smelled the caramel to ensure the ultimate balance of smoky, almost-burnt sugar; or scraped off the untidy "feet" of my truffles so they were perfect.

I picked up the bottle of gold cocoa butter. It looked a little like gold paint now, but once I melted it down and airbrushed it across my chocolates, it would look amazing.

We scheduled the weekly cook-off meeting for right after our regular early Sunday closing. I was setting up when Erica lugged her ever-increasing Great Fudge Cook-off file box to the largest table in the store. Located in the back corner, it was where high school students crammed for tests, or pretended to, retirees met to plan their day trips, and an endless supply of PTA moms coordinated school events.

Even the always-put-together Erica looked a little drained from balancing the twin terrors and customers.

Without comment, I handed her a Balsamic Dream, her favorite truffle—dark chocolate ganache with a rush of balsamic vinegar. "How did the recital go?"

"Colleen said it was delightful," Erica said, enjoying her treat.

"Did Mark make it?"

"Yes," she said. "He had a miraculous recovery just in time to see it."

Denise Coburn walked through the open back door of the shop, tiny magenta shorts emphasizing her incredibly long legs that always made me feel like a hippo. A pygmy hippo. And she was the giraffe undulating across the African plains.

Undulating? I was hanging out with brainy Erica too much. "Hi, Denise," I said as she slouched into a chair across from Erica.

"Hi," she said as part of a long-winded sigh. She'd pulled her thick auburn hair into a huge bun that magically stayed in place on the top of her head with only one clip, and once again I cursed my own wispy strawberry blond hair that behaved only as long as it took me to leave the salon.

Denise's photography studio, next door to our shop, catered to families and smaller businesses in our town. She'd recently landed the contract for the local high school's senior portraits, but everyone knew she dreamed of selling her artsy work to galleries in Washington, where people had more money to spend on that stuff. Personally, I thought her creative photos were out of focus and just a bit odd. Who wanted a blurry photo of a shiny penny in a gutter hanging on their wall?

"Tough day in the photography trenches?" Erica pulled out more files and a color-coded spreadsheet.

"I guess," she said, picking up a truffle. "Another delay by that gallery owner I told you about." She bit off one tiny corner and put the rest down. How do people do that? Of course, she couldn't resist my Amaretto Palle Darks, the only candy I'd ever seen her eat in one bite, but I'd sold out of those earlier in the day.

"The gallery in DC?" I popped a whole Mayan Warrior in my mouth and let the chocolate melt on my tongue, the spicy cayenne tickling the back of my throat just like it was supposed to. "What happened?" I asked as I sat down.

Denise shrugged. "He left a message telling me he had a family emergency and had to reschedule our meeting tomorrow. And I'd cancelled all my sessions for the trip up there."

"I'm sorry," Erica said. "Why not email them? Once he sees your photographs, he's going to just adore your work."

The eternal optimist.

Denise sighed dramatically again. "He said he has to meet me first. He believes my montage of work is an inward expression of my outward view of the world."

What a load of BS. I was about to warn her that this dude might just have a casting couch when the final two members of our committee walked in.

Steve and Jolene Roxbury arrived in their usual geek chic: Steve, the high school science teacher, wore an ancient T-shirt of the periodic table, and Jolene, the math and drama teacher, wore a shirt that read, "Half playwright. Half ninja."

"Love the shirt," I told her.

"Thanks!" Jolene said. She gave a little "Hi-yah!" along with a karate chop. "Gift from Steve-o when I got my black belt in tae kwon do." She and her husband both put a few Bacon-and-Smoked-Salt Truffles on their plates and sat down while I retrieved the coffee.

Jolene tasted her chocolate and moaned. "Oh, Michelle. I *love* this new concoction."

"The only perk of being on this committee," Steve agreed. He pulled out his smartphone. "Look!" he said, showing us photos of Jolene in her karate *gi*, the white fabric vibrant against her dark skin. Her proud grin as she held her black belt made us all smile.

Ever-efficient Erica started to hand out notes just as some teens loitering upstairs noticed the Roxburys. "Yo, Mr. and Mrs. R!" they yelled, hanging dangerously over the wooden balcony. Erica obviously hadn't kicked out her comic-book-section regulars.

When Erica had found out that teens drove all the way to Frederick to buy their comic books, she'd started stocking them. And since she loved comic books as much as any of them, she'd started a book club named the Super Hero Geek Team.

"Yo," Steve yelled back. "Stay away from my issue of *Justice League International*."

One of the inmates of West Riverdale High waved a comic book back and forth and taunted in a singsong voice, "Got it right he-re."

"You bent it!" Steve barked. "I don't want that one."

One of them noticed the time on the huge clock at the front of the store and yelled, "Dinner!" as if an emergency was happening, and then they all ran out the front door.

I let out a little "Whew," and Erica smirked at me.

"Just go over your notes." I got up to lock the front door. "And give us our marching orders."

"Yay!" she said. "I love obedient minions." She passed out copies of the action items list. "We have a lot to do in less than two weeks, but everything seems to be coming together."

She opened up a tri-fold display board and pointed to a color-coded, minutely detailed project plan that looked like it could win the high school science fair. "First the book launch and Boys and Girls Club fundraiser. Michelle has graciously volunteered cupcakes for that evening," Erica said without a hint of sarcasm. "I made a list of some of the Boys and Girls Club volunteers for other food items."

"I can make my world-famous guacamole," Jolene offered.

Erica said, "That'd be great, but we need to focus our resources on our top priorities. The most pressing issues right now are more donations of silent auction items and getting the word out to ensure high attendance at both of our events."

I whispered to Jolene, "You're a 'resource.' "

Erica ignored me, moving on to talking about chair rentals and hosting duties that night. She looked right at me. "Let's talk about the fudge contest," she said, smiling with excitement. "I have an announcement." She paused for dramatic effect. "Hillary Punkin is judging!"

"What?" I gasped.

"Hillary Punkin, star chef of the TV show *Life by Chocolate*, has agreed to be a celebrity judge for the West Riverdale Great Fudge Cook-off!"

Oh. My. God.

Hillary Punkin at the West Riverdale Great Fudge Cook-off?

Hillary was the Grand Chef Network's premiere pastry chef who traveled the country "discovering" local chocolatiers. Panic welled up in my chest. Hillary either loved or hated the chocolate and her opinion never made sense. In one show, she adored lavender essence in her truffle. In the next, it made her gag on-screen. She seemed to have no clue of her own irrationality. But she had a huge audience and could make or break a business.

"Is she doing a show here?" My lips felt numb.

"No," Erica said, oblivious to my dismay. She barely watched TV, let alone cooking shows, and had no idea what she might have set in motion. Just like the beginning of any horror movie.

"She heard about your chocolates winning that blind taste test," Erica said, sounding proud. "She'll be in DC for a show, so she has time only for the contest. But ever since she hinted at it on Twitter, our website hits have gone through the roof!"

"Cool!" Steve said. "That should help attendance for the whole weekend."

I pasted a weak smile on my face, and Erica's eyebrows drew together as she figured out I was less than ecstatic. She continued with her action items, which included everything from confirming the balloon arch orders for the festival to getting more volunteers to help set up chairs for the book signing.

Yes, my chocolates had won the prestigious *Washington Food Scene* magazine's third annual blind chocolate taste test, and now Erica insisted on putting "award-winning" in front of any mention of my products. But Hillary might just be contrary enough to want to prove them wrong.

Even if Hillary wasn't doing a show here, she always had a "Yay or Nay" segment at the end, and it was particularly brutal—just a shop's name and location with a happy yellow "Yay" or nasty red "Nay" after it and no explanation as to why.

Maybe it wasn't too late to call off Hillary, I thought as panic fluttered in my chest. I'd built a nice business making chocolates for a ritzy hotel in Georgetown, bed-and-breakfasts in Virginia, and gift basket companies that sent my chocolates to clients all over the East Coast. Much of my sales were due to word of mouth, and if Hillary Punkin slammed my chocolates, I would be in trouble.

On the other hand, if she loved my chocolates and gave them a "Yay," who knows how much my business would grow? It was a dilemma.

A knock sounded on the front door and I tensed when Gwen Ficks waved at us through the window. I stood up to let her in, the usually cheerful bells on the front door now sounding like a warning. Gwen had been West Riverdale's mayor for five years, winning her second term easily even though the town's economy had taken a hit along with the rest of the country's. She'd lost a ton of money when the bad economy had completely stopped sales of the new housing development she'd invested in, and she was working hard to try to turn the town's fortunes around.

She was the one who'd convinced us to hold our Great Fudge Cook-off during Memorial Day weekend. And somehow the whole thing had snowballed into the beginning of her "Save Main Street" effort, the result of four struggling shops closing up in the last year.

West Riverdale was probably the one town in the country not named after an actual river. Founded by the River family centuries ago, we were close enough to Antietam National Battlefield to pick up a few lost tourists rambling their way back east. The only building of any historical value we had was the Rivers Mill, which had been used to store artillery during the Civil War and was now an artists' cooperative. The River family had settled what was then known as River-dale back in colonial times, but other than some Main Street buildings that were considered "historical" just because they were old, people in search of history had a heck of a lot of other towns to visit instead of ours.

West Riverdale's Memorial Day parade used to be a big event for our town, as people came from all over to experience historic small-town life. Like a vacation in the 1950s before they returned to their high-tech lives. But parade attendance had declined in recent years and Gwen was determined to do something about it.

As a Main Street shop owner, I supported anything to increase business, but every time the mayor stopped by our meeting, she added to our workload. Her single-minded attention to the town's revenues during this weekend made me think that maybe our town was worse off than she maintained in her speeches. Especially since she'd railroaded a sales tax through town council that went into effect for Memorial Day weekend only. It was an accounting nightmare for any business in town.

"I wanted to stop by and personally give you the good news," Gwen said as she buzzed over to stand beside Erica's chair, her light citrusy perfume drifting by in her wake. She wore her trademark suit jacket and Ralph Lauren scarf over jeans, straddling those "I'm-so-professional" and "I'm-just-like-you-folk" impressions that politicians have to do.

"The Best Western by the highway is at full capacity for the entire Memorial Day weekend!" Gwen said.

"Whoo boy!" Steve pumped his fist in the air.

Gwen went on. "I knew that new slogan would do the trick. We may have to change our name to Mayberry."

Gwen "Fixit" Ficks believed any problem could be solved by throwing a slogan at it. Erica had used *West Riverdale: The Mayberry of Maryland*, in her latest press release, touting our extremely low crime rate in a time when the rest of the country seemed to be going crazy.

"This is due to all the hard work of you gals—and guy." Gwen winked at Steve. "I'm so excited I can barely contain myself! This weekend is going to be a huge success."

While Gwen was saying all the right things, she seemed a little subdued. For her, anyway.

"That's great news," Erica said, with a little wrinkle in her forehead that indicated her mind was already thinking of all the ways the news affected our plans.

"And I thought of one more little push we could do," Gwen said.

Inside I groaned. That was why she wasn't as cheerleader-bouncy as usual. She knew piling more work onto our committee wasn't cool.

"I'm sure you've heard about the new solar project at West Riverdale High," she said. "Principal Palladine has been so forward thinking! It will save the school district a ton of money. How do you feel about: 'West Riverdale: The Greenest Town in Maryland'?" She smiled as if delighted with herself. "See? It's a play on words. Our lovely rolling green hills and the fact that we're helping the planet by using our sunshine for clean energy. It'll appeal to a totally new demographic. The company we're working with is called Get Me Some Solar. Isn't that cute?"

Gwen turned her smile wattage up.

Here it comes, I thought. Even gung-ho Erica seemed worried about what Gwen would ask us to do next.

"And it would be great if you could give them an excellent spot at the Arts Festival. You know what they say. 'Location, location, location!' "

West Riverdale's first Arts Festival was fast turning into the West Riverdale Flea Market. We'd started off with the best intentions, limiting the booths to only quality artists, but when we'd run out of those, anyone with a check and something to sell could buy a spot. Now one side of the park would have artists selling their work, plus a few booths I'd have to categorize as "crafts," but on the other side, customers could buy tools from Duncan Hardware, organic cheese from Farmer Henry, and hubcaps of questionable lineage from Frank's Finds.

I would be one of the food vendors, along with Zelini's Italian Kitchen, Bubba's Southern BBQ, and Sweeney's Weenies.

Of course, the highlight of the day would be the Great Fudge Cook-off right after the grand opening. Kona and I had narrowed down forty entries to the top ten in a blind taste test. These entries would be judged by Mayor Gwen and the chefs of two highly respected restaurants in Frederick, the closest "big" city to West Riverdale. And now Hillary.

"I'll let you busy bees get back to work. I'm heading up to DC tonight for some meetings tomorrow. Working hard to get funding for more solar projects." Gwen headed for the door. Just as she opened it, she turned around and the whole group inhaled. "I told Get Me Some Solar that we'd include their flyers in the bags we're handing out. Thank you all so much. This is going to be amazing!"

After she was sure Gwen was truly gone, Jolene said, "If that woman didn't work so hard for this town, I could hate her." She sighed. "It could've been worse. At least the math team and drama club volunteered to help stuff the bags."

"Well, *we* volunteered them," Steve corrected. "And they'll be around all weekend for anything we need."

"Michelle," Erica said. "Can you contact the other hotels? If they're selling out as well, we have to be prepared."

I nodded, now worrying if I had enough supplies for an

influx of tourists. That wasn't a bad problem to have but I'd still have to deal with it.

"Steve," Erica said. "That solar project is an amazing opportunity for you and your students to study green energy."

"You bet," Steve said. "We already have a weather station, so we're going to compare how much energy the solar panels produce given different weather patterns."

"Speaking of weather." Erica was in total efficiency mode. "What's the latest prediction?"

"We're keeping an eye on a tropical depression that could head this way, but so far, so good." He went on to talk about the latest results of the campus weather station.

Tropical depression? In Maryland, that often led to rainstorms that felt like monsoons. Which would suck. Tourists were notoriously finicky. A prediction of rain could cause a lot of them to change their plans.

Worrying about how to plan for an unknown number of potential customers made me miss Erica's usual rah-rah speech at the end of the meeting, but given the expressions of happy resolve on the faces of Denise and the Roxburys, it must have been effective.

After the good-byes, I escaped to my storage room to evaluate my supplies. Being surrounded by my chocolate and sugar and spices made me feel like the possibilities were endless.

I counted my bags of Felchlin dark chocolate, smelling their cocoa richness through the sturdy wrapping. Would I use them to make simple but amazing caramels, filled bonbons or elaborate truffles decorated with airbrushed designs? I could decide. I was queen of my little chocolate world.

Wizard of the magic I'd create in my kitchen. Some people thought of chocolate as an expression of passion and love, but to me chocolate was food and family and friends. It meant kindness and giving.

I estimated that I could create several thousand truffles from my stock. Should I make that many? We also had to keep up on my hotel and website orders.

Emergency supplies were an option. Already prepared little chocolate cups, ready to be filled. Or gourmet cream centers waiting to be dipped. It was cheating, but they were delicious in their own way, just not a true Michelle chocolate.

I was working out different scenarios when Denise surprised me by opening the door and sliding in, closing it behind her to keep out the humidity even though it wasn't yet horrible for May. I held up my finger and then completed a calculation.

She waited, a troubled frown on her face.

"What's up?" I asked.

She shrugged. "Not ready to go home."

"I'm sorry," I said. Denise's mother had moved in with her while she had fought cancer. She had died two months ago. Denise must not want to face her empty apartment.

Too bad Colleen wasn't here. She was Denise's best friend and confidant. And I was terrible at making people feel better.

"Good news about our weekend, right?" I tried.

She nodded, still preoccupied. "I found some black-and-white photos my grandpa took of Memorial Day parades from a long time ago. Do you think if I made copies people would buy them?"

"Sure," I said. "Sounds like you're having the same

problem I am—figuring out how to plan for attendance we can't predict."

"I know, right?" She ran a finger along a metal shelf filled with silicone chocolate molds.

"Are you okay?"

"Yeah," she said, but then bit her lip.

"Are you worried about something?" With Denise, it was better to be direct. While we'd developed a courteous working friendship, she held a lot of herself back. "Thinking about the break-in?"

Two weeks earlier, I'd arrived at the building to find the security alarm turned off and Denise's studio torn apart. I'd called 911 and then Denise. Stacks of photographs had been tossed around, as if someone had been searching for something. Denise had looked scared to death and then mad as hell. She'd told the police that nothing was missing and that she had no idea who could've broken in, but no one believed her.

Erica and I hadn't figured out how much to push. We all used the same security code for the back hallway Chocolates and Chapters shared with Denise's studio, but we had different security codes for our store and our storage rooms.

The security company said someone who knew the code for the back hallway and the specific code for Denise's area entered the building at three in the morning and searched her studio. We had our suspicions. Denise had a tendency to fall for bad-boy looks, and her last boyfriend had the bad-boy habits to go along with them, including a history of burglary and car theft.

"No," she said. "That was nothing."

"That's so weird that nothing was stolen with all of your expensive equipment," I said.

She turned to face me. "Do you ever just want to get the hell out of West Riverdale?"

"What?" I asked, confused by her abrupt change of subject.

"Out of this town. 'The Mayberry of Maryland,'" she added with mocking finger quotes.

"Not really." I'd spent my whole life here and never felt the urge to try a more exciting way of life. "It's my home. You should talk to Erica. She's the travel fanatic."

"I don't know how she lives with herself, having to come back here." She scowled. "If I got out of West Riverdale, you'd never see me again."

This was getting weird. "Did something happen?" I asked her. "You sound really upset."

She took a deep breath and tried to sound more upbeat. "I just don't think I can take another winter like we had. If I had the money, I'd move somewhere that was warm all the time."

"You could take some awesome photos of a tropical beach." I played along. "Maybe after you sell a bunch of photos in that gallery, you can afford a great vacation."

"Yeah," she said. "Like *The Eighties at Echo Beach*."

"What's that?"

"A photography book," she said. "Erica knows it." She opened the door. "Thanks."

I felt an "I guess" after it, maybe because I knew I hadn't helped. I should've called her back, but I had to finish my projections. I love making chocolates, but planning to make chocolates was not nearly as much fun.

3

"I'm heading out," I told Erica in my most innocent voice. No way did I want to let anyone in West Riverdale know about my top-secret project: making X-rated chocolates for my cousin's bachelorette party. Luckily she lived in Washington, DC—far enough away that no one would find out. Not only would these chocolates alienate the pious folks in town, but I'd never live it down with my friends. And I really didn't want to be called on to make adult chocolates for every bachelorette party in the area.

I'd hid the risqué molds at home, but for some reason, I felt like a criminal sneaking out my airbrush equipment and going back in for the chocolate and flavorings. These bridesmaids didn't want to buy the crappy bachelorette chocolate they could order online; they wanted high quality chocolate in a variety of flavors, and they wanted them sprayed with gold. I didn't even want to know why. What would the rest of that high-end bachelorette party entail? Channing Tatum dancing out of a cake?

I shut down my side of the shop and waved to Erica, who was doing the final walk-through. The weather was cool enough that I could take care of this special order at home, package it up and send it off before anyone knew what I was doing.

I heard a meow as I pulled the back door shut.

A brown-striped cat sat at the edge of the wooden porch behind the store. It stared at me with green eyes that caught the glow of the setting sun.

"Hi, kitty." I took a step toward it. "Are you lost?" It didn't have a collar.

I looked around as if I could figure out where it had come from. Had it escaped from the Pampered Pet adoption event? "Hold on," I said to the cat, and then felt foolish for telling it what to do as if it could understand me. The haughty expression on its face didn't help.

I put the last of my supplies in the car and called the pet store to see if they were missing a cat. No one answered, so I left a message. Most of the Main Street shops closed early on Sundays until after Memorial Day. The cat waited on the porch. Should I take it home?

I'd never had a pet growing up. My mom always said my brother Leo and I were enough to clean up after. Looking at her fur, a name popped into my head. Maybe I could keep it and name it Coco.

I leaned down to pet it and it pushed back against my hand and purred. But when I tried to pick it up, it squirmed away like a slippery ferret.

Ah, trust issues. A cat after my own heart. "It's okay." I

sat down on the edge of the porch and it started rubbing against my leg, purring once again. "Coco," I tried.

It seemed to like that and I melted a little. What a cutie. After petting it for a few minutes, I tried again to pick it up, still not sure what I would do with the poor thing.

"Meow!" This time it swatted at me as it twisted away, as if to teach me a lesson.

"Okay, okay," I said. "You don't want to be picked up." I couldn't take it inside. The health department would have a fit. "Wait here."

I opened the door and the warning alarm came on, letting me know that Erica had locked up and activated the security system using the front door panel.

Coco hopped off the porch, and by the time I went in to disarm the security system and came back out, the cat had disappeared.

It probably belonged to someone in the neighborhood, but just in case it actually was a starving stray too scarred by life on the streets to trust me to return, I went into the kitchen and scrounged around for cat-friendly food—a bit of cream poured into a small plastic tub and a chunk of cooked bacon. I reset the alarm and left the treats against the wall on the porch.

The lights were on in the Duncan Hardware store across Main Street and I made a quick decision to buy a new air hose for spray-painting with my gold cocoa butter. Almost all of the parking spots were open so I whipped my minivan into one of them and headed for the aisle I knew well. I still hadn't figured out how to keep my air hoses from clogging regularly.

Principal Peter Palladine was stocking shelves halfway down, wearing the red apron of Duncan Hardware employees.

"Moonlighting?" I asked him. If I'd known he was here, I could've brought him some Black Forest Milks. My accountant always complained that I gave away too much of my product, but trying one or two made almost everyone buy more. Except for the cheapskates. And most of the time I liked sharing my yummy chocolate with them too.

He chuckled. "Just helping out Sammy on his new expanded Sunday evening hours," he said, sounding a little like a commercial. "Plus, with a kid in med school, I could use all the extra pennies I can get."

I couldn't help but smile back. Principal Palladine was so proud of his daughter that he fit "kid in med school" into any conversation he could. "How's she doing?"

"Great!" he said. "Actually loves working with a cadaver." He shook his head in wonder.

"Following in her mom's footsteps," I said. His wife was a physician's assistant who almost single-handedly ran a free clinic in one of the poorest areas of DC.

"Anything I can help you with?" he asked.

"Just need a new hose for my airbrush machine." I picked one off the metal hook.

"Let me know if you need some help," he said. "Those buggers can be tricky to change."

"Thanks," I said. I'd been maintaining my equipment for years and wouldn't have a problem.

"You working on something special?" he asked. "Anything else you need?"

"Nope," I said quickly. "Just maintenance."

He gave me a funny look, that principal intuition always working.

"Thanks Mr. Palladine."

"Peter, dear," he insisted.

Old habits die hard.

Beatrice Duncan was manning the checkout. She and her husband, Harold, had helped her son, Sammy, buy the hardware store when his boss retired but they hadn't realized that business acumen didn't necessarily go along with tool enthusiasm. Sammy was great when you needed to find the right ratchet wrench but wasn't so good at balancing a bank statement.

"You guys are open late," I said. "For a Sunday."

"Don't I know it." She pushed her fist into her lower back. Her short gray hair was gelled to stand straight up. "Sammy thought it could bring in some new business."

"Good idea," I said, even though I was the only customer in the store.

She shrugged. "It was worth a try. We just need to hang on until Memorial Day weekend," she added with a hopeful expression that made my stomach sink. "We put coupons in your Fudge Cook-off program and ordered a ton of flags and souvenirs for the tourists."

"Cool!" I handed over the cash for the hose, resisting the urge to tell her to keep the change.

Worry ate at me all the way home. This wasn't the first time I'd learned that a lot of people were counting on that weekend. What if we didn't pull it off?

It was dusk by the time I pulled up in front of our house, but our next-door neighbor, Henna Bradbury, must have been looking out for me. Henna had gone through some kind of metamorphosis when her husband died a few years before, letting out her inner hippie and changing her name from

Carol. She now spent her days painting elaborate neon designs on fabric and wire to create butterflies of all sizes that she sold online.

Henna stomped over, her long gray hair pulled into a side ponytail and her rainbow skirt swirling angrily around her legs. She stopped beside my car as I got out. "Michelle. You have to do something about that Denise."

"I do?" I asked.

She went on like I hadn't spoken. "She is the biggest thorn in my side. How dare she tell the Arts Guild that I'm not a real artist!" She was so mad, she was actually shaking.

"Denise wouldn't say that." Although I had a recent memory of someone mentioning that Denise liked being president of the guild a bit too much.

"Oh no?" Henna drew herself up to her total height of five feet, two inches. "Are you telling me my best friend Sadie is a liar?"

"Oh, of course not," I rushed to say. "Is there any chance she misunderstood?"

"No." Henna was adamant. "At last week's guild meeting, I petitioned them yet again for membership. I told them all about my beautiful art flying all over the world. Then they asked me to leave for their discussion, and today I got a note saying that they regret to inform me that I wasn't accepted." She scrunched up her hand like she had most likely scrunched up the note. "I needed a unanimous vote, and Sadie said Denise was the only one who voted no."

"I'm so sorry," I said. "But do you really need that stupid guild?" I picked up my air compressor and chocolate from the minivan, trying to indicate that I needed to get moving.

Henna's look of shock made me realize how important this was to her. "It's more than just an honor to belong to that guild," she said more quietly. "They do group advertising that results in sales. Real sales. And there's a beautiful sense of community."

"I'm sorry," I repeated. "But your work is finding its audience without them. Maybe even more of an audience than some of the members have."

"You can say that again," she said. "Including your friend Denise."

"What?"

"Sadie told me. Denise was close to losing that store but somehow came up with the money." She frowned. "If she's having that much trouble making ends meet, she might not be around too much longer. Once she's out of the way, I'll get in for sure." She turned around and trudged back to her home.

"I really am sorry," I called after her. What did Denise have to gain by blocking poor Henna's membership?

I hadn't taken two steps when a motorcycle zoomed up to stop beside me, forcing me to jump back. As I was about to swear at the idiot driver, I recognized him through the tinted visor.

Leo.

What was my brother doing riding a motorcycle?

He turned off the bike, put the kickstand down and stabilized himself before swinging his prosthetic leg over to stand up.

He grinned. "Hey, Berry," he said. His nickname was due to my insistence as a child that strawberry blond hair was far prettier than his dark brown. "You like it?"

I was speechless. "How the . . . ?" My voice trailed off but he knew what I meant.

"Harold Duncan modified it for me." He pointed to some equipment that meant nothing to me. "He put the gear shift and kickstand on the other side. Cool, huh?"

To say I was conflicted was an understatement. Leo had returned from the war in Afghanistan vastly changed from the happy-go-lucky adventurer he'd been his whole life. And it went much deeper than the loss of his leg.

I'd hoped that getting out of Walter Reed and coming home to West Riverdale would help him, but depression had followed him. And when he wasn't depressed, he was angry. At the war. At the world. At himself.

I'd forced him to see West Riverdale's only psychiatrist, who was helping Leo fight his demons. He was getting better, but every once in a while he slid back toward the precipice, which was even more terrifying to me than his early episodes of depression.

We'd lost our parents in a car accident when Leo was eighteen and I was fourteen. His whole life he'd dreamed of being a Marine, and he put that dream on hold to take care of me. Once I turned eighteen and got a "real" job, I'd convinced him that it was his turn, and he enlisted.

And look what that got him.

I tried to talk, but all I did was sputter a little, and he laughed. A real laugh.

"Wow." My voice was faint.

Luckily, Erica drove up in her electric car and saved me. "Cool ride, Leo," she said as she got out. "A Harley?"

"Sure is," Leo said, and they launched into a discussion

in another language of pingel shifts, hand clutches and other mechanical nonsense.

I remembered what I was holding. "I'll be right back." I took my supplies into the kitchen and came back out.

Leo gave me a wave as he drove off.

"He knows you're not too happy with him and that bike," Erica said with sympathy as she plugged her car in. Since we didn't have a garage, she'd had a special charging unit installed in our miniscule driveway.

"How could it possibly be safe for him?" I asked.

"Maybe that's what he likes," she said.

We walked up the wooden stairs. "Has he responded to that veteran's organization?" Erica asked.

I shook my head. While the whole town wanted to rally around their hometown war hero, Leo had blocked himself off from anything having to do with the military. Lately, he'd been ducking the parade committee who wanted to include him in their Memorial Day celebration.

"It takes time," Erica said and headed upstairs. We split a rambling hundred-year-old house with a wraparound porch that needed a paint job. The house had been converted into two apartments decades before. Erica had her own space on the second floor, with a kitchenette that was fine for the basics. We shared the living room on the ground floor whenever we had company, and she used my much larger kitchen when she needed to cook a big meal. Erica didn't need much sleep and sometimes took on research projects in her free time for a number of professors. I found it reassuring to hear her pacing long into the night, as she thought about some problem she was working on.

Erica's floor was like a different country from mine. She had about a thousand books scattered all over and interesting art and other novelties from around the world. Her bed belonged in some kind of ad for a five-star hotel on an exotic beach somewhere, with wispy curtains hung between the four posts. It certainly gave away her secret that she was a total romantic.

My apartment was the very definition of functional. I had only a few things on the walls that I had bought at garage sales, a photo of my family when I was twelve, and a huge beanbag chair in the shape of a Hershey's Kiss in the corner of my dining room. I certainly didn't have a bed that was appropriate for a romantic comedy set in the Caribbean.

I looked forward to playing with my gold cocoa butter, like a toddler with a new toy, and tried to think of another use for it. Something other than for bachelorette party favors. I bet my exclusive hotel in Georgetown would love me to add a gold sheen to the logo chocolates they placed on customers' pillows every night.

I closed the door to my apartment, which was the "do not disturb" code Erica and I used, and started tempering the chocolate. Even X-rated chocolate was going to be smooth and delicious if I was making it.

First, I chipped away at a brick of my gorgeous dark Felchlin chocolate and tossed the pieces into a double boiler. I took my time bringing it to the perfect temperature and then removed the pot from the flame, adding more chunks to reduce the heat.

I squeezed gold cocoa butter into the small cup of the electric warmer and turned back to the chocolate.

With my expensive, but indispensable, infrared thermometer,

I monitored the chocolate until it dropped to exactly eighty-four degrees, and then I put it back into the double boiler for reheating.

Like any chocolatier worth anything, I instinctively knew when the chocolate was ready—when it hit that rich brown color and that perfect combination of flat and shiny on the surface. But I liked the confirmation of my thermometer.

Leaving the chocolate to heat up, I poured a tiny amount of the now-melted gold cocoa butter into the paint holder and turned on the airbrush machine.

I sprayed a light dusting across the first mold, held it up to the light to make sure it was even, and set it aside to cool down, the risqué outlines still jarring me. I repeated the process with the first three molds, stopping in between to stir the chocolate.

The hints of vanilla, citrus and smoke in the chocolate were released by the heat. As soon as it was ready, I poured the perfect amount in each mold, tapped gently to remove the air bubbles and set them in my refrigerator.

As I was spraying the next mold, my door opened and I jumped, fumbling the airbrush and shooting a spray of gold across my chin before grabbing it out of the air with both hands.

A blast from my past had walked right into my kitchen.

4

Benjamin "Bean" Russell. The middle brother of Colleen and Erica. One of my brother Leo's best friends. And unbeknownst to anyone, including Erica, the star of my high school fantasies. Okay, college as well. And maybe ever since I found out he was visiting. I'd had quite the dry spell lately, romance-wise.

"Hi," Bean said, looking not much like the hero I remembered. While his hair always had the disheveled look of a distracted writer, it now seemed to be plastered to his head in a weird "I just woke up" smush on one side. He hadn't shaved in days, and his clothes looked as slept in as his hair.

"Hi, Bean." I turned off the noisy compressor and tried to hide the molds behind me. "Erica's apartment is upstairs." My words sounded too loud in the sudden quiet.

"I know. I followed my nose."

I raised my eyebrows.

"I knocked but you didn't hear me." He cleared his throat. "And I go by Ben now."

Of course. He wasn't the sixteen-year-old wunderkind of West Riverdale anymore, shattering every academic record—that is, until Erica came along and shattered them all again. Now he was a world-renowned journalist and author coming home for a book launch at his sisters' store before jetting off to another exotic part of the world to do an exposé that rocked whatever political or business enterprise he investigated. I'd read an advanced copy of his first book and it was intimidatingly brilliant.

"Sure." I paused. "Bean." Couldn't let him get a big head.

His eyebrows came together but he let it go. I wiped at the gold on my chin, even though I was probably making it worse. He hadn't been home in the two years since I'd become friends with Erica. "I'm Michelle."

"I know," he said. "You look different."

"I'm not thirteen anymore." It came out more defensively than I intended, probably because I flashed back to a fumbled kiss in a dark closet, the unfortunate result of a spin-the-bottle loss. Or win. I was sure he didn't remember it at all.

"You weren't gold-plated back then either." He stared at my face. "What is that?"

"Gold cocoa butter." For some reason, that sounded ridiculous. "I spray-paint it across a mold then pour chocolate on top of it so it looks like it has a gold sheen. So it's like edible gold, but it's not, you know, real gold."

A flash of amusement crossed his face, his brown eyes crinkling in the corners. "Okay." His gaze went to my mouth. "Edible you say."

Whoo boy. I could feel a flush building and looked away. "Yep. So, Erica?"

Again the amused look. "Yes."

"Is upstairs." I pointed a little too emphatically out the door but he leaned back against the counter as if he was planning to stay for a while. I couldn't figure out how to usher him out without revealing the molds behind me.

"If I didn't know any better, I'd think you were hiding something."

"Nope," I said too loudly. "Not hiding anything."

"I don't know. I'm a reporter. I have finely tuned instincts for that kind of thing."

"I'm just making chocolate. I'm sure Erica is waiting for you."

"No, she's not," he said. "I'm surprising her. Nice try." He feinted right and I leaned my body to make sure he couldn't see the molds. Then he moved left for the refrigerator. "Got any food in there?"

"No!" I said, but it was too late.

He pulled open the door and stared at my project: gold-painted, anatomically correct chocolates. Tiny, but definitely male.

"Whoa. What are you going to do with those? You can't," he grimaced, "*eat* them."

I felt a giggle rise in my chest. "Okay, you found me out. I'm making chocolates for my cousin's bachelorette party. I've never made X-rated chocolate before. Don't tell Erica."

"Oh, I won't. I'm sure she'd make you move out or something," he said. "Got any others that aren't shaped like that? Erica said your chocolates are like tasting heaven. And I haven't eaten anything except protein bars in about twenty-four hours."

"Yuck." I got up and opened the wine cooler I used to store chocolates at home. Two of them held thousands of chocolates in my kitchen at the shop. I pulled out a batch of red-white-and-blue painted chocolates molded into flags.

"Try these." I arranged a few on a small plate for him.

He tossed one in his mouth. "Mmm," he said. "Amazing." He swallowed and ate another, closing his eyes for a moment.

It was hard not to stare.

He smiled, revealing the same David Letterman gap in his teeth that Erica had. Both had ganged up on their parents, refusing to get braces to correct it. "That's the best thing I've tasted in my life. You actually made those?"

"Yep," I said. "Glad you like them."

"Got any more?"

"Take the whole batch," I said. "And make sure Erica feeds you some real food so you don't go into a diabetic coma. And don't tell her!"

This time he headed for the door. "I don't know. You might have to buy my silence with more chocolate."

My alarm went off in the middle of a dream in which my poor young staff was forced to toss chocolates out to crowds pushing through the doors while I was in the back, frantically wrapping chocolates from a fast-moving conveyor belt like Lucille Ball in that candy factory episode.

I usually couldn't wait for Mondays, which I dedicated to inventing and tasting new concoctions. But after tossing and turning much of the night, it took two cups of my strong French press coffee to get me into my running clothes and out the door. If I wanted to eat my own products and not gain weight, running had become nonnegotiable.

The foggy morning didn't help my energy level. I couldn't even see past the next hill, and we had plenty of those. Our house was on the outskirts of town, right where the sidewalks ended, so I ran on the side of the road. Houses appeared like ghosts in the gloom before falling behind as I trudged along. It took until the second mile for me to get up to my normal pace, but as I finished my four-mile route, I felt great. Invincible. I was going to kick some major cooking butt.

I showered and put on brown chef's clothes that stayed cool and, more important, didn't show chocolate stains. I packed my secret chocolates in a large box with special chilled dividers to keep them cool and layers to cushion them, then loaded my contraband and drove to the store in my minivan emblazoned with my logo.

The houses and businesses got closer together as I drove toward town. Most of Main Street was narrow, packed with buildings from colonial times. Some of them looked like they held each other up, their bricks and mortar seeming to bind together. The town kept up the old cobblestone sidewalks to complete the historic appearance.

Our section of Main Street was somewhat more modern. In 1954, a fire had raged, destroying the whole block. Tales were still told of the bravery of the firefighters who made a stand in tiny White Stone Alley, preventing the fire from decimating the whole street and possibly the entire town.

Back then, people around here weren't as into preserving historic buildings, so the owner of a few of the stores bought out the rest of the block and built what he called the West Riverdale Town Center Mall, a long wooden building that fit the needs of shops more than colonial families.

As I passed Chocolates and Chapters in the middle of Main Street, I was surprised to see a dim light in the dining area. I definitely didn't leave that light on.

I parked in the gravel lot behind the store and saw the brown cat sitting by the empty food containers as if waiting for me to refill them. Maybe it hadn't been such a good idea to feed it. I couldn't have a cat in a chocolate shop. One stray hair in a truffle and the health department would slap me with some kind of fine. And what would the customers think?

"Good morning," I said to the cat. What did I know? "Coco?" I tried. Green eyes followed me as I walked over and unlocked the door.

Shoot. It was already unlocked. Everyone knew that Monday mornings were my time. Colleen usually opened up the bookstore while Mark dropped their kids off at daycare, but this was early even for her.

Kona always opened up the front without interrupting my creative flow, and my other assistant Kayla didn't come in until noon. I got the whole back kitchen to myself to decide what chocolate magic or madness we'd create that week.

"Wait here," I told the cat, and went inside. As I walked down the short hall toward my kitchen, I smelled Denise's perfume, Samsara. She loved it, even after Erica told her the Hindu definition of samsara: the eternal cycle of birth, suffering, death and rebirth. Sounded creepy to me, but it did smell glamorous on her.

One reason I was good at creating new recipes and knowing if they'd appeal to customers was my highly developed sense of smell, which translated to my ability to distinguish between subtle flavors. Unfortunately for my parents, it had made me a picky eater as a child, but it turned out to be a great asset for a chocolatier.

I couldn't believe that Denise was at the store so early. She'd perfected the art of walking in five minutes before her first client and looking like she was ready and waiting to take their photos. And hadn't she told us she'd cancelled all of her appointments for the day?

I dropped off my purse in the kitchen before making my way to the front of the store to investigate the light. The scent of perfume grew even stronger.

Denise's break-in popped into my head, filling me with an ominous feeling. Should I call the police? Instead, I went back to the kitchen and picked up my cell phone. And an extra-large, extra-heavy copper ladle. Just in case.

The light came from a small reading lamp we'd placed on a side table. I flicked on the overhead lights, which were the superefficient kind that came on slowly as they warmed up. I paused, ready to pounce, or run away, if anything moved.

The perfume was even stronger in here, mixed with something almond-tinged that I'd never smelled before, medicinal on the surface but dank and dark underneath. When I moved closer, I saw very long legs sticking out from a high-backed chair with oversized wings facing the bookstore. Denise was the only person I knew with legs that long.

"Denise?"

Nothing.

I walked over and saw that she was leaning her head against the right side wing and holding on to her stomach as if she'd fallen asleep in pain. A box of my chocolates sat in front of her on the coffee table and I couldn't help but notice they were all Denise's favorites, Amaretto Palle Darks, and that three were missing. "Denise?" I touched her shoulder.

Still nothing. My heart started to pound.

I shook her shoulder this time and her head dropped forward, chocolate froth falling from her mouth.

5

screamed, just as Erica came through the front door, the bells attached to the handle ringing. "Erica! Something's wrong with Denise!"

Erica whipped out her phone, dialed 911 and handed it to me. She checked Denise's neck for a pulse and then pulled her awkwardly to the floor.

"West Riverdale Police. State your emergency."

I recognized Maxine's voice, the older lady originally from New York who bought a small box of Black Forest Milks every Friday night before her shift. "I have an emergency." My voice shook. "At Chocolates and Chapters."

"Michelle?"

"Yes. I think Denise is seriously sick." I watched Erica start CPR and added, "Maybe dead. Please send an ambulance now!"

Her training must have kicked in because she said, "I'll have someone there right away. Please hold on."

"Michelle." Erica used her no-nonsense tone while she pushed on Denise's chest and counted. "Go into the kitchen and find something to suction out her airway."

I ran to the kitchen and set the phone down, ignoring Maxine's voice when she came back on. I wrenched open a drawer, grabbed a turkey baster and ran back to Erica as sirens sounded in the distance. Luckily, the town's police and fire stations were only a few blocks away.

"Perfect," she said, continuing to count and push down hard on Denise's chest. When she paused to check her pulse, she told me, "Now clean out her mouth, but don't touch anything. That foam may indicate poison."

Poison? My eyes went to the box of my chocolates on the table. Oh. My. God.

A police car screeched to a halt in front of the store and Lieutenant Bobby Simkin ran in. He dropped down beside Erica and took over CPR. "Anything?" he asked her.

She shook her head and moved me aside, grabbing the turkey baster from my hand. "Sorry."

"You did great," he said, completely focused on Denise.

We backed up out of the way when the fire truck arrived and two firefighters rushed in.

I grabbed Erica's hand which started to shake violently.

The firefighters stepped in and Bobby joined us. "What happened?" he asked, breathing hard from his effort.

"I don't know," I said, feeling powerless. "She was here when I came in."

"Let's go." Bobby directed us outside as the ambulance

arrived, the EMTs rushing in with a gurney. "I'm sorry but I have to separate you two while I secure the scene."

We both stared at him, stunned that he was treating us like suspects.

Erica and Bobby had dated in high school, and he was one of my brother's best friends. Sometimes it was still hard for me to believe he was a policeman.

"It's procedure." He glanced sideways at Erica, but she followed directions and moved to stand on one end of the building and I waited by the other. It seemed ridiculous.

Bobby retrieved crime-scene tape from his car and secured it between trees in front of the store. Another policeman, who didn't look old enough to drink let alone wear a police uniform, arrived. He pulled out his own yellow tape and went around to the back of the building.

Chocolates and Chapters was a crime scene.

I tried to catch my breath, leaning back against the wall. Erica looked like how I felt—shocked and bewildered.

Tires screeched and we stood up as Colleen jumped out of her car.

"Colleen!" Bobby grabbed her arm as she attempted to come inside the tape. "Erica is fine."

She watched as the emergency workers placed Denise on the gurney while continuing CPR.

"You can't go in," Bobby said.

Erica's face crumbled when she saw her sister and she rushed over to grab her, the tape between them. I pushed back tears as a flood of emotion hit me. The grim faces of the emergency personnel told me the truth. That Denise was dead. Maybe poisoned. Maybe by my chocolates.

Chief of Police Eric Noonan drove up in his own car, his

pace sedate compared to Colleen, and my heart began to race. He got out, seeming unhurried even though he must have rushed to get dressed and looked like he'd just run a hand through his shock of gray hair.

Usually I appreciated his deliberate air. Somehow it inspired confidence in his ability to do the right thing, although people sometimes grew exasperated when it seemed to take so long. Even choosing which chocolates to order took him forever and he always chose Simply Delish Milks. Every single time.

The chief watched Denise being loaded into the ambulance and took in the entire scene before directing the other officer to widen the secure area. He strolled over to us. "Report," he ordered Bobby as he opened a well-worn notepad.

Bobby had transferred home over a year before from the Baltimore Police Department, where he'd been a decorated officer, but Chief Noonan still acted like he didn't quite trust him. It might have something to do with Bobby riding his motorcycle through our high school graduation, narrowly avoiding hitting a lot of parents. But it was an awesome memory for our class.

Bobby spoke in a respectful tone. "The nine-one-one dispatcher informed us of an emergency at this address at zero seven hundred. I arrived to find Ms. Russell performing CPR on Ms. Coburn, with Ms. Serrano helping. I proceeded to take over. The patient was nonresponsive. The firefighters arrived and continued CPR."

Noonan nodded to Bobby. He turned to me. "Who found Ms. Coburn?"

"Me," I admitted in almost a whisper.

"What happened?"

"I don't know." I shook my head. "I came in early as always, but the door was unlocked. I was distracted by this cat outside and Denise was here ahead of me. I thought it was weird when I smelled . . ."

"Smelled what?" he asked.

"I smelled her perfume."

He stared at me.

"It's Samsara," I said, my tone defensive.

"Michelle's borderline hyperosmic," Erica said. "In a good way. Smells aren't stronger for her than the average person. She can just smell variations of scents others can't."

"I'm not hyperosmic," I told the chief. "It's part of being a chef." He wrote down a note. I could just imagine it. *Thinks she smells well.*

The chief asked, "So you walked straight back to Denise?"

"Yes." I remembered my side trip. "Well, no. I remembered the break-in Denise had last month, so I went back to the kitchen and picked up a big ladle. And my cell phone."

"A ladle?" Chief Noonan sounded like he couldn't believe what he was hearing. Lieutenant Bobby tried to hide a smile.

"It was heavy!" I said.

"So you thought you might be going into danger, so you picked up a *ladle*, and continued on." He shook his head like a disapproving parent. "What happened next?"

"I, uh, found her." My throat closed up and I began again with effort. "She wasn't moving."

Erica took a step toward me and I shook my head. I told him everything, my voice shaking. The chocolate on the table. The froth in her mouth. Erica's CPR attempt.

He stayed quiet, taking copious notes and nodding at times. "Anyone you know have a beef with Denise?"

"Enough to want to . . ." I couldn't finish the thought as the ambulance drove away ominously slowly, the siren on low.

"I know it's difficult to consider, but just think about it. Was anyone mad at Denise?"

Erica jumped in. "Larry the Loser. I mean Stapleton. Her ex-boyfriend. He has criminal tendencies."

Holy cow. Could Larry have done this? "And we think he's the one who broke in here," I added.

"You didn't tell us that at the time," Noonan said, exasperation coming through.

"Um, no," I admitted. "It was Denise's studio. We let her handle it. And she said nothing was stolen."

Erica dropped Colleen's hand and started pacing, which always got her brain juices flowing. "But we changed the security codes after the break-in. How could he possibly get in here and poison the chocolates?"

Colleen and I gasped together. She thought the same thing. That my chocolates were poisoned. And they killed Denise.

"Okay, that's enough speculation." The chief's voice was firm. "Colleen. If you must stay, please wait across the street and don't discuss anything you heard."

Colleen nodded, blinking as if she couldn't believe what was happening and moved to the other side of Main Street, where other neighbors were starting to gather.

"Sorry," Erica said, but continued pacing. "Maybe he had an accomplice. Perhaps you should investigate—"

"Whoa, whoa, whoa," interrupted Noonan. "This is a job for the police."

The sound of a motorcycle came from down the street, becoming an ear-pounding roar, and Leo drove right up to us, the front tire stopping past the tape as if dismissing its power. I felt my chin quiver before tears broke through. I went up to him as he swung his leg off the bike. He wrapped his arms around me, both of us a little unsteady.

"Is she done?" Leo asked the chief.

Noonan paused and then said, "For now."

"Then we're leaving," Leo said, pulling the crime-scene tape over my head and tugging me away.

Noonan scowled but didn't stop us. "I'll need a formal statement down at the station. This morning."

Leo nodded curtly and ushered me out.

The crowd across the street was growing. Bad news spread fast.

Back at home, Leo used my cow-painted kettle to make me tea with too much sugar and milk. "I'm not going into shock," I told him. He'd left his motorcycle behind the shop and driven me home in my minivan.

"Sorry," he said mildly. "That's the way you used to like it."

"When I was eight," I said, but drank it anyway. The sun came through the kitchen window, highlighting my hands on the cup.

"You want to talk about it?" he asked.

I told him what I'd seen, leaving out the whole ladle thing.

"So you think someone poisoned Denise?" he asked.

I shuddered. "I don't know. I can't see how poison could get in my chocolates otherwise." My voice trailed off. It sounded dramatic but those chocolates were a part of me. I couldn't bear to think of them causing a tragedy. In the world of good and evil, my chocolates had always been solidly on the good side.

Kona called, and I told her everything I knew and that I'd let her know when she should come to work again. I also called Kayla. She'd been sound asleep and hadn't heard anything about Denise.

Erica drove up. She came into my kitchen, stress causing her face to pinch. "Hey, Leo." She helped herself to tea. "Crazy morning, right?"

"For West Riverdale," Leo said.

Of course. He'd seen a lot worse than one dead person. He'd lost fellow soldiers, his own friends and colleagues, in situations a heck of a lot worse than this.

"So is she . . . ?" I asked Erica.

She nodded.

I took in a deep breath, letting go of the little ray of hope I'd had. "What happens now?"

"They called in the Baltimore crime-scene techs and the state police." She sent a sympathetic glance my way. "And the health department may investigate as well."

The health department. Words that strike fear into anyone who sells food.

The health inspector I'd worked with when the store opened was a doll who loved my truffles, but I was sure she had procedures to follow that would keep my store closed for too long. And what if they found poison in more of my chocolates? My business would be done. My reputation shattered.

I fought off worrying about my livelihood. At least I was

alive. Poor Denise was dead. She'd never get to move to the beach like she dreamed of.

"I made my statement to the homicide detective," Erica said. "He'll probably be out here pretty soon."

"So we just wait?"

"We can't work today," Erica said. "Do you have any special projects you want to work on?"

Oh no! My bridal shower chocolates were still in my minivan. Not only did I have to get them in the mail, I had to do it before anyone saw them. "I have to mail a package." I tried to be casual. Wait. How could I know they were safe? I had to get rid of them. Shoot! I couldn't throw them away. What if someone, or something, found them? I'd have to treat them like toxic waste or something.

Then a larger realization hit me. "Oh my God," I said. "My four-packs of truffles and chocolate bars are all over this town. The drugstore. The diner. I have to let them know . . ." I felt heartsick, finally realizing what had probably already happened in my shop. "Oh my God. They're destroying all of those caramels I made." I thought about the hundreds I'd stored in the wine coolers—the Lemon Meringue Milks that I'd just perfected. The Chai Darks. I imagined strange men throwing my creations into plastic bags like cheap Halloween candy corn and felt sick to my stomach.

How much money had I just lost? How much time?

I dropped my head into my hands. "My hotel." My biggest client, the upscale hotel in Georgetown. If I lost them, I'd be so screwed.

What was wrong with me? Denise was dead. That was so much more important than my dead business.

"I'll call them," Erica said. "While you run your errand."

"No," I said. "I need to do it."

"You should stick close to home," Leo said. "So far, it isn't clear who the intended target was."

"What?" I hadn't even thought of that.

"Erica?" Bean's voice came from the doorway. He stood there in navy plaid pajama pants and a Baltimore Orioles T-shirt, looking all just-woken-up sexy. He pushed his hand through his hair, his shirt lifting to show a tantalizing flash of muscular stomach. "Good morning," he said sleepily.

"Um, not really," I said.

"Bean!" Leo walked by me to give him a man-type hug, with lots of backslapping.

Bean must have picked up on the tension in the room because he stopped the reunion to ask, "What's going on?"

6

It took forever for Erica to tell the whole story to Bean and for me to kick everyone out so I could make my phone calls. Erica went upstairs to consult with our lawyer on the press release and letters to our customers, while I brought up my sales information on my laptop and took a deep breath.

It was early enough that some of the businesses who bought my chocolates weren't open yet, and I was able to leave a few messages before talking to live people. But my voice choked up when I called the diner and got Iris, my favorite waitress in the world, who gave advice worthy of a mafia don in a southern accent while serving scrambled eggs and grits. "What y'all gotta do," she told me, "is find the critter who dun 'nat and twist his little neck like a chicken."

I laughed through a few tears. "Thanks, Iris. I'll consider that."

"And you tell that Chief Noonan that if he don't get off his fat butt and find that a-hole, I'm gonna do summin' awful to his griddle cakes."

I asked her to return any chocolate to me and to let any customers know of the recall as well.

The hardest call was to the food buyer at my biggest customer, the hotel. She had visited my shop right after it opened and took a chance on me. It didn't matter that in two years I'd never let her down; her responsibility was to her customers. She listened to me for a minute and then asked, "Any other victims?"

"No," I said.

I heard the hard, fast tapping of her pen through the phone. "Here's what we're going to do. I'll stop distributing your chocolates in our hotel until we learn the findings of the health department. We will make a determination at that time whether to return our recent purchase."

I breathed out a sigh of short-lived relief.

She continued. "If the findings are that your shop is responsible, then I will have to find another supplier." Her voice softened. "I'm sorry."

We said our good-byes and I hung up, a heavy weight on my chest, and moved on to my next issue.

No way could I send this box to my cousin. I'd have to make another batch of adult chocolates completely from scratch, with new ingredients, and get it to the maid of honor by Saturday. Although once I explained the delay, they may want to just buy Internet crap.

I'd already decided to ask Tonya Ashton for help. She'd been the only other female on my adult coed softball team, playing on and off when she could. She'd gone through the

Frederick community college's nursing program, studying long hours in my shop while I poured her tons of free coffee refills and gave her discounts on the Green Apple Indulgences she loved. She'd mentioned on Facebook that she was now working at the West Riverdale Urgent Care, which was on the other side of town. I hoped she'd be willing to help me.

I texted Tonya before I left to make sure she was working. She'd texted back a bunch of questions about Denise, but I told her I'd tell her when I saw her. I felt crazy nervous driving through West Riverdale, although I avoided Main Street. I even thought someone was following me for a while, until the car pulled into the gas station right by the clinic.

My cell phone buzzed in my pocket as I pulled around the back of the building. It was a text from Jolene Roxbury. *How ya holding up honey?* Her southern charm came through the phone. *I'll call you in between classes.*

No need, I texted back.

Want Steve and me to stop by after school?

No, that's okay, I typed at the same time my phone buzzed again.

No I can't. Drama club . . . We should hold an emergency meeting asap.

No kidding, I started to text and then decided to answer a simple *Yes*. Then I added, *There was a stray cat hanging around the store. Can you let me know if it's still around?*

Tonya came running out as soon as I let her know I was there and gave me a dramatic overly squeezy hug. "Oh you poor thing!"

Tonya had become famous on YouTube a few years before for documenting her travels with her boyfriend to follow the Baltimore Orioles to every home and away game, and using her college fund to pay for it all. Everyone loved her energetic enthusiasm for the team, and her expressive face when they won or lost was priceless. Her parents had not been pleased.

I guess she'd sowed all her wild oats because now she was happily married to her travel partner and had a kid just a few months old. Their birth announcements had featured a squirrely looking baby, of course wearing an Orioles onesie.

"It was terrible," I admitted. "They think Denise was . . ." I unexpectedly teared up and had to clear my throat. "Poisoned."

She gasped and clasped my arm. "No!"

"I imagine that they'll throw all of my chocolate in the shop away." My heart clenched. "But I made these at home for my cousin and now I can't send them to her." I told her about my special project. "They're probably fine. But I can't risk it. I can't throw them away—what if a kid found them, or a little squirrel or something got into them and they were poisoned?"

"Of *course*," she said, her mouth in a perfect little frown like a computer icon for "sad." "That would be terrible."

"But I just can't let anyone know I made them. It'd be too embarrassing." I ripped up the tape on the box and pulled up the divider, showing her the chocolates. They looked so harmless.

She met my eyes and started laughing. "They're so tiny!"

"I know," I said. "They're ridiculous. I wanted to see if you could just throw them in your medical waste bin or something. I don't know how it works—"

Suddenly, Reese Everhard, owner and executive editor of the *West Riverdale Examiner*, jumped from behind the corner of the building. "Stop her!" she said. "She's trying to get rid of evidence!"

I looked around as if she meant someone else and Tonya skipped back as if I'd handed her a live rattlesnake. Reese ran over and grabbed the box, tearing at it with her wickedly long nails. I instinctively tried to take it back from her and then the tape broke free and the box of gold, X-rated chocolates glowed in the morning sunlight, before spewing across the ground.

For the second time in my life, and the second time in one day, I was surrounded by police officers. While Tonya and a group of urgent care workers looked on laughing their fool heads off, Reese, who had called Chief Noonan when she saw me meeting with Tonya, insisted on having the police "collect the evidence."

With all of the cell phone videos in action, the whole world was going to have plenty of "evidence" that I made bachelorette party chocolates. Maybe that'd be my new career.

After Tonya had stopped laughing, she'd yelled at Reese to leave me alone and find a real scandal to investigate. Someone besides me was finally losing patience with the loony reporter.

Everyone knew that Reese had bought the newspaper as some kind of compensation. It was horrible: she and her husband had been trying to have children for two years and found out she couldn't. So the jerk left her. He'd been forced to leave town after the reason for the split became known and everyone had frozen him out. Reese had earned a heck of a lot of sympathy. But that was fast depleting with her outrageous attempts to increase circulation.

Even in crazy Reese world, how could she be proud of her journalistic accomplishments? Like the time she broke the heartbreaking story of the missing Girl Scout cookies. Or the article about the horribly underserved population of vegetarians at high school football games. And, the one that got her the most Google hits for its hysterically overblown prose, the rampant corruption of the town council who received, wait for it, free coffee at their meetings, supplied by the West Riverdale Diner.

She needed to get a life.

Reese and I went way back. We'd been on opposing recreational basketball and softball teams throughout elementary and middle school, trading championships along the way. Most people assumed we were sports buddies, but Reese was monstrously competitive even when we were on the same high school team. When she was injured halfway through the basketball season, I replaced her as point guard and took the team to the state championships while she sat on the bench in her cast. She'd never forgiven me.

I checked her out from head to toe—she'd already been suspected of using recording devices without letting her targets know. Was that pen in her pocket actually a tiny camera?

"Those chocolates could be poisoned too," Reese said, sticking her neck out and looking remarkably like a stork. "It was murder, wasn't it?" She leaned her chest toward Lieutenant Bobby. Definitely a camera.

"No comment," Bobby said, making notes.

I t wasn't even noon by the time I made it home and I was already exhausted. Bean leaned back on the porch with Leo, trying hard not to laugh. He had his shirt off, enjoying the sunny day. Erica had told me that his back was scarred from a horrific police interrogation in Afghanistan early in his career, but all I could see were abs too well-defined for someone who spent so much time in front of a computer.

"Worst day of your life?" Leo asked, which had become our way of checking in with each other ever since our parents died—the true worst day of our lives.

"Not yet"—I trudged up the wooden steps—"but the day's still young."

"I know what'll cheer you up," Leo said. "You're trending on Twitter."

"I am not," I insisted, appalled.

"I'm kidding," he said, "but look at this." He showed me his phone with a video of me grabbing at the box and the X-rated chocolates flying in slow motion. You could almost hear me yelling, "Nooo!" It was definitely taped by the camera in Reese's pocket and she'd uploaded it to her blog as soon as she could. The bitch.

"I'm never going outside again," I said, and stomped to my room.

I burrowed under my mother's quilt and went to sleep until I could face the world again, something I did when life got to be too much. This was the perfect time for such an escape.

By the time I woke up, the sun was no longer coming through the front of the house. I looked at my phone and listened to a bunch of messages checking in to find out if I was okay. A few of them worriedly asked if Memorial Day weekend was still on. Beatrice Duncan's message held the strongest plea. "I'm so sad about Denise, but please tell me we're still carrying out all of the plans for Memorial Day. We're all counting on you and Erica."

I walked out to my kitchen, and Bean looked up from his laptop. "Feeling better?" he said. He'd obviously showered and changed.

"Are you babysitting me?" I asked, suddenly worried what I looked like. I went to the sink and rubbed a wet paper towel over my face. I knew my hair was unfixable.

"Not really," he said. "Leo just wanted someone here when you woke up."

"As fine as I can be now that my friend is dead and my X-rated chocolate business is public knowledge."

"So, good, right?" he said, smiling.

I smiled back, not feeling so bad with him so cheery.

Then Lieutenant Bobby drove up in his cruiser with a state police car right behind him.

I groaned.

"I'll get rid of them," Bean said, his smile disappearing into a scowl. I remembered that Bobby had broken Erica's heart at the end of high school. Some big-brother animosity was probably at work.

"No." I went to the door. "Time to get it over with."

Lieutenant Bobby apologized for bothering me and paused at the doorway when he saw Bean. He nodded stiffly. "Benjamin."

"He goes by Bean," I said, which made Bean shake his head in exasperation.

Bobby gestured to the man standing behind him in a state police uniform. "This is Detective Roger Lockett. He's in charge of Denise's investigation."

"Really?" I asked him. "Like lock-it-up-and-throw-away-the-key?"

"No," Bobby said with a straight face. "Like L-O-C-K-E-T-T."

Detective Lockett smirked. "I've heard 'em all before," he warned in a strong western Pennsylvania accent.

"Challenge accepted," I said. "Are you from Pittsburgh?"

The detective was actually pretty cute in a rough-and-tumble kind of way. Short dark hair and a crooked nose that had definitely been broken. Where Bobby was tall and lean, Lockett was wide and muscular, his shoulders pushing at the seams of his uniform. "Haaja know?" He emphasized the accent.

"Yinz guys want coffee?" I said, using one of the Pittsburgh-ese words I'd heard a lot. "I used to work with someone from the North Side. Her accent was so contagious."

"South Side for me." Lockett's smile didn't reach his eyes as he and Bobby joined Bean at the table.

"I used to go to Kennywood with my folks," I said. "Best roller coasters *ev-er*."

"You bet." This time Lockett's eyes smiled too.

"You staying?" I asked Bean.

He leaned back in his chair as an answer. "Does she need a lawyer?" he asked them both with a challenging glare as they sat at the table.

I rolled my eyes as I poured coffee for everyone and set up the creamer and sugar.

"Only she knows that," Bobby hedged.

I joined them. "I didn't do anything wrong."

Lockett pulled a battered notepad out. "Let's go through what happened this morning."

I launched yet again into the saga. Bean kept a watchful eye on all of us, making me feel safe and somewhat less stressed about it all. Or maybe I was just getting used to being questioned by the police.

Lockett took careful notes, asking questions when I stalled and not pushing when I got emotional. Even Bean seemed to have a grudging respect for him at the end of our conversation.

Bean went into reporter mode as I wrapped up my story. "What do you know so far? Were the chocolates poisoned?"

Instead of answering, Lockett asked, "Did you store rat poison in your kitchen?"

"No!" I said. "I don't use rat poison and I certainly wouldn't have it anywhere close to my products."

Lockett made a note and my impatience got the best of me. "Were they poisoned or not?"

Bobby waited for Lockett to nod and answered, "We won't be sure until the tests are complete, but it looks like a needle was inserted into the bottom of the chocolates and then smoothed over. And the symptoms point to poison."

My hand shook as I put my mug down, sloshing coffee on the table. Bean touched my arm.

"I'm sorry," I said, shocked that our suspicions were most likely true. I shook my head. "I just can't believe it."

I looked up to see Lockett watching me closely. Of course. I was a prime suspect to him. "I'll have to ask you not to make any of your products until the testing is complete." He looked around the kitchen. "Including at your home."

I sucked in a breath.

"Was Denise the target?" Bean asked.

Lockett was reluctant to answer. "Yes. The chocolates were left on the counter in her studio."

"But why did she come into our store?" I asked. "She wasn't even planning to work today."

"Why not?" Lockett asked, his voice intense.

I explained the cancelled visit to the gallery owner in DC. "I can't remember the name, but Erica probably does." Then I flashed back to our weird conversation the night before. "I don't know if this is relevant, but she talked to me last night about wanting to get out of town. To live somewhere that was always warm."

"Did she say where?" Lockett asked.

I shook my head. "No, just that if she had the money, she'd move."

He nodded. "Can you think of anyone who had something against Denise?"

"Her ex-boyfriend, Larry Stapleton, was not a good guy." I told him about the break-in and our suspicions. And then my gaze went to Henna's house.

"What?" Lockett asked.

I would have been fine telling Bobby, but somehow it felt like a betrayal to tell a stranger. "This is probably just nonsense, but yesterday Henna Bradbury stopped me to complain about Denise." I told him about our conversation outside the house. "But Henna would never *hurt* her."

"Stranger things have happened," Lockett said.

"Are you going to question her?" Bean asked.

"Yes," Lockett said with a firm nod.

"She's just a little old lady," I insisted. "I shouldn't have said anything."

"I'd like to gather more information before I talk to her," he said, "so don't discuss this with her if you happen to see her."

"Of course not," I said. Like I'd admit to Henna that I'd tattled on her.

He flipped his notepad closed and stood. "Thank you for your time."

"Do you think this will be . . . figured out in time for Memorial Day?" I asked.

A flash of exasperation crossed the state policeman's face. "That's certainly a big deal here. Let me be clear. We don't work according to some artificial deadline. We will follow our procedures and find out who did this in due time."

"Really?" I asked. "Did you just say 'in due time'?"

Lockett raised his eyebrows but seemed amused at being called out. "Sees ya." He deliberately used the comical way to say "good-bye" in Pittsburgh.

Bobby nodded and followed him out.

"This isn't going to be fixed anytime soon," I said to Bean, who now had the same expression that Erica used when deep in thought.

Bobby knocked briefly and came back in. "I told Erica this earlier, but you should make sure not to be alone in that building until we figure out this thing."

"How long is that going to take?" My voice was just a little bit whiny.

He hesitated. "Off the record?"

We both nodded.

"I knew Lockett in Baltimore. He's a good cop. And he won't be rushed."

"Meaning he's going to take forever."

Bobby didn't argue.

"Did you see a brown cat around the store?" I asked.

He shook his head. "You have a cat at the store?"

"No. There was a stray." I stopped. "So any chance of this being solved by the time we get to the fudge contest?" I asked, thinking of my phone messages.

Bobby twisted his mouth in a your-guess-is-as-good-as-mine expression.

I sat up straight. "Do you know how many people in this town are counting on that weekend? No way will visitors come here if they think they could be killed."

"We'll all do what we can," he said, "but Lockett's running the show. And the most important thing is finding the killer."

7

Erica must have been waiting for Bobby to leave because she came down as soon as he drove away.

"Chicken," I said. "You have to stop avoiding Bobby."

She ignored that. "What did they say?"

I was about to launch into a play-by-play when Bean closed his laptop and stood up. "I told Leo I'd meet him at the Ear."

The Ear was the nickname for O'Shaughnessey's, a bar at the edge of town. Decades ago, the curvy parts of the neon B had burned out to make the *Bar* sign look like *Ear*, and the owners had kept it that way ever since.

"Good," I said. "Let us know what people are saying."

I filled Erica in on everything Bobby and Roger Lockett had said, starting to choke up when I told her I was banned from making chocolate. Her expression held so much sympathy, I couldn't take it.

"What the hell am I going to do with myself?" I couldn't imagine a whole day going by, especially a Monday, and not making chocolate. And then I felt ashamed again. Denise was dead. I shook my head.

Erica seemed to read my thoughts. "We all have different ways of coping with loss. Your business is your baby," she said quietly.

"My way of coping is to make chocolate." I couldn't even work on the bridal party chocolates until I was cleared.

She put a hand on my shoulder and I felt the urge to turn into her and hide my face like a child. "I hate to say it, but we need to move ahead on the fudge cook-off and the other Memorial Day weekend events."

"I know," I said quietly. "Are you getting the same kind of phone messages I am?"

She grimaced and nodded. "It's not our call whether to cancel or not. So let's do what we can." She looked away. "And I've been thinking about the store. Maybe we should hire a hazmat company to completely scour the place."

My breath caught in my throat. "But wouldn't that be like admitting that we had a problem? That I somehow—"

"Not at all. It would demonstrate that we care about the safety of our customers." She pulled her laptop out of her backpack. "I have a plan."

"Why am I not surprised?"

She opened a new document. "I drafted a press release. Based on my research, the crime-scene techs will most likely be done tomorrow, which means we could have it cleaned on Wednesday and maybe we can even get back in there by Thursday."

Thursday. I could make it until then.

"Which means we could reopen this weekend."

The relief I felt was immense, even if it was balanced on too many "ifs" to hold steady for long.

She wasn't done. "While I'm working on this, why don't you figure out what you need to order?"

"Okay." Then an idea jumped into my head.

It was a terrible idea.

"What?" Erica asked, seeing my expression.

"Nothing." Maybe it wasn't such a bad idea.

"Tell me," Erica insisted.

"We know this town better than Lockett," I said.

"Of course," Erica said.

Maybe it was kind of an exciting idea. "You're really smart. And I'm . . . determined."

"That second part's an understatement," Erica said drily.

"What if we tried to find out what happened to Denise? Kinda helped the police a little?" Just saying it made me feel uneasy.

She did her thinking thing, where her face went blank as she dove into her brain to assess all of the possible variables to the situation. "That's a great idea. We have time now, at least until we can get back in the shop. Let's see what we can find out."

She jumped up. "Be right back."

She brought down a large roll of white butcher paper, different colored markers and masking tape, dumping them all on the table and then taking down my Walmart-special artwork of a steaming cup of coffee in neon colors hanging on one of the walls.

"Are you creating a project plan for a murder investigation?" I knew how she worked.

"Of course," she said, surprised. "How else are we going to figure out where to start?"

First I went crazy on my suppliers' websites, placing a serious hit on my credit card to rush order chocolate and other ingredients so that it all would arrive by Wednesday. Lockett didn't say I couldn't order my supplies. The rest I'd pick up at the grocery store when I was allowed to get back to work.

Then I joined Erica as we created the beginning of our murder investigation project plan—a huge interconnected spreadsheet of any details we thought might be important.

Erica began her investigation online. The Internet truly did have everything. What she learned about potential poisons was particularly enlightening.

"According to her symptoms, Denise may have been poisoned with cyanide."

"Where would someone get cyanide?" I asked.

"It's not that hard," she said. She raised her eyebrow. "It used to be commonly found in photographic development chemicals. But I've never known Denise to develop film. She's all digital."

I shrugged. "And wouldn't she need a special lab for that?"

She read from another page. "It's also in some kinds of

rat poison that only farmers use," she said. "Also, manufacturing plants, old chemistry labs, even in antique shops."

We had all of those around West Riverdale.

We created a profile for the perfect suspect: someone who had motive, means and opportunity, according to Erica's research into murder investigating. And then more specific categories: knowledge and access to poison, our security system and my chocolate. There couldn't be very many people who fit all of these.

We made lists of everything we could think of: who was mad at Denise; who had the knowledge to break into our store; who bought Amaretto Palle Darks recently. Although that was almost impossible to figure out. I kept only loose track in my own store and my four-packs of truffles were sold all over town, placed right by the cash register for impulse buying. Most of them had one Amaretto Palle included, and I had no idea who bought them on the other end. Store owners just kept track of the number of boxes sold and gave me a check every month.

"I have a question and I don't want you to take it the wrong way," I said.

"No problem." She sounded distracted. "What is it?"

"Why did you come in so early on a Monday?" She blinked at me and I quivered inside, feeling like I might be risking our friendship. "I totally know you didn't do anything . . . bad. I just think I should know in case anyone asks."

"Of course," she said. "I received a distressing email about some research I'd finished a while ago and was too upset to stay at home, so I came into the store to work on the next press release."

She was so matter-of-fact that I felt relieved. "I'm glad you were there." It would have been way worse alone.

She stared at the plan. "What has changed recently in Denise's life?"

I remembered my last conversation with Denise, when she'd stopped into my storage room and talked about leaving town. "Do you have some kind of photography book that Denise liked? Something about a beach?"

Erica knew it right away. *"The Eighties at Echo Beach?"*

"Yes!" I said. "Denise mentioned it Sunday night after the meeting. She was a little weird about it." I relayed the conversation.

"It's in the photography section of my used books," she said. "We'll find it when we can get back in." She made a note in her computer.

I was standing at the window with a cup of coffee, trying not to think about the nasty effects of poison, when I noticed Henna walking to her studio. Today she was swathed head to toe in purple, from a scarf covering her hair to purple striped socks and lavender sandals.

"What do you think about visiting Henna?" I asked Erica. So far we had only two suspects: Henna and Denise's ex-boyfriend Larry.

She looked up from her color coding, a pink highlighter in her hand. "Really? We're starting to interview our suspects now?"

"Why not?" I said, feeling adventurous.

"Lockett said not to mention anything to her," Erica pointed out.

"We can pretend it's just a friendly visit." I probably should be embarrassed that I'd never seen the inside of her studio. She'd been my next-door neighbor for a year, for Pete's sake.

"What should we ask her?" Erica started typing on her laptop.

I raised my eyebrows. "You're taking notes?"

"Of course," she said. "We have to be scrupulous in documenting our investigation. We've already established a potential motive for Henna. Let's try to find out if she had the means and opportunity."

"So we're looking for someone who bought my chocolate, used a needle to stick cyanide in it and gave it to Denise." Saying it out loud made me feel ill. "We're just going to go over there and see if she has rat poison and a hypodermic needle just lying around?"

"I think just you," said Erica, getting to her feet. "Two of us in that small room might be intimidating." Erica paused to think for a minute. "Tell her that you've always wanted to see her art process and you finally have free time because of the shop being closed. Flatter her work. Then figure out if she uses a rodenticide."

"A lot of people in this town own rat poison," I said.

"That's not true," Erica said. "You don't."

"Because I pay someone to get rid of them," I said. "And I pay extra to never see them or know anything about the process."

"Right," Erica said. "You pay the exterminator extra to use catch-and-release traps." She thought for a moment. "It's even more difficult because it's not something that's sold in regular stores. Maybe we can get a list from the Department of Agriculture."

She added a note to the rapidly expanding plan on the

wall. The sprawling, highlighted columns looked peculiar on the kitchen wall surrounded by the ornate, antique wainscoting. "Just see if you can find anything suspicious."

"Okay." I took a deep breath and picked my way through the yard, cutting through the break in our overgrown hedges.

Henna had let her grass grow long in the fall. It had trapped stray leaves, now all brown and fused together, and new growth was struggling to break through. Her son lived at least an hour away. Maybe he hadn't been helping recently. I followed the solar fairy lights she'd placed along the path to her studio.

She'd done her best to disguise the fact that her studio used to be a chicken coop. The outside was painted sky blue, with dozens of butterflies drawn in garish designs not found in nature. A huge oak tree towered over the studio, keeping the small building cool in the summer. The cracks between the wooden slats allowed the cold in during the winter, but she still worked away in all seasons.

I knocked on the door, the scent of patchouli not quite masking the stench of old chicken poop. "Henna?" I asked. "It's Michelle."

"Michelle?" She sounded confused.

I pushed the door open a bit. "Can I come in?"

"Sure." She didn't sound very sure.

"I've always wanted to see your studio," I lied. If I'd thought the outside was garish, the inside was like the psychedelic nightmares of a butterfly collector. Three of the walls were covered with drying butterfly parts—painted wings in various stages of completion and wooden rod heads with imaginary butterfly faces painted on.

She smiled. "How nice! It's small but it works."

"It sure does." I pretended to admire a blue wing with wide swishes of black paint on it. Shelves covered the last wall, holding buckets of paint and glitter glue, rolls of material and wire, and wooden dowels of different widths. "Look at how efficient you are."

"I have to be. I don't want to get behind on orders," she said. "I'm sending this one to Seattle." She held up a red-spotted creature that was more like a ladybug than a butterfly.

"Seattle," I said as if it was someplace exotic. "Awesome." I struggled to find a way to begin. "So how long did you train before you were able to do all this?" I asked. "Since I have no idea when they'll let me back in the shop, I was thinking I should take up a hobby so I don't go crazy." Something that doesn't involve adult chocolates.

"Given your career choice, you obviously have an artistic bent," she said. "You just need to experiment and practice. I developed my own technique, and you can do the same."

"Thanks. That's so nice of you. I have to figure out something to do with my time, since . . . " I let my voice trail off. "It's terrible what happened to Denise." I felt another jolt of sadness that must have shown in my face.

Henna's expression changed, but she turned away before I could tell if she was sad or mad. "I can't believe that happened right here in West Riverdale. That's like something from DC or Baltimore."

"Do you know anyone who may have had a problem with her?" I kept my voice light and then held my breath. Was I too obvious?

She stiffened and said defensively, "No. Not enough to *kill* her."

"I didn't mean you," I reassured her. "You wouldn't hurt a fly."

She seemed mollified.

"But maybe she pissed off other people," I said. "Maybe someone who didn't have the moral code that you do."

"That's absurd," she said, but then she looked uncertain.

"You have an idea? Who is it?" I pulled up a stool, trying to make it seem like I wanted her to dish the gossip rather than betray a confidence.

"Well, there were other people she kept out of the guild," she admitted reluctantly. "And Opal Wilkinds was not happy Denise got that senior portrait gig."

"Really? Why?"

"Opal's been the only senior portrait photographer for years," Henna said. "She makes most of her income from that. Some of those crazy parents spend up to a thousand dollars on those things."

I couldn't hide my shock. "A thousand?" Our school pulled from nearby towns and had over two hundred seniors. "She makes two hundred thousand dollars?"

"No," Henna said. "Some just buy one and copy it at the drugstore. But Opal makes a pretty penny anyway. And sharing that with Denise was going to be a major hit." She poured a bit of white paint onto her artist palette and dabbed a tiny paintbrush in it. "But she'd never do anything like, like kill someone."

I didn't know Opal very well, although she occasionally bought chocolates for her customers during the holidays. She was part of a middle-aged party crowd that drank a lot and lived to have a good time at the local bars. Occasionally, they'd go too far and I'd hear the gossip in the shop. Like when they tried to pick up married men, or when one of them threw up outside the all-night diner, or the time they went streaking on Lady Godiva Day. Supposedly, that was a sight to see. Or not see.

I remembered that I was here to check out Henna. "So have you had any problems with mice or rats or anything out here? I thought I saw something move when I put the garbage out last week."

Henna gave me a weird look for my awkward change of subject. "There's nothing for them to eat out here. I had one hide in my material roll once—just plugged the ends and drove it down the road."

"So you're like me and use the humane traps," I said.

"Gotta watch out for karma," she said.

My cell phone rang in my pocket and I silenced it.

Henna looked alarmed. "Get that out of here!"

"What?"

She stood up and made a shooing gesture with her hands. "Those EMF waves are terrible for your health. And they mess with my creative process."

I took a step back to the doorway. "You don't have a cell phone?"

"No," she said. "You should get rid of yours. You're young. You really don't want those things messing with your immune system. Or your lady parts. They cause damage to your very DNA. And your babies' DNA. No one has any idea how we're affecting our future generations."

My cell phone rang again as if on cue. Henna's eyes widened in horror. "Out!"

I covered the phone as if protecting her from its dangerous rays and didn't answer until I was outside.

"Michelle," Erica said in a way-too-friendly voice. "Mayor Gwen is here and needs to talk to us."

"Really?" I asked. "I'm on my way."

Gwen lived in the middle of the almost empty housing development she'd lost her shirt on, way on the other side of town, so she certainly hadn't stopped by on her way home. As I rushed back, I wondered if she had any news about Denise.

Gwen jumped to her feet as soon as I opened the door. Erica had put her in our shared living room. "I'm so sorry for your loss," she said grabbing my hands and holding on. "I rushed back as soon as I saw the news."

"Thank you." I extricated my hands and gestured for her to take the couch. Erica and I sat in chairs facing her. "Have you talked to the chief?"

"Oh yes." Her hands fluttered when she talked, which wasn't like her. "That was the first thing I did. I told him that he had to figure this whole thing out a lot faster than he usually works."

I noticed a layer of dust on the end table. This room normally got cleaned when we had a party but we'd been too busy to host one in months.

"It's terrible that you two had to find her," Gwen said. "You're so brave."

"We're fine," I said.

"I hope this doesn't dim your zeal to produce the best cook-off and arts festival this town has ever seen," she said.

Ah, the real reason she was here. My dismay at her insensitivity must have shown on my face because her hands fluttered again.

"No dimmed zeal here," I said lightly.

"We wouldn't want to disappoint all of your neighbors who've been working so hard on their fudge entries, or all of the town businesses who are counting on those tourist dollars," she said.

She continued. "I was telling Erica that I *begged* the chief to get this mess cleaned up as soon as he could, so Memorial Day weekend can go off without a hitch. We all admire his methodical way of approaching his job, but this time he just has to move things along a lot faster."

"What did he say?" I asked.

She pursed her lips. "That this is the first murder our town has seen in more than a decade and it's up to the state police to determine how long it will take. But the chief will be working closely with them and I'm sure he can speed up the process. Especially after I educated him about how vitally important those tax dollars we expect to earn that weekend are to this town, the town that employs him."

"Did he say when we'd be able to get back in the shop?" Erica asked.

"Yes, that's the good news," the mayor said. "The crime-scene investigation will be done tomorrow. I thought that you should wait until the weekend to reopen, to be respectful of course. Plus, there will be some cleaning to be done."

I shuddered and then removed that thought from my mind. "Do you think people will want to eat my chocolate if the investigation isn't complete?"

She looked so outraged that I felt heartened. "Of course they will! And I'll be first in line when you reopen."

8

After the mayor left, I filled Erica in on what Henna had said, especially about Opal Wilkinds, photographer to the stars. The West Riverdale Stars that is.

We were updating the investigation project plan when Bean came in the front door. "Hello?" he called from the open doorway.

"Come on in," Erica said absentmindedly as she typed into her laptop and I wrote on the paper on the wall.

"Erica!" I pointed with my pen. We wouldn't be able to let anyone into our kitchen until this whole thing was over.

"Oops," she said.

Bean seemed surprised by our new artwork, but understood it immediately. "Is this a good idea?"

"Why not?" Erica asked at the same time I insisted, "Yes," both of us with the same defensive tone.

He raised his eyebrows. "Denise was intentionally murdered. Whoever killed her might kill again."

"We won't be doing anything dangerous," I said. "We'll just be asking questions. Discreetly."

"As discreetly as your project for your cousin?"

I scowled at him. Erica smiled. She'd obviously seen the video.

"Nevertheless," Erica said. "There's no reason we can't make a few inquiries. Just to help the police." She lifted her shoulder as if to say "no biggie."

"What's the news from the Ear?" I asked. "Was Opal Wilkinds there?"

"Why? Is she one of your suspects?" He sounded like an older brother teasing his little sister.

Erica pointed to Opal's name in the suspects column.

"People were talking about her," he said. "Something about how she was hitting the Scotch hard lately."

Hmm. Maybe because she was guilt-ridden.

"Spill it all, Bean," Erica said. "I know you had to be asking questions. Who are the top suspects according to the townspeople?"

"Okay boss," he said. "Harold and Beatrice Duncan think it was the big box store that's been trying to get the town council to approve their building application."

"What possible motive could they have?" I asked.

"Something about how Denise must've caught them doing something illegal, maybe paying off a town councilman. They think anyone who voted yes should be looked into."

"Who else?" Erica asked.

"Your buddy Tonya thinks it was Reese, trying to get a real story to work on."

"I wouldn't put it past her," I said.

"And some other customer had used her Ouija board to learn that it was ghosts. Or vampires. She wasn't very clear."

I didn't fall asleep until after one in the morning and was woken up at five a.m. to the sound of two people running around upstairs. I made it to the door just as Erica and Bean pounded down the stairs.

"The state police just brought Mark in for questioning," Erica yelled.

Colleen's husband? "About what?" That made no sense.

Bean's face was grim as he rushed by. "Meet us at the police station."

I changed out of my pajamas, a small part of me glad that Bean hadn't seemed to notice my comfort clothes of flannel pants with a hole in one knee and a West Riverdale High T-shirt so threadbare the seams were peeling away.

My brain woke up on the way to the station, and I thought about how Colleen had been acting recently. She'd been even more strained than her usual three-kid stress level; had something else been going on in her life? Something to do with Mark?

Main Street was still asleep, dawn just starting to show over the horizon. I turned onto Cedar. At the end stood the police station, a white clapboard building that used to be the home of the mayor in the 1960s, normally sleepy, but now alight and buzzing with activity. I took a deep breath and let myself in.

Erica, Colleen and Bean sat together on wooden chairs in the waiting area, looking so much alike and yet so different. Same nose, same Irish skin and serious hazel eyes. Colleen's face was more round, softer somehow. But all three were worried.

Lieutenant Bobby stood behind the counter with a grim expression. I sent him a nod while I sat in the chair opposite the siblings.

"A lawyer on the way?" I asked.

Erica nodded. "Bean called a friend. He'll be here soon."

"Did you tell Mark not to say anything until he got here?" I asked.

"I didn't have time," Colleen said, her exasperation making me realize she must have already been asked that.

"What happened?" I asked.

Erica threw an accusing glance over her shoulder at Bobby. "Bean doesn't want us to talk here. All I can say is that Colleen called me crying to tell me Detective Lockett was taking Mark in for questioning about Denise's murder."

"Holy cow," I said. "Based on what?"

She shook her head. "Later."

"Was Bobby there?"

"No. Just Lockett and Noonan."

Chief Noonan must know about their family history—no secret in this small town—and kept Bobby out of it. But what was up with the harsh early morning tactics?

Bobby had his hard I'm-a-cop face on. I wondered if that meant he was mad at the chief or Mark.

Erica started to say something else just as Antony Marino, the famous criminal lawyer to top-level DC politicians, walked in with a freakin' entourage. As I'd seen on TV, he strolled in with his fedora and tailored suit as if he owned the place. The only thing missing was the ornate cane that he usually carried. I half expected to see 1920s paparazzi behind him with their old-time flashbulbs exploding.

Colleen looked alarmed when she realized who Bean's friend was. "I can't afford . . . " she started to stutter.

"Don't worry." Bean put his hand on her arm. "He's doing this for free. He owes me."

That must be an interesting story.

"I'd like to see my client immediately," the lawyer demanded, his courtroom voice echoing in the small hall.

Bobby sent a wry glance toward Bean and led the lawyer back to the "interrogation" room, a small office that was nothing like they have on cop shows. No two-way mirror, a table made of carved mahogany and, since it also served as the lunchroom, super comfy, ergonomic chairs the West Riverdale Chamber of Commerce recently bought the police department.

A few minutes later, Mark was escorted out by Detective Lockett, Marino walking behind with a satisfied smirk. Mark was all disheveled, probably at being woken up at the crack of dawn. When he looked at Colleen, his face changed, becoming red with shame. There was no doubt to any of us that he was guilty of something.

Some kind of unspoken married-forever communication happened between them and Colleen flushed with anger. Not just anger. Rage. Right when she was about to lunge toward Mark, Bean grabbed her by both arms and steered her outside, talking urgently into her ear.

Only so many things made a woman that mad. Was Mark having an affair?

We followed, Marino and his staff taking Bean aside to

talk by a waiting limo, and the rest of us stood by the cars. Colleen stared daggers at Mark while he found something fascinating on the ground to explore and Erica clasped her hands together, her face tight with worry.

How awkward could it get? I worried that Colleen would erupt into violence like on those reality cop shows. She was tall but I could probably hold her back. I'm short but tough, and I'd been an athlete my whole life. Oh wait, she wrangled those twins all day. She'd probably be able to take me. And she had fury on her side.

Marino walked over with Bean at his side. "I'll clear a time in the next two days. No one talks to the police, including that Lieutenant Simkin."

He continued. "As soon as a local judge wakes up, the chief will have his warrant to search your home and office. I'm *sure* there is nothing present to implicate you. Be there and cooperate."

The lawyer jumped into his limo and his entourage followed, one of them opening his laptop before the door was closed by the driver.

Bean took in the murderous expression on Colleen's face and seemed at a loss for what to do next. But just for a moment. "Michelle, please drive Colleen home. Mark will ride with Erica and me to discuss what Marino's next steps will be."

He put his hand on Colleen's shoulder. "I'll call you when we're done. Don't worry. We'll figure this out together."

Mark looked plenty worried about going with Bean but probably realized Erica's car was the lesser of the two evils. Bean slammed the door, the only indication that he was pissed as hell.

I was definitely getting the short end of the stick. I had the infuriated woman. A brief vision of the Hulk breaking out of my van crossed my mind before I shook it off. Colleen got in and shoved her seatbelt into the lock.

As I started driving, Colleen sat silent, her hands shaking with anger, or maybe adrenaline.

"I just want to say that if there's anything I can do, let me know," I ventured.

Somehow my innocent sentence opened up the floodgates and she punched the dashboard with both hands so hard I thought the airbags would explode in our faces.

"That cheating sonofabitch," she yelled. She let out a string of curses, punctuating each one with more pounding on the dashboard.

I should've kept my mouth shut, I told myself just as she burst into tears and hugged her hand to her chest. It must have hurt like hell.

I drove a little faster then, feeling helpless and over-whelmed. I'd never had the kind of commitment she had from Mark, and couldn't imagine the pain he'd caused her.

We arrived at her house and she didn't get out right away. It looked idyllic—a two-story redbrick ranch house, with toys in the driveway and even a white picket fence. "How could he ruin that?" she asked.

"You don't know for sure that he . . ."

She nodded, still staring at the house. "I know. The wife always knows, even if she tries not to."

If I hadn't seen his guilty look, I'd never have believed it. If Mark could have an affair in our small town, then anything could happen.

"So he was having an affair with Denise?" I asked, confused.

"No!" she scoffed, as if that was absolutely idiotic. "I knew something was up with him. Two weeks ago, Denise was going to be at some camera trade show in the same hotel that Mark's company was hosting a convention. So I asked her to check up on him."

I imagined giraffe-tall Denise watching him at the hotel bar, trying to stay hidden, maybe behind a fake tree in the corner.

"Not follow him or anything," she said defensively. "Just to peek in and see if he was misbehaving. She came back saying she hadn't seen him, but now it seems like she did catch him. That sonofabitch." She shook her head, sadness edging out the anger in her voice.

"It's one of his clients," she said. "Or that bitch assistant of his. She's always so condescending to me."

She was getting away from the major issue. That Detective Lockett believed Mark was a viable murder suspect. And that the murder victim was Denise, her best friend.

"So you think he . . . did something . . . to Denise?"

She whipped her head around to stare at me and I back-pedaled. "I mean. Chief Noonan . . ."

"Are you crazy?" she asked, turning her anger onto a more convenient target. "No. Never."

I couldn't imagine plump, hair-receding, exhausted-from-parenting-three-kids Mark having an affair. And I didn't want to.

"Oh good," I said, as if reassuring myself. "Why did Lockett bring him in?"

"Something about text messages Denise sent," she said. "She sent me one asking me to come in early but I didn't get it until this morning. When it was too late."

She turned to stare at her house, as if not sure she wanted to go in. The sun was rising quickly, dissipating the red clouds in the distance. Her anger seemed to be gone, replaced with uncertainty.

Then she firmed her chin and opened the door. "Time to call the locksmith."

9

arrived at my own home and looked at it as Colleen probably did. No bikes littering the front lawn. No one waiting for me in my apartment. A pang of disquiet hit me for the first time ever. Wow, was I growing up?

I shook off the wistful feeling and went in. Look where all that got Colleen. Lights were on in Erica's apartment but my natural desire to avoid emotional conflicts still warred with my curiosity of what the heck was happening up there. Or more accurately, what the heck did it have to do with Denise's murder? Did Mark really kill Denise? And use my chocolates to do it? It was hard to believe.

Plus, Erica and I were a team, and that team was in trouble.

I climbed the stairs quietly and peeked into her home office. Erica was near tears. Bean was scowling in anger. Mark sat slouched in a chair seeming defeated and defiant at the same time, like a teenager rebelling against the tyranny of curfew.

"I didn't kill Denise," Mark said as I walked in. He turned to me. "How is she?"

I ignored his intent. "Meeting with Fitzy the locksmith about now."

Bean smiled with a little pride for his sister, and maybe a little nastiness for Mark. "Okay. You didn't kill Denise. So you weren't having an affair?"

Mark slumped down again. "No, that part is true."

Bean made a disgusted sound and walked to the window. Erica looked shattered, feeling terrible for her sister.

"With your assistant?" I asked, taking over. Maybe for our project plan on the kitchen wall. And for Colleen. And a little bit for betrayed women everywhere.

"What? No," he protested and then shook his head. "She's in sales, like me. We met at a convention a year ago."

"This has been going on for a year?" Bean asked, outraged.

"No," Mark said. "We were friends. She was . . . fun."

No one thought of Colleen as fun anymore.

"And a month or two ago, it became," he paused, "more."

He blushed and I realized it was worse than an affair. He was *in love* with her.

"So when you were getting 'additional training,' you were with her," Erica said.

He nodded. "That's what I told Colleen."

Much as some nosy part of me wanted to pursue the sordid story, our main concern was the police. "Why did Lockett bring you in for questioning?"

He groaned and dropped his head into his hands. "Denise

got photos of me with Gretchen at a conference a couple of weeks ago. She told me I had to tell Colleen or she would. She's been texting them to me all week and gave me an ultimatum. She said she was going to tell her yesterday morning."

Erica stared at him, wide-eyed. "Yesterday morning?" she asked. "When Denise was killed?"

His eyes darted to all three of us. "I didn't do it!"

He must have seen doubt in our eyes. "I was going to tell Colleen this weekend, but then the twins were crazy and Pru was already nervous about the dance recital and I just . . ." He made a helpless gesture with his hands. "I decided to let whatever happens, happen. Then at least . . . it would be over."

Bean took a step closer. "You didn't have the guts to do it yourself. You'd let Denise, Colleen's best friend, tell her that you were having an affair."

"Yes," Mark said, defeated. "And then Colleen could decide what she wanted to do."

Bean's hands clenched as if he wanted to beat him to a pulp, and then he headed for the door. "I guess it's a good thing you have such a good lawyer."

"Where are you going?" Mark asked, desperation creeping into his voice.

"To get one for Colleen," Bean said grimly.

Erica and I walked Mark downstairs, past Bean who was pacing the living room with his phone pressed to his ear. "Don't leave town," Bean called out, his hand over the phone. "And do everything, I mean *everything*, exactly the way Marino tells you to. He's your best chance of getting out of this mess."

Erica waited with Mark for his friend to pick him up. I watched him through the window and wondered what the hell he was thinking. An affair? In this town? How long did he think he'd get away with it? And if Mark *was* having an affair, what else was going on in West Riverdale?

I decided to be useful and update the project plan on my kitchen wall, saving Erica from listing her brother-in-law as a suspect. He fit our little profile pretty well. He knew the security codes. He had access to my chocolate. And he certainly had a motive.

But I still couldn't see mild-mannered Mark as a cold-blooded murderer.

I made breakfast, since it was still morning and cooking always helped me to think. I whipped up a batch of my pancakes and fried extra crispy bacon. Erica just picked at her food, worry creasing her forehead.

I'd never realized before just how entrenched we were in each other's lives. Business partners, housemates, friends.

People believed that super-intellectuals like Erica were less feeling, but it wasn't true. Erica felt things intensely, even if she didn't show it. Like her brother, she had a deeply ingrained sense of justice and worked to make the world a better place.

I know she was scared for what her sister and the kids would have to go through. Horrified that Denise had died. And, just like me, worried for the future of our business.

I'd been selfishly allowing her to do all the consoling. "I'm sorry," I said.

Her eyes met mine. "You didn't cheat on my sister."

"Not that," I said. "I mean, for not realizing that this whole thing is just as hard on you as it is on me."

"I understand," she said. "It's your chocolate, your babies, under scrutiny."

"Which affects your business," I insisted. "And now your sister . . ."

She nodded, somber. "We are going to be fine. Both of us." She looked over at the plan hanging on the wall. "And we're going to find out who did this, so those angels don't grow up believing their father was a murderer."

I let the angels comment slide.

Bean walked in as he hung up the phone, grabbed a piece of bacon and sat down. "Anything new?"

Erica shook her head and jumped to a new subject. "Did you know that some experts think a relationship can get stuck at the developmental stage it started?"

"So Colleen and Mark got stuck when they were just college kids?" I filled a mug of coffee for Bean and set it in front of him.

He nodded his thanks. "Others believe each partner can develop but sometimes in different directions."

"So anything can happen?" I asked. "Is this about you and Bobby?"

Erica scowled. "No."

I went on. "Because from what I saw this morning, Colleen just unstuck herself."

We all looked out the window when a car drove up with Reese the loco reporter. She walked right up to the door and rang the doorbell. Of course we ignored her.

"I know you're in there, Michelle," she said.

I half expected her to cup her hands on the window to see inside.

"A source has told me that the police found poison in

your store," she called out, obviously enunciating for her own camera. "Wouldn't you like to tell the public your side?"

"Lying bitch," I muttered. "No way did they find poison in my store." Then I remembered Detective Lockett asking if I kept rat poison there. Had the police really found something? Had someone tried to make it seem like I was responsible?

"Interesting," Bean said, talking quietly as if Reese might overhear. "Maybe she knows someone in the police department. Or Lockett leaked that to her on purpose to see what she could dig up."

After a few more determined knocks, she left, with a purposeful grimace on her face.

I turned to Bean. "Do you know something I don't?"

He shook his head. "Just wondering if Lockett is using her."

"What do you mean?" I demanded.

"He asked you about the poison for a reason," Bean said. "Don't underestimate him."

Ten minutes later, Erica got a call from Colleen that Reese was knocking on her door and wouldn't leave.

"Where is she?" I asked.

"On her front porch," Erica acted as go-between.

"That's private property," I said. "I'll call the police."

Bobby threatened Reese with trespassing and she left under protest. Sure enough, a half hour later a video of her visits to our homes and interaction with Bobby popped up on her blog with the headline, *Local Police Protecting Murder Suspects*.

And of course she repeated the video of my X-rated chocolates flying through the air.

"Bitch" was too nice a word for her.

A little later, Colleen called to say the Baltimore crime-scene techs had arrived at her house with the warrant. The schools had some kind of teacher in-service day and she had taken the kids to daycare so they didn't see anything.

"That was fast," Bean murmured.

I looked around my own house. How horrible to have someone searching through every single item in your home, no matter how personal. Erica left to stay with Colleen while Bean went upstairs to make more calls.

I dusted the living room and then went back to the kitchen, not sure what to do with myself.

It made me realize how all-consuming my shop was, and how happy I'd been just yesterday morning.

I'd bounced around to a lot of jobs: lifeguard at the YMCA until they said I had to teach kids how to swim; a waitress at the diner until I couldn't get time off for the Labor Day softball tournament; apple picking in the summer until my hands were red and raw; and working the front desk in an auto shop.

I wasn't qualified for much, and just one class at the Frederick Community College convinced me college wasn't for me. That caused the biggest argument Leo and I ever had. I didn't know what I wanted to do, but I was pretty clear on what I didn't want to do. To his credit, he'd never used guilt to get me to go, and with what he had given up to raise me, he certainly could have.

With all the idealism of any eighteen-year-old, I knew I'd figure it out.

Still, I lived for the times I wasn't working and could just hang out with friends. It wasn't until I begged my way into becoming a salesperson at a chocolate shop in the next town that I found what I was meant to do.

At first, I wanted to work there so I could eat the chocolate. But then I took one chocolate-making class and I fell in love with the artistry of creating something beautiful *and* delicious.

I apprenticed under the shop owner, Astrid Trenton, who loved my enthusiasm and taught me to use my weird sense of smell to my advantage. When she retired, I returned home and opened up my own shop. I got to make happiness for a living.

The project plan on the wall called to me. I texted Erica that I was going to track down Opal. She texted back. *Try her studio. Tell her we need someone to photograph Hillary Punkin for the fudge cook-off and she'll get the photo credit.* Erica was even giving me my cover story.

Opal's studio was in a small strip mall at the end of Jasper Street. It was centuries newer than a lot of the buildings in town. According to a lot of people in town, that meant it lacked character. But since it was built in the early eighties, it probably didn't need to have the whole electricity system rewired to handle a state-of-the-art humidifier, like our store.

Our renovation was way more expensive than it should've been. I swore our building inspector was really working for our landlord, Yuli Gorshkov. When we'd made the deal with Yuli to pay for the renovations ourselves in exchange for a rent reduction for two years, we didn't realize all kinds of new code requirements would be lumped in, codes he was aware of and hadn't yet implemented.

As soon as I pulled into Opal's lot, I realized my mistake. Her studio was directly across the street from a coffee shop that the local police frequented and Chief Noonan was staring right at me through the front window. Since I'd driven by the coffee shop's parking lot, and the other stores in the strip mall ranged from a discount DUI lawyer, a tax accountant who closed up shop for a few months after tax day and an eyebrow threading salon, Noonan could only assume that I'd come to see Opal.

"Lost?" he said as he ambled over.

"Um." Erica's clever cover story got jumbled around in my brain while he stared at me over his reading glasses.

"I just wanted to ask Opal if she'd take photos at the fudge cook-off." I tried to send out innocent vibes but they obviously didn't work.

"Oh, really." He tucked his thumbs into his pants pockets and leaned back, which shouldn't have looked threatening, but was.

"I've learned that it's usually more effective to ask someone to volunteer in person rather than over the phone," I said as if passing on sage wisdom.

He made an "after you" gesture. "Go ahead."

I walked toward Opal's studio door with the chief at my side. "We need a professional photographer to take photos when Hillary Punkin's here," I lied. "It's part of the deal with her."

His face softened. "My wife loves that Hillary."

I tried the door. It was locked, so I knocked. No answer. Which was good because no way was I asking Opal questions with the chief breathing down my neck.

"Oops. Look at that." I pointed to her *Sorry, we're closed* sign. "I'll try again another time."

"Okay, then." He watched me leave, still wary.

10

We hosted an emergency meeting of the Great Fudge Cook-off Committee in our now dust-free living room. Heavy clouds had moved in and light rain was falling, just teasing us with the deluge that was predicted for later.

The mood was understandably somber. Seeing the group together made me realize even more that Denise was gone.

Erica had asked Beatrice Duncan if she could spare time from the hardware store to help, and she had graciously accepted. Truly, I didn't know how Beatrice could fit one more thing into her schedule. Besides the parade committee, she regularly volunteered at the library, her church and the Humane Society in the next town, in addition to working in her son's store. But Erica believed that when something needed to be accomplished, it was best to ask a busy person; they knew what they were doing and how to make it succeed.

Beatrice wasn't happy at the moment. "I don't know what to do with that Fitzy. He's only seventy-five and would forget his head if it wasn't bolted on." She chuckled and tugged her blue Duncan Hardware golf shirt out of the elastic waistband of her beige capris. "Did you get that? He's a locksmith and I said his head was bolted on."

Erica smiled, trying to be polite but she didn't like mean humor against her elders.

"Anyways," Beatrice went on, "he just shouldn't be in charge of the parade this year. Everyone's bending over backwards for him because he's getting up there and his palsy is something awful sometimes, but I don't know if he's gonna be able to handle it."

"Then he's so lucky he has such a great team to make sure it all goes off without a hitch," Erica said, smoothing feathers and being bossy at the same time.

Jolene sat beside me. "I looked for that cat like you asked, but it wasn't anywhere around."

"Thanks anyway," I said, thinking about the coming rain. The cat couldn't have appeared out of nowhere just a few days ago. Obviously it had a home and I should stop worrying.

I didn't have any chocolate to serve, so I busied myself with the pizza as Erica sat down and pulled out some notes. Any normal person would be exhausted after spending the day with her sister in such a difficult time, but she seemed as energetic as ever.

"No matter what anyone says," Erica began, "we're holding this cook-off and it's going to be awesome."

That brought tentative smiles to everyone's face.

"I do have some good news and some bad news," Erica said. "What do you want to hear first?"

Jolene raised her hand. "I always want my bad news first." Today she and Steve had rushed over after karate, Jolene in her white *gi* and Steve in another ratty T-shirt, this one reading, *DFTBA. Don't Forget To Be Awesome.*

"The lesser of the bad news is that all of the hotels had some cancellations," Erica said. "The story ran on one Baltimore station and they're worried that the news of Denise's murder has made West Riverdale less appealing."

Less appealing? No kidding.

"What's the worse news?" Steve asked.

She paused. "Hillary Punkin is rescinding her offer to judge the contest."

"What?" I screeched. Even though a little bit of relief hit me first, outrage won.

"Her 'people' follow our social media and because of Reese's blogs, they aren't sure Hillary should be associated with . . . tainted . . . chocolate," Erica said.

I flushed deeply with embarrassment. *Tainted.*

"They hadn't made it definite yet that she would attend, so they aren't making any kind of announcement that she's not," Erica said. "They said something about keeping her schedule open, so it's not definite either way."

"What's the good news?" Beatrice asked.

"The health department is holding off on investigating and will wait to decide once the tests from the police are complete."

"When will that be?" Steve asked.

"Unofficially? I heard the tests on enough of the samples taken by the crime-scene techs should be completed tomorrow. Assuming they're clean, we can make more solid plans for reopening." Erica flipped through her notes. "Possibly as early as Saturday, as the mayor was hoping."

She went on to the next topic. "I'd like to hold a special meeting and press conference with anyone associated with the cook-off and festival—sponsors, artists, vendors, advertisers, any press who would like to come, even contestants. I already passed the idea by Gwen and she's more than happy to help us reassure everyone. Can we pull it together by tomorrow night?"

"Where would we hold it?" Beatrice asked. "The community center?"

"Good idea," Erica said.

"Maybe the chief would make a statement as well saying their investigation is moving forward," Steve suggested. "Help everyone to feel better."

I escaped into the kitchen while they discussed more details. *I probably shouldn't even attend that meeting*, I thought, as I loaded more pizza slices on a tray. I'd just be a reminder of the reason we were in this mess.

Steve followed me into the kitchen, pretending that he needed more water. "How ya holding up?"

I sighed. "Probably about as well as can be expected." We'd tacked a sheet over our investigation project plan on the wall. Luckily, Steve was too polite to ask about it.

"We all know it's not you," he said. He took the tray from me. "You run a clean shop."

Unexpected tears threatened.

"Ah, don't go getting all mushy," he said, but his brown eyes were a little wet too. "You know this town is behind you one hundred percent."

He headed toward the door. "We all just gotta make sure the police find this asshole," he said, whispering the last word.

"Steven Roxbury, are you cursing?" Jolene demanded as we joined them.

I t was barely seven by the time the meeting broke up, and Erica and I decided to have a drink at the Ear. If we happened to learn something about Opal, then yay for us.

"Guess who wants X-rated chocolates?" I asked Erica on the drive over.

She laughed. "Who?"

"Beatrice."

"Really? For what?"

"She wants to surprise her bridge club." I tried imagining a bunch of little old ladies sitting around card tables playing bridge and eating tiny anatomically correct chocolates. "But I'm not supposed to let Howard know."

"I can imagine he wouldn't be pleased," she said. "What did you tell her?"

"I said I'd think about it."

"Wait," Erica said. "Is that what Jolene wanted to talk to you about by the door?"

"Yep." I laughed. "She wants them as a gag gift for her teacher friends."

"That's why she was talking about girl power?"

"Yeah," I said. "She wants me to just own the whole X-rated chocolate thing and be proud." We turned onto the Ear's street. That was so not going to happen.

After talking to Henna, I understood why Opal bought rounds of drinks every fall. She made a freakin' fortune once school started and parents ordered their senior portrait packages. I'd overheard the gossip from customers that she spent a lot of time at the Ear, claiming it was her "Cheers bar" where everyone knew her name. Every month or two, she'd go too far and end up making some kind of drunken scene that I'd hear about in the shop the next day. She'd stay away for a week or two until she could face her bar buddies again. She'd drink diet soda for a while, but soon she was putting away the tequila and returning to her partying ways.

The rain was falling a little heavier now, making the half-full asphalt parking lot black and shiny. Erica backed her electric car into a spot close to the exit.

"Think we're going to have to make a fast getaway?" I asked.

"Just want to be prepared." She got out and looked at the other cars as if trying to figure out who was there. Knowing her memory, she probably deduced a bunch of them.

The Ear was set back from the road, a low, white wooden building that snuggled in amongst huge gnarled trees now protecting a bunch of patrons on a smoking break from the rain. The Ear sign blinked in its old-fashioned red-neon glory. Paint was peeling in some places, but it almost seemed deliberate, as if it was pretending to be a sleazy bar. Like a suburban kid walking out of his McMansion wearing his pants pulled down like a rapper.

A banner flapped in the wind encouraging people to *Get Your Preak On at the Ear!*

I opened the door to the sound of people talking and

laughing over Carrie Underwood singing about taking a Louisville slugger to her cheating boyfriend's car, and the smell of stale beer, peanuts and sweat.

The bartender, Jake Hale, smiled as we walked in and said, "Welcome." He gave me a wink, letting me know he hadn't forgotten the time I'd tried to buy a six-pack of beer from him when I was sixteen.

Opal sat hunched over in the back of a booth with a bunch of women in their forties or fifties. She stared into what looked like a glass of soda while she poked at the ice with a tiny red straw. Her friends seemed to be oblivious to her self-imposed isolation, laughing uproariously at a joke and clinking their margarita glasses.

The rest of the bar had a sprinkling of tables and booths filled, but a lot of noise came from the pool room in the back.

By unspoken agreement, Erica and I sat down at the corner of the bar as far from Opal and the raucous pool room as we could get.

"What can I get for you two lovely ladies?" Jake looked like a casting call for a friendly neighborhood bartender. Tall and handsome in that easygoing way, with unstyled brown hair that needed a cut and an untucked green flannel shirt over weathered jeans.

I checked the beer labels on tap. "How about 1634?"

"Excellent choice," he said cheerfully. "Good for you for supporting our local businesses. And it's delicious. And for you, milady? A chardonnay perhaps?"

Erica ignored his teasing and tried not to stare at Opal. "The same."

"How's your brother?" Jake called to me from in front of the tap.

"Good," I said. Jake had played football with Leo way back in high school. "Getting back in the swing of things."

"How're Sydney and Alex?" Erica asked. She was also the encyclopedia of everyone and anyone's names, relatives and history of any significance, but I was still amazed that she remembered the names of Jake's kids.

"Great!" he said. He gave us our drinks and pulled a framed photo of his family from a shelf that held liquor bottles. "Here's a picture from our last trip to Florida."

"Beautiful," Erica said, while I murmured some nonsense.

He returned it to its place of honor and took a few minutes to handle the order of a waitress who looked a lot like him. Jake had a huge family and usually employed at least a few cousins at a time.

"How are we going to talk to Opal?" I whispered to Erica.

"I don't think we can." She frowned as she peeked over at her table. "It'd be too obvious in front of all those women."

"Maybe if she goes to the bathroom," I said right before Jake returned.

"I was real sorry to hear about Denise," he said. "I still can't believe it. She was sitting right there just two weeks ago." He pointed to an empty cane-backed chair by a small table close to the door.

"Really?" I felt a shiver run down my spine, as if her ghost sat there now. "Did she come here a lot?" I tried to keep the surprise out of my voice. She seemed more likely to go to the brass and fern bar with a dance floor in the next town.

He shrugged. "Once in a while."

"Was she with someone?" I asked.

I guess I wasn't being subtle enough for Erica, because

she changed the subject. "I was thinking that you should put a coupon in the fudge cook-off program," she said. "It doesn't cost that much and you'd get a lot of tourists stopping in. Did you hear the Best Western is sold out for the whole Memorial Day weekend?"

Jake looked surprised. "You're still going ahead with that?"

"Of course," Erica said. "Too many businesses in town are depending on it."

"People were saying that maybe it'd be cancelled, because of, you know . . . Denise," he said.

"I'm sure Chief Noonan will find the perpetrator and that will allay everyone's concerns," Erica insisted. She always sounded more snotty when she was upset.

"Any speculation going on about who did it?" I asked. "You must hear a lot, being in the center of things here."

He picked up a pint glass with an etched Bass label and started drying it. "She had an argument with someone when she was here," he said reluctantly, as if worried about breaking some kind of bartender code.

I tried to hide a quiver of nervousness. Or excitement. "With who?"

Erica sent me a look. She was just dying to correct me and say "whom."

"Some guy," he said. "He was pretty pissed off."

"Did you recognize him?" Erica asked. "Was it Mark?"

"Of course not," he said. "He and Colleen come here for their date nights."

I asked, "What did they argue about?" at the same time Erica asked, "What did he look like?"

We stared at each other for a minute and then she nodded, letting me go first. "They argued?" I asked.

Jake smiled at our little control issue. "She showed him some photos and he blew a gasket," he said. "He grabbed them and she laughed at him. That really drove him nuts."

A loud cheer echoed out from the pool room and I had to raise my voice. "What happened next?"

"He told her she was out of her mind and then he lit outta here."

"Did he threaten her?" Erica asked. She must have been itching to pull out her fancy murder investigation notebook, but restrained herself.

"I couldn't hear much of what he said—it was three-dollar-beer night and this place was packed—but she looked pretty shaken up. Like, she was acting all tough in front of him and as soon as he left, she kinda collapsed."

"Collapsed?"

"Not really, like, on the floor, or anything." He struggled to explain. "Like she had psyched herself up to do something and it went worse than she expected."

"Did you ask her what was wrong?" Erica asked before I had a chance to.

"Of course." He seemed a little offended. "But she didn't want to talk about it."

"What happened next?" I asked.

"She asked me to walk her to her car."

She was that worried? "Was he hanging around?"

He shook his head. "Nope. Long gone."

"Did you see what was in the photos?" Erica asked.

He tilted his head as if realizing we weren't just gossiping. "I was too far away."

Erica didn't slow down. "What did the guy look like?"

"Kinda normal," he said.

"Nondescript?" Erica asked. She couldn't take it anymore and pulled out her notebook.

Jake seemed amused. "What are you guys doing? Helping the chief?"

"No," I said. "Of course not."

He gave me that "you tried to buy beer from me when you were underage" look. How did bartenders know when you're lying?

Erica tried to appear less intense. "We're just trying to understand it. It was terrible finding her like that."

From the disconcerted look on Jake's face, deflecting attention by playing the sympathy card worked. "What was that guy like?" I asked.

"To tell you the truth, he looked a little like a weasel. And had those scars on his face like that actor. Mickey Rourke, maybe?"

"Pockmarks? Like from acne?" Erica asked.

"Yeah. Like that. And he wore a big diamond earring. Probably fake, given the rest of him." He walked away to serve two guys in cowboy hats who'd just walked in.

"Does that sound like Larry?" I asked. I realized I'd only seen him from a distance, when he waited for Denise outside in his car, but he did have that weasely look.

"Could be." Erica looked over at Opal, who hadn't moved, and from the way she was nursing that soda, she wasn't headed for the bathroom anytime soon. "Let's get back to Opal another time," she said. "I want to research Larry."

We finished our drinks, left some money on the bar and waved good-bye to Jake.

"Well that was productive," Erica said as we walked across the wet parking lot. She hit the button to unlock the doors. Heavy rain clouds gathered, blocking out any light from the moon.

Out of the corner of my eye, I noticed the curtain move in one of the Ear's windows. A man stood behind it, but with the light behind him, I couldn't tell who it was. He moved away and I shook off my uneasy feeling.

"Too bad we don't have a photo of Larry to show Jake and make sure," I said.

We got in the car and looked at each other. "But I'm sure Denise had some," Erica said.

"Maybe you can ask Lieutenant Bobby," I said. "He has to have a mug shot somewhere."

She scoffed. "Right."

"Or maybe we can check out her apartment ourselves." I dug my keychain out of my purse and held up the key Denise had given me the time she asked me to water her plants when Colleen was also out of town.

"Oh, we shouldn't," Erica said in a voice that meant, "Oh we should," and started driving toward town.

The clouds spit rain on the trip over, with occasional heavier outbursts as if to warn us away. Denise had lived just a block from the store, in a second-floor apartment above the Knit Wits yarn store. It hurt my heart to see our store, even from a block away, and know I couldn't go in.

"Wait," I said. "Can you drive by the back of the store? I want to see if the cat is out in the rain."

She drove by slowly, but Coco was out of sight.

Except for the restaurants, the rest of Main Street was closed. We parked behind the yarn store and pulled our hoods up over our heads. We probably looked like bad actors in a TV cop show the way we were skulking around as we approached the building. I was so nervous that I was breathing fast and I had to keep myself from giggling.

From the bottom of the steps leading to Denise's apartment we tried to see if there was some kind of sticker that sealed it as a crime scene, but since we couldn't tell, we started up. I'd been to her apartment only a few times, but I'd never noticed how much the ancient stair boards creaked, even wet with rain. My keys jangled abrasively in my hand, and Erica shushed me before chuckling at her own nervous response.

As soon as we made it to the top of the stairs, I heard a large bump from inside. Erica's eyes widened like a cartoon character, and we both turned to get the heck out of there when the door burst open. Larry the Loser, with Denise's laptop in hand, looked as surprised to see us as we were to see him.

"Larry?" I ventured, before he stuck out a straight-arm just like a football player and pushed me out of the way.

11

stumbled against the wooden railing and then instinctively ran down the stairs after him, yelling, "Bring that back!" Erica was right behind me.

Larry looked back at us and tripped over the wet curb, and the laptop flew out of his hands and hit the street with a loud crunching sound. I cringed. Whatever was on there had probably disappeared into cyber heaven. He moved toward it as a police car came flying around the corner, then he took off through the trees.

Lieutenant Bobby tore out of the car after him, yelling to us, "You guys okay?" as he ran.

"Yeah," I yelled back and waved him on. "Go get him!"

My breath was heaving, as if I'd run for miles instead of down some stairs. Erica was staring at the laptop.

"We can't," I said, knowing she desperately wanted to see what was on it. "Bobby'll kill us."

Oops. That was the wrong thing to say. Her eyebrows came together in a scowl. Just as she moved toward it, Bobby stepped out from the trees.

"You lost him?" I asked. Maybe Larry was as weaselly in action as he looked.

"He had his car right over there in the alley," he said a little defensively. Then he radioed in what had happened, staring at us as if he didn't trust us.

"What the heck were you doing here?" he asked after he ended the call.

"Um," I started, but then the chief arrived in his cruiser.

He approached slowly. I felt like I was a child and he'd caught me playing hooky. "Twice in one day I find you snooping around, Ms. Serrano. And this time with Ms. Russell. You two playing Scooby Doo or something?"

"No, sir," I said. "We just—"

Erica interrupted. "We were anxious to find out if Denise's apartment had been cleared by the police. We had an emergency meeting of the cook-off committee and realized we need photographs Denise had taken for the event."

That girl sure thought fast on her feet.

"We had no intention of entering if the crime-scene seal was still intact," she said, as if offended he could think anything different.

Somehow her snotty words made it more believable. I peeked up at Bobby, who didn't appear at all bamboozled.

"And then that horrible man pushed Michelle and she practically fell down the stairs," she said with a tiny shudder.

Had she taken acting lessons at college?

I stayed silent. The chief grunted and seemed to relent.

"So, in some small way, we assisted your investigation," Erica said. "If we weren't here, he would've gotten away with that." She pointed to the computer.

"Was her apartment searched already?" I asked.

The chief grimaced. "Yes it was." He spoke to Bobby. "Call that state cop buddy of yours and get him over here."

He pointed a finger at us. "You two get on home. I'll stop by for a statement later."

Bobby smirked at us, probably knowing it would give us time to get our stories straight.

t didn't take long for Detective Lockett and Bobby to arrive, Bobby knocking but not even bothering for us to respond before coming in. We were waiting on the couch in the living room to make sure they didn't see our new artwork in the kitchen.

They shook off the rain that had started in earnest, hanging their dripping coats on an antique coatrack Erica had found at one of her estate sales. Lockett sat down in an overstuffed chair while Bobby stood leaning on the doorjamb.

Lockett leaned forward with his hands on his knees. "What are you gals up to?"

We'd already agreed that Erica would do the talking. "As I explained to the chief, we were hoping you were done in there and we could retrieve photos of the different fudge entries that Denise had taken. We need them for the press release."

Lockett stared at us as if about to call "bull," and I had to look down. Then he shifted in his chair. "How 'bout this. You two stop turning up where you're not wanted, and I won't slap you in jail for the next coupla weeks to keep you out of my way."

I pushed my hands together to stop them from trembling, but Erica stared at him calmly. "Why are you threatening us?"

What the heck was she doing?

"Excuse me?" he said, his tone menacing.

"We haven't committed any crime. You have no legal basis to arrest us," she said, "so you must have another reason."

Bobby shifted his feet around. I think he was trying not to smile.

Lockett's eyes narrowed. He didn't like being called on his bluff.

"I'd like to offer a service to you," she continued, as if he'd agreed with her and we had all moved on. "I have an assistant who's a whiz at computers. Maybe he can take a look at that computer you found and see why Larry was so determined to get it."

Lockett chuckled. "We have very talented techs who will get what we need."

"Fair enough," she said. "But in the event they can't, he's at your disposal."

"I'll keep that in mind," he said. "So, what do you think is on that computer?"

"I suspect it's something Larry didn't want the police to find," she said. "Perhaps his motivation for killing her. And given that she was a photographer, photos of some kind."

His expression was calculating. "Anything else?"

She leaned forward in her chair. "By showing up at Denise's tonight, he seemed to believe the police wouldn't find the laptop, so it had to be very well hidden. Some of these old buildings have unexpected nooks and crannies, and perhaps due to his relationship with Denise, he knew her hiding place. Once you figure out why he wanted the laptop so badly, I believe you'll find your motive."

"Which would be?" he prompted.

"Now that I don't know," she said. "But I believe your accomplished techs will find out." She turned to Bobby. "How'd you get there so fast tonight?"

Lockett answered for him. "A neighbor called when Larry broke in."

Erica tilted her head. "Do you have any results from your testing of our store?"

He gave Bobby a "can you believe this girl?" look but Bobby remained impassive. "Okay, this is preliminary. I'm tellin' ya only because we're releasing this info in the morning. The only poison found was in the chocolate on the table. Your shop is clean. You can get back in there tomorrow."

The relief I felt was so overwhelming, tears popped into my eyes. Detective Lockett noticed; he noticed everything.

I was about to stand and let them leave when Erica pushed. "Reese Everhard stopped by earlier to say you'd found poison in the store. Was she lying to get a reaction, or does she know something you don't?"

Lockett's face tightened. "Did she now?"

Erica's eyes widened. "So she told the truth. You found poison in the store."

"That's not public information," he said.

"We certainly won't tell anyone," she said. "And you're smart enough to know that it didn't belong there. It was planted." She paused. "How . . . premeditated."

My mouth fell open, and it took a moment before I could talk. "Someone tried to frame me?"

"Not necessarily," Lockett said. "They were most likely trying to make it look like an accident."

"An accident?" I stood up. "That I'd be so stupid, so negligent, that I'd somehow allow poison into my chocolate?"

Erica put her hand on my arm. "Well, that's better than a cold-blooded murderer."

"Where was the poison?" I demanded.

"I'm not going to tell you," the detective said. He had a gleam in his eyes, like he was enjoying the hunt for this particular killer.

Bobby shifted in the doorway, and the detective looked down at his notebook.

Erica sat for a moment. "Anything else that didn't seem to belong?"

Lockett stood up. "We're done. Keep this to yourself."

We followed him to the front door.

"We'll deal with Ms. Everhard," he said as they both shrugged into their coats.

"Good night," Erica said, as if this had been a social call. "Careful driving in that rain."

After we were sure they were both gone, we rushed to fill in more information on our wall chart. Larry was certainly suspect number one. Since the police had the computer he was after, and a lot more resources than we did, they'd find Larry first.

It took until bedtime for me to realize that it could've gone badly for us tonight. Larry could have tried to hurt us. Or worse.

What kept me tossing and turning was how much we had

misjudged him. If Larry had pulled off Denise's murder, along with planting evidence to create a smoke screen, even if it didn't fool the police, he must be smarter than we assumed.

I hoped Wednesday would live up to its nickname of "hump day" and that we were on our way over it. While some kind of top-of-the-line hazmat company that Erica found was scouring our store, I shopped for everything I needed to restock and reopen on Saturday, and Erica organized the fudge cook-off reboot meeting for later in the day. She'd already heard that a ton of concerned citizens were attending to find out how the investigation and plans for the cook-off were progressing.

Kona had called, anxious to start working the next day. I called my other assistant, Kayla. "Please tell me you're free to work in the store tomorrow."

"I'm free to work in the store tomorrow," she said, sounding like a robot.

"Oh good," I said. "Wait. Are you really free or are you telling me what I want to hear?"

"Calm down," she said. "I'm free. I'll be there." I heard a car changing into high gear. "Wait. Tomorrow's Thursday, right?"

Kayla always said she was too ADHD to stick to one job at a time, so she split her time between the shop, teaching yoga and driving high-end sports cars to wealthy collectors.

"Where are you?"

"Coming up on Savannah, Georgia," she said. "This car's going to Fort Lauderdale, and I'm flying back tonight."

"Then what are you doing on the phone? Hang up and pay attention to the road!"

"Always," she said and hung up.

Colleen had stepped in to plan Denise's funeral for Saturday afternoon, including taking up a collection for the costs, since there seemed to be no record of a will. Denise had told her that she came from a long line of couples with only one child and her mother had been her only family before her death from cancer. Denise had hoped to break that curse and have a bunch of children when she married. It made her death even more sad; she was the end of her line.

We heard a few whispers asking why Colleen, who was married to a "person of interest" in Denise's murder, was coordinating the service. But they were drowned out by most of the town pointing out that Denise and Colleen were best friends.

We planned to open at our normal time on Saturday and treat it as a trial run, closing by one, in time for the funeral.

Saturday evening was the running of the Preakness Stakes at the Pimlico Race Course in Baltimore, which was a big deal in West Riverdale. Every business that didn't have televisions to show the race just closed down.

I'd driven all the way to Frederick to buy my cream, sugar and other supplies to avoid running into any neighbors. I even threw in a few cans of gourmet cat food for Coco, in the event she made her way back to the store. I'd welcomed the long drive alone through the rolling hills that surrounded our town. On the way back, I noticed that solar panels were popping up on a bunch of West Riverdale homes. How cool that West Riverdale residents were so into green technology.

A scowling Henna stormed over as soon as I parked in front of my house. "Michelle Serrano!"

Whoa. It was like being yelled at by my mother. "Henna? What's wrong?" Playing dumb rarely worked but it was worth a try. I got out and grabbed a grocery bag full of cream and sugar to use as a buffer.

"Did you tell the police that I was mad at Denise?" She was so furious, her hands were fisted, as if she was holding back on hitting me.

"Me? Of course not," I tried.

"Because I told you that in confidence," she said. "And then they came here and questioned me about where I was Sunday night. Me!"

"I'm *so* sorry," I said. "They must have misunderstood me. I was in such shock that I don't remember a lot of that day, but they did ask if anyone had an issue with Denise."

Her mouth dropped open and I rushed to finish.

"I told them that of course you had nothing to do with it, so I'm sure it's just procedure or something."

She seemed to calm down a little, so I picked another bag up. "I have to get these into the refrigerator." Then I paused. "So you must have been working Sunday night."

She looked disconcerted for a moment and then said, "Yes. Yes I was."

Was she hiding something? "I'm sorry if I caused any problems," I said. "I wasn't thinking very clearly."

She nodded, not sure whether to forgive me.

I leaned back against my minivan. "Did they tell you if they had any leads?"

She shook her head. "No. Just gave me a hard time."

"Well, you have nothing to worry about," I reassured her. "They'll catch whoever did this and it'll work out."

I hoped I wasn't telling her a huge lie.

. . . .

Neighbors were pouring into the West Riverdale Community Center, which was a big name for the simple building on Peach Lane that was basically a large, barnlike, only somewhat insulated room with a wooden floor. A small metal shack in the back held tables and chairs that had to be moved by whomever used it. The usage fee was often waived if the renter cleaned up afterward, unless they were a company that had deep pockets.

My store was only two blocks away. I'd walked close to it, telling myself that I was looking for Coco, but I also just wanted to see it. It made me ache, like I was experiencing nostalgia for a long-lost home.

It seemed like most of the town was here as well as a lot of people I didn't know who probably weren't actually involved with the festival. I'd been standing by the cookies and coffee table when the first few people came in and veered away, sending me speculative glances. Did they think I'd poisoned the cookies? I was probably being paranoid, but in the event they were not on carb-free diets, I slinked to the opposite corner in the back.

I was surprised to see a bunch of Erica's Super Hero Geek Team club members coming in the back door, holding money. Erica pulled out a box from under a covered table and handed out comic books, collecting money and accepting her thanks. They must not have been able to wait until we reopened for their comic-book fix.

Henna sat up straight in the front row, as if to prove her innocence. Right beside her sat Reese Everhard, which added to my anxiety. She was obviously willing to say or do anything for a story. Beatrice Duncan was a few rows back, in a one-sided discussion with Sammy, haranguing him about something having to do with the hardware store, while Howard stared off into the corner. Principal Palladine walked in with a guy in an expensive business suit and slicked-back hair. The guy was giving him a friendly smile but seemed unhappy with whatever they were discussing. The principal seemed displeased as well, although his face lit up when he saw me. He left the businessman behind and came over.

"How are you, Michelle?" He always used the prettiest pronunciation of my name, "Mee-shell," with a little French lilt at the end. He gave my shoulder a small squeeze in support. "Holding up okay?"

"I'm fine," I said. "Ready to get back to work."

He nodded approvingly. "Sounds like you."

Principal Palladine had been one of my favorite adults after the death of my parents. He hadn't fawned all over me like some, trying to be the one who saved me from my grief. He hadn't attempted to take over for Leo and be my parent. He'd called me into his office once to offer any help when I needed it. I didn't realize it until much later, but he'd most likely intervened when teachers had become tired of my acting out in classes or when I skipped doing homework. I'd always been somewhat of an academic slacker and my grief at my parents' death had only intensified my you-only-live-once mentality. It was a miracle I graduated, which may also have been because of him.

"Who is that guy?" I asked. "I haven't seen him before."

"He's the president of Get Me Some Solar, the company installing the panels at our school," he said.

"Seems like you weren't getting along so well." I sure was getting nosy.

"Nah, it's fine," he said. "Just trying to nail down some details."

"What a great project," I said.

"Yep," he said. "It's going to save us a ton on electricity."

An older lady who had been the secretary when I was in high school waved from the chairs, and the principal excused himself.

I felt a little alone for a moment, and then Leo was standing beside me.

"You sneak in the back?" I smiled my delight in having him there.

"Seems like the place to be tonight." He looked around the fast-filling room. It could only help to have the visible support of my decorated war veteran brother. I moved a little closer to him as the police contingent—Chief Noonan, Lieutenant Bobby and Detective Lockett—came through the door right on time and stood against the wall by the entrance.

Erica nodded to them and then moved to the podium on the small stage. The banner announcing the Great Fudge Cook-off and highlighting all of the sponsors hung behind her. We'd created a whole new category—Titanium Sponsor—for Get Me Some Solar so that they could have top billing. Now that I'd seen the thousand-dollar suit the president was wearing, I wished we had charged them more.

Erica welcomed everyone and reminded them that we were all on the same team to make Memorial Day weekend go off without a hitch. She gave a wonderful little introduction of the mayor, who added her peppy speech to the momentum of the feel-good meeting.

Then Gwen introduced Chief Noonan, and the mood changed.

"Thank you all for coming." He introduced Detective Lockett and Lieutenant Bobby. "I know you must have a lot of questions about this terrible crime. I just wanted to let you know that we are working closely with the state police and will find out who did this."

Noonan cleared his throat. "I'll take your questions, but please know that I won't be discussing any details, since this is an active investigation."

"Do you have any leads?" Someone asked from the front. "We hear locals have been brought in for questioning."

He meant Mark. I tensed until the chief said, "We've interviewed several persons of interest and so far, no suspects have been identified."

Bean appeared on the other side of me, his whole focus on the spectacle while I couldn't help but notice how cute he looked in a black T-shirt that pulled across his shoulder, oh-so-close to mine.

A man with a digital recorder and notepad did a double take when he saw Bean and jumped up to talk to him. "Hey, Russell," he said, shoving his glasses up on top of his head and shaking Bean's hand. "You on this?"

"Oliver," Bean said. "Nah, I live here. They got you on the crime beat now?"

He chuckled. "Nope. I'm here checking out your mayor."

Bean's eyes narrowed. "What's going on with her?"

"Not sure yet. I got a tip that some super PAC is interested in her potential run for the House next year."

I tried to keep the surprise off my face, as if I wasn't eavesdropping on their conversation.

"Why would a super PAC be interested in a small-town mayor?" Bean asked.

"You tell me," he said. "From what I understand, the party is having a hard time getting people to step up to the plate this time around. Bad political environment. I'm just following the money to see what's up." He got a calculating look on his face. "You know the players here. Who should I talk to?"

Bean shook his head. "I don't know yet. Just got into town." He thought for a moment. "I'll give you what I find out, okay?"

"You got any dirt on her?" The reporter's voice was eager.

Bean shook his head. "Clean as a whistle. I don't think you'll find anything."

The reporter snorted. "There's always something," he said. "Gives me job stability." He moved back to his chair and asked, "Mayor Ficks, there have been rumors that you're considering a run for the House of Representatives. How would the recent violence in your town affect that?"

A small murmur went up in the audience, but the mayor didn't even look surprised. She took a step forward and the chief handed her the microphone. "Right now I'm focusing on keeping West Riverdale as safe as it's been during my whole tenure." She stepped back and the next question was directed to the chief.

Look at our Gwen, being all mayor-ly. I felt proud that our little town of West Riverdale might have someone in Congress. Maybe she'd even buy my chocolates to give away to all of her hotshot DC friends.

Reese decided she'd been waving her skinny spider-monkey arms long enough without a response and stood. My stomach dropped. "It has been reported that Ms. Coburn died from poisoned chocolates made by Michelle Serrano." She turned to point to me in the back. "And she is planning to open her store again in a few days. How safe are her chocolates?"

"Well," the chief began before Detective Lockett moved in front of him at the podium.

"After thorough testing by the state crime lab, we verified that only the chocolates in the box and those ingested by the victim were poisoned. It was not accidental poisoning. The shop in question has been cleared because there are no safety issues."

Actual tears came to my eyes and I had to sniffle a little before Leo handed me the bandana hanging out of his back pocket. I was so grateful for Lockett's very public show of support. Leo put his arm around my shoulder for a manly hug.

"Interesting." Bean's eyes stayed on the detective.

But Reese didn't give up. "Would you eat her chocolate, detective?"

Mayor Gwen spoke up so loud she didn't need the mike. "Why Reese Everhard, are you ever gonna grow the heck up?" A little bit of her southern twang came through. "You're still mad that Michelle led the basketball team to the state finals all these years later?" She took a step forward to address the whole crowd. "People, this is the problem with our government right now. They're all stuck in high school like Reese here. It's time to *move on*."

"She's good," Bean's friend muttered. "Homey, loyal and professional all in the same package."

If his buddy was right about Gwen's intentions, it sounded like she had her campaign slogan. I could see the banners now: *Move On with Gwen Ficks*.

12

drove home in a hopeful daze that even the wild wind that was always a preview for a storm couldn't dim. I'd be back in my shop tomorrow. A lot of my neighbors, and customers, had come over to say good night, this time without the speculation that had been apparent earlier at the meeting. Leo had left as soon as he could, but Bean had stayed right by me. Sometimes our arms touched, which generated totally inappropriate zings through me just when the pastor of the local church offered me his warm wishes.

Reese had escaped right away, obviously cowed by the mayor's words. Maybe she'd leave me alone from now on.

Detective Lockett had been out the door as soon as the formal presentation part was over, skipping the cookies, coffee and gossip part of the evening. Bean had kept an eye on him as he left, as if he didn't quite trust him.

Already planning what chocolate magic I'd be whipping up the next day, I completely ignored the car parked across the street from my house. That is, until Reese got out and stood by my minivan door, blocking me in. I could either whack her out of the way, which I considered, or wait for her to say her piece and leave.

"Why is the mayor defending you?" she asked, her face tight with annoyance. And maybe embarrassment. "What do you have on her?"

"Oh, so that's the only answer?" I scoffed, trying not to feel intimidated.

"What?"

She couldn't hear me through the window and with the wind blowing through the giant oaks around my house. I lowered the window an inch. "You're losing your mind, Reese. The only reason the mayor said those things to you is because you sound like an idiot. You can't make up a conspiracy where there isn't one."

"Right," Reese said. "And that's why the state cop told everyone your chocolate was safe when he knows they found poison in your kitchen. And why the mayor threatened to take away my community education grant if I didn't leave you alone."

My disbelief must have shown on my face because she ramped up to yelling. "And why they're not talking about needles hidden in the Harris house." She flinched, as if she hadn't wanted to tell me that.

What? Needles found in Colleen's house? "How would you know what they found?" I asked. "Do you have a mole in the police department? Is that what they taught you in your online journalism class? Or maybe *you* planted the poison in my kitchen." I opened the minivan door, forcing her to jump back as I got out. "Did you kill Denise just to have a real story for once? And try to implicate me for some stupid revenge?"

To say she looked shocked was an understatement. She rocked back on her heels and her mouth opened and shut a few times. Not a good look for someone who already resembled a stork. More like a pelican now.

Then she slammed her jaw shut. "You listen to me, Michelle Serrano. You may think you can hide behind your bigwig friends, but I have the power of the press on my side and I'm going to prove you did it."

"You're barking up the wrong tree," I said. *And barking mad.* "And losing your chance to find the real killer." The "you idiot" was implied in my tone.

She stomped back to her car just as Erica drove up.

"What was that about?" Erica asked as she joined me in watching Reese drive away.

"She thinks we're in some conspiracy with the mayor and Lockett to hide what really happened with Denise," I said, my anger turning into confusion. "She said the police found needles at Mark and Colleen's." Worry tingled at the back of my neck.

Erica was stunned. "That's crazy."

"I know," I said. "Why didn't Bobby tell us?"

"You have to talk to him," she said. "Or maybe have Leo ask." Her voice trailed off and then she seemed to regroup. "Let's put that aside for now." Erica held out something shiny in her hand. "Guess what this is?"

I looked at it closely. "A flash drive?" I asked, with a sarcastic tone.

"And guess where I found it?" She tugged her backpack out of the front seat and threw it on her shoulder.

"I hate guessing games," I said. "Just tell me."

"In that book Denise mentioned to you," she said, a little smug. "*The Eighties at Echo Beach.*"

"What? You went in the shop? How does it look?" I was consumed with a desire to go to my home away from home, combined with an equal amount of dread at having to face the spot where Denise died.

"It looks great," she said. "The cleanup is done. We're on track to get in there tomorrow and open on Saturday. I'm using what Detective Lockett said tonight for the press release, and you'll need to send it out to all of your clients too."

Another bit of stress leaked away at her words.

"Did you see Coco?" When she looked confused, I explained. "I saw a stray cat there a few days ago, before all this happened. I named it Coco."

"Is it a brown tabby?"

"Yes," I said. "Was it there?"

"Its name is Puck."

I raised my eyebrows. "From Shakespeare? Really?"

"Really," she said, probably feeling defensive about such a silly name. "I fed it and gave it some water."

"Tonight?" I felt weirdly snubbed.

"Yes," she said. "When I found this." She held up the flash drive.

"What's on it?" I asked.

"I don't know," she said, "but let's find out."

We walked into the house, and I ran right into Erica's back as she stopped at the doorway of the kitchen.

"Uh-oh," she said.

I peeked around her. Our kitchen was trashed.

"Uh-oh," I repeated. My stomach dropped at the sight of something—sugar? flour?—tossed all over the counters and floor, and the words "Screw you!" written across the remaining pieces of the torn-up investigation project plan.

"I'm calling the police," Erica said and pulled her phone out.

"No, wait." I tried to make sense of this. "Let's figure out who this could be first." When she looked unsure, I said, "What if it was Mark?"

She put her phone back in her pocket and took a shaky breath. "What if it was Reese?"

"Could be," I said, being the calm one for once. "Let's think about what we want to have happen here. If we call the police, they'll see our project plan and they won't be happy."

Erica nodded. "But that message is rather threatening."

"It could be Larry, in which case we want the police to collect the evidence. And help to prove that Mark is innocent." I was arguing the other side now.

Both of us took in the scene and then Erica pulled her phone out again. "I'll take photos and video."

"I'll call Mark and ask him if he did it," I said. "And warn him that we're about to call the cops."

Mark denied knowing anything about the mess in our kitchen.

We called Bean first. He'd gone out with his reporter buddy after the meeting, but agreed to come home immediately, no questions asked.

Erica stayed close to the wall and took a ton of photos. I didn't know what we'd do with them, but it seemed like a good idea. "Michelle," she said. "Where's your computer?"

"What?" I rushed to the dining room, which I used as an office. It was easy enough to scoop everything off the table when we had a lot of friends over. My computer was where I'd left it.

Bean walked in and stood in the doorway. "Wow," he said mildly. "Someone's pissed."

"We've been debating calling the police," Erica said.

Another car drove up and parked in front of our house. "Oh, lovely," I said. "We're having a party." I looked outside and panicked. "Damn. It's Bobby."

Bean shrugged. "May as well let him in."

"You're not the one with a murder investigation project plan all over the wall," I hissed.

"I expect he'll break the door down if you don't answer," he said.

Bobby knocked. I took a deep breath and opened the door, standing in the way so he couldn't just walk in. "Hi Bobby," I said, oh so casually. "What's up?"

Bobby looked tired but his eyes became more alert as he noticed Bean standing in the doorway to the kitchen. "Is Erica here? I have a few questions for her."

"Now's not a good time," I said. "Can you stop back tomorrow?" I started to close the door and his hand shot out. His eyes went to the flour footprints on the floor leading from the kitchen. Damn those cop observation skills.

"What's going on?" he said.

"Nothing," I said in my high-pitched I'm-lying voice. I really had to work on that. "She'll call you."

With one hand, he pushed the door open and walked in, making sure not to disturb the footprints. "Where is she?"

Bean made an "after you" gesture toward the kitchen.

Bobby froze when he saw the mess. And Erica standing at the edge of it.

"What the hell?" He took a step inside and saw the project plan. His face darkened and he turned back to Bean.

"Did you know about this?" he asked him.

"This?" Bean pointed to the mess on the floor. "Or that?" He pointed to the wall. "Oh yeah. I knew about that."

"You see," Erica started, but Bobby held up his hand for her to stop. He closed his eyes as if trying to contain his temper.

She ignored him. "We came home and it was like this. We were just thinking of calling the police, but . . ." She caught the look on his face and trailed off. Very unlike her.

"Erica wanted to call," I backed her up, "but I talked her out of it because . . ."

"You didn't want the police to see that you're investigating a *murder*," he said.

"Well, when you put it that way . . ." I said.

Erica scowled at me as if I were jumping sides. "Look Bobby. You know this means more to us than it does to Lockett. We're just asking people some questions."

"Did you think that maybe we're asking the same people the same questions?" he asked. "Or are we too stupid to figure out what you can?"

Erica flinched, which seemed to cause him to lose steam. He took a step toward her and she looked down.

I felt like I was watching a Spanish soap opera without subtitles. Something was going on but I couldn't decipher the explanation. Too bad I could never get Erica to tell me what had happened between the two of them in high school.

I stepped in. "We're not cops. People might tell us things they won't tell you."

Bobby shoved his hand through his hair and put his cop face on. "This has got to stop."

I let out my breath. "We're not doing anything wrong. That plan is just to help us organize our thoughts. But we don't want Lockett or the chief to know until we have something to show for it."

He gestured toward the mess. "This looks like you have something to show for it," he said. "Someone obviously knows what you're up to."

"That's why we were going to call you, to get fingerprints or something," I said. "Because maybe it was Larry."

Bobby pointed to the "Screw you" message scrawled across the plan. "Apparently, it was someone on your list. What if it was Mark? Are you going to press charges?"

"It wasn't him," I said.

"So you called him to check?" His jaw tensed. "You know we can get a warrant for your phone records, right?"

"I just wanted to make sure he didn't get mad at us and do something stupid," I said.

"He's not *that* much of an idiot," Bean said.

Erica spoke up. "I think we should take this down now and invite Bobby's crime-scene techs to take fingerprints."

"They'll know you removed something," he said. "And how are you going to get over there?"

"Like this," she said, and walked right through, leaving narrow shoe prints in her wake. She threw a laughing glance over her shoulder to Bobby and his face softened as if against his will. "Don't tell."

I t was hours later when the last tech left. Detective Lockett was busy doing something else, and after being drilled by the chief, I was allowed to leave to purchase more flour and sugar. Erica had explained the footprints by saying her cell phone was on the other side and she didn't realize she shouldn't walk through. We hid the remnants of our plan in my minivan. I was grateful our intruder hadn't found my chocolate supplies still in their boxes; it would've taken another day to have more delivered and made it impossible to open on Saturday.

Bobby was about to get in his car when I arrived back at home, and I decided to ask him something that had been stuck in the back of my mind. It went along with what Reese had told me, and I couldn't discuss it with Erica or Bean. "I know we've caused you a lot of trouble," I started and he gave me a look that said "ya-think?" loud and clear.

"Can I ask just one more question? Is Colleen a suspect?"

"Off the record?" He glanced at the house as if making sure Erica wasn't watching.

"Sure," I said. Luckily I wasn't a reporter and didn't have to worry about journalistic ethics.

"She's on the list, but we verified that she didn't open Denise's text until morning," he said. "As far as we know, Denise was about to tell her about her husband's affair, but was giving Mark one last chance to tell her himself."

"Okay, thanks," I said. "What a mess, huh?"

"You said it," he said as he got in his cruiser.

"Is this," I gestured toward the house, "something we should worry about?" I immediately felt like a wimp.

He hesitated and got out again. "The reason I stopped by is it's clear someone is trying to implicate Mark. Additional evidence was found in his house. So any information you guys know, you need to tell us."

"You mean the needles?" I asked.

"How do you know about that?" he demanded.

"Reese yelled it to me when she was pissed," I said. "I don't think she meant to. So it's true?"

He nodded.

"Bobby," I said. "You guys have to realize that no one is stupid enough to leave needles they used for a murder in their own house."

"You'd be surprised."

"Okay, Mark and Colleen aren't stupid enough," I insisted. "Someone tried to frame them, very clumsily, I might add. And that was after trying to implicate me."

His eyes smiled. "You gotta stop playing detective." He looked up when Erica's shadow fell across the window. "I'll let you know if an arrest is . . . imminent."

I watched him drive away but a small part of me wondered what the chances were that Colleen had seen Denise's messages on Mark's phone. And what she'd be capable of if she did, even if Denise was her best friend.

When I went inside, Bean and Erica had started cleaning. We finished quickly, but I knew we'd be finding flour and sugar in odd places for a long time. Ant season was sure to be a killer.

Bobby and the crime-scene tech surmised that someone

had come in and scouted out the ground floor, stopping to search my computer, where the techs had found fingerprints not belonging to any of us. They wouldn't tell us if the prints were Larry's.

If it *was* Larry, and he was searching for the laptop he'd dropped outside Denise's apartment, he'd be able to tell very quickly that it wasn't the same computer. Mine was plastered with stickers of mouthwatering truffles all over it.

I reminded myself to back up my data as soon as the techs left. Although sadly nothing had changed about my business since it had auto–backed up on Sunday.

At some point, the prowler had gone upstairs, taking two hundred dollars in cash from Erica's desk, rifling through her papers and then finally ending up in the kitchen.

There he or she had made the kitchen a disaster area, and left, according to the flour and sugar-filled footprints. Bobby knew, but the techs didn't, that our little project plan was most likely what caused him or her to go nuts.

If it was Larry, he must be pretty desperate to get that computer if he'd risk breaking and entering when the whole town was looking for him. Or maybe he knew that everyone who was anyone would be at that meeting.

Luckily, Erica had her laptop with the whole investigation on it, and we were able to rebuild the plan on the wall after Bean went upstairs.

"The flash drive!" she said. "I can't believe I forgot it." She pulled out the drive from her pocket and stuck it into the side of her computer. I finished taping up the last sheet of paper and looked over her shoulder.

A pop-up asking for a password appeared on the screen.

"Shoot," she said. She tried a few different words but nothing opened it. "Maybe Zane can crack it. You know, he worked on her website. People use the same password for lots of things. He may even know what hers was." She pulled out her phone to send a text. "I'll have him meet us at the store tomorrow."

"We could always give it to Bobby," I said.

She gave me a "yeah right" sneer. "Maybe after we copy it. If he's nice."

"So what the hell happened with you two?" I asked her.

"Who?" she asked, but her face stiffened.

"Nice try," I said. "With you and Bobby. It seems like you guys have some unfinished business."

Erica's face closed down. *"There is no past that we can bring back by longing for it."*

"Is that a quote or something? Does that mean you're longing for your past with Bobby?" I asked. "Tell me."

"It's not important." But her stressed tone made that a lie.

I went for the big guns. "Denise is dead. We worked with her for almost two years and hardly knew her. Don't you wish you'd straight out asked her why she wanted to be a photographer so bad? Or what the deal was with all the bad boys? Or how she got all that hair to stay in place with one little pin? And really, any of us could have found those chocolates and eaten one." I gave a fake shudder and paused.

"I'd never have known why you two broke up." I was shameless. But it was time for her to spill. "It must have been pretty bad if you can't forgive him so many years later."

She thought for a second and then took a deep breath, as

if she'd made a decision. "So it was our senior year," she began. "And I got that full-ride scholarship to Stanford."

"What did Bobby do?" I, like the rest of the town, believed that he was the one who'd screwed up.

"Nothing."

"What?" I said, surprised. "Really?"

She paused. "Everyone assumed he did something wrong." She looked a little lost, so unlike her. "But it was me."

"What happened?" I asked.

"There was this admitted student weekend on campus," she said, "and my parents let me fly out there."

"Okay," I said.

"And." Her voice got quiet. "I met someone."

"Oh." And then a longer, "Oooh."

"Actually, I met a lot of people, from around the world, who were so smart and accomplished." She paused. "And sophisticated."

"Hmm," I said encouragingly.

"And I got this stupid idea that I didn't want to be held back by my state-school boyfriend." She sounded thoroughly disgusted with her eighteen-year-old self. "So I broke up with him."

"Ah."

"Right before graduation."

"Uh-huh," I said.

"And then he drove his motorcycle through the stands, ended up in jail, and lost his scholarship to UM," she said. "So when you say he looks at me, he's not looking at me the way you think. He's looking at me because I ruined his life."

"Hmm," I said. "His life doesn't seem very ruined to me.

He's perfectly happy being Lieutenant Bobby here in West Riverdale."

She looked like she didn't believe me.

I went on. "And when he's looking at you, I *know* he's not thinking you ruined his life. He's thinking he'd like to ruin those clothes you're wearing." She looked confused. "Like rip them off and haul you off to that goddess bed of yours."

Erica flushed.

"But you'll never know until you ask him."

She avoided my gaze, but I think I saw interest flare. "Maybe I will. So what's going on with you and Bean?"

"Nothing!" Turnabout was not fair play.

13

The next morning I sat in my car outside the shop. It was dawn and for the first time ever, I wasn't sure I wanted to go in.

The shop felt threatening, all dark and closed up in the early morning gloom, instead of full of possibilities. Who killed Denise? Someone I knew? Why did they use my chocolates? Could it really be Mark?

I took a deep breath.

Erica had warned me that the store would feel different. She'd taken all of my equipment from home to be part of the cleanup and they'd told her that my kitchen shelves and drawers would be empty and my spic-and-span utensils, pots and bowls would be piled up on the tables for me to put away. My storeroom was bare. I didn't want to think about what they'd done in the dining area where Denise had died.

Then Coco leapt up onto the porch, as if waiting to welcome me. I got out of the car and sat on the porch that was damp with morning dew. Coco climbed into my lap, purring loudly and making me feel better. After a minute of petting, she nipped my thumb as if to say, "Where's the food?" Erica drove up. The cat took one look at the car and ran off.

Erica got out, wearing a Chocolates by Michelle T-shirt. "I thought you were running," she said, "or I'd have been here sooner."

I jumped up to hug her, and heard another car approach. It was Kona, in her decade-old Honda decorated with Hawaiian hibiscus flower decals, with Kayla in the front seat.

Tears popped into my eyes at the unwavering support of my friends.

Kona yawned as she got out and threw her peace bag over her shoulder. "Are we ready?" Her brain kicked in. "Oh my God. Did they throw out the coffee?"

I laughed and shoved a new five-pound bag of Dublin Roasters coffee beans into her hands. "Your first duty is to make the strongest coffee you can. We're going to need it."

"I second that motion," Kayla said, pushing back an adorable curl that had fallen into her eyes. Her mop of blond ringlets was even more disheveled than normal.

Erica did the honors and opened the door. I noticed right away that the scent of chocolate was missing. But by the time we'd emptied the minivan of the bags of chocolate and other supplies that had heavily damaged my credit card, it was starting to smell more like it should. My home away from home.

The four of us moved to the dining area and stood silent for a moment. The cleaning company had taken away the couch and rearranged the furniture. Most people wouldn't notice the new arrangement but it was jarring to me. "I don't like the flow," I said.

"It's fine," Erica said, but her voice was gentle. "Let's get to work."

Even though I knew everything was clean, I felt the need to wash it all again. First I put out food for Coco, expecting it to be back at some point. I started tempering my new batch of chocolate on the stove while we scrubbed, and then began to put everything back in the kitchen where it belonged.

When it was time to cook, I told Erica she should work on what she needed to do to reopen the book store. Kona and I had developed a rhythm long ago that worked well, and Kayla was beginning to understand how the process flowed.

Erica wasn't known for her attention to detail in the kitchen, and cheerfully left to work with her books. "Zane should be in soon," she said on her way out. "He found a first edition of *A is for Alibi* at an estate sale yesterday. It's not in the best shape, but may be worth a lot."

We'd decided not to make a big deal of our little side project and didn't mention the flash drive to my assistants.

As if summoned by her words, Zane strolled in from the back door, dressed like an eighties Ralph Lauren commercial. With his argyle sweater, Bermuda shorts and boat shoes, he looked like the kind of rich kid from the Eastern Shore who'd be voted "Most Likely to Take Over Daddy's Business" in his yearbook.

Since his dad was an organic goat farmer, I doubted that was Zane's plan. I think he'd do anything to avoid goats.

He'd found the perfect job as Erica's assistant and all-around techie for her used and rare book business. His mother had been the town librarian for years, so maybe loving books was genetic. He was also getting his computer science degree and had built our very cool website that included everything about my chocolates, Erica's new books and an auction site for her rare books. He'd created websites for a lot of the Main Street shops.

Maybe the preppy look was a thing among computer kids. The older I got, the more I realized that tons of sub-cultures existed out there that I knew nothing about.

Erica jumped up from her stool. "Did you bring it?"

"Of course," he said. "Let me get my gloves." They headed off toward his office, which was basically a reno-vated storage closet.

After tucking her long sleeves in her oven mitts to avoid the often spattering caramel, Kona poured the sugar into the hot pan and began stirring, the most backbreaking job in the kitchen. It required single-minded attention. The slightest mistake could send it into a smoking mess. A bigger mistake could result in a fire that would stink up the place for days.

I checked the temperature of the tempering chocolate and then put a huge pot onto the second stove to work on the ganache. I poured in the cream and stirred. I'd been a little worried that the chocolate would somehow feel toxic to me, but I was at peace for the first time all week.

Every two hours we took a break to stretch our backs, arms and shoulder muscles and get off our feet for a while. We'd made enough caramel for hundreds of our standard sized Fleur de Sel Caramels and several hundred more of my tiny giveaway "gateway drug" caramels. The caramel filling would need to cool overnight so we could finish them in the morning, including sprinkling my special sea salt on top.

Since the secret was out, I assigned my cousin's bachelorette chocolates to Kona, who thought the project was hilarious. She even volunteered to ship them and get them out of sight.

We'd also finished batches of the tangy Raspberry Surprise Darks and Milks and refreshing Mint Julep Milks, which were cooling on my shelving unit. All was right in my little world.

Erica joined us for the second breather. Of course, our conversation turned to Denise's murder.

"So who do you think did it?" Kona asked and took a drink from her chai tea.

"Killed Denise?" Erica asked matter-of-factly. "What do you think?" She'd taken me aside a little earlier to let me know that Zane had tried all of Denise's passwords that he knew and none of them had worked on the flash drive. Now he was using some kind of program that hackers use to crack passwords. I didn't even want to know if it was legal.

Kona pulled her sandwich out of a paper bag. "People keep talking about her ex-boyfriend from Westminster."

"He's at the top of the list for me," I said.

"He's a strong suspect," Erica said, taking a sip of her coffee. "But maybe we're all just trying to reassure ourselves that it's not someone we know in West Riverdale."

"Anyone else people are talking about?" I asked Kona.

She looked sheepishly at Erica. "Well, everyone knows about . . . Mark."

Erica nodded. "Of course. Who else?"

Kayla jumped in. "Well, Opal saw Denise taking photos in the Giant Eagle parking lot and went off on her. It was a few days before she died," she said. "She even knocked over Denise's tripod and her camera broke."

"Was Opal mad about the senior portrait job?" I asked.

"That's what I heard," Kayla said. "She accused Denise of sleeping with someone on the school board to get that gig. Then Denise yelled back saying she didn't need to get the job like Opal did."

"That sounds intense," Erica said. "Is that true about Opal getting the job that way?"

Kayla shrugged. "It was forever ago. Who knows?"

"Anyone else?" Erica asked.

Kona gave me a sideways glance.

"Me?" I asked, horrified. "What possible reason would I have?" It was barely palatable for crazy Reese to have her conspiracy theories, but my neighbors? People I see every day?

"Not really." Her words rushed out. "They just watch too many cop shows where anyone remotely attached to the victim is a potential suspect. And, you know, they say poison is a women's weapon."

"What possible motive do I have in this fictional world they live in?" I asked.

She looked down, obviously not wanting to answer.

"Tell me," I insisted.

"Well," she started reluctantly. "One story is because you were secretly in love with Larry."

I rolled my eyes. "Even Denise wasn't secretly in love with that scumbag."

"Another is that you wanted to take over her space." She rolled her eyes like that was ridiculous.

"And I'm willing to kill for it?"

"People are idiots," she said, with the cynicism of a twenty-year-old.

"Who else?" Erica asked.

"That angry butterfly lady," Kayla said. "Everyone knows she was mad at Denise for keeping her out of some dumb art group."

"What do *you* think?" Erica asked.

Kona frowned. "She was a photographer. I think she got photos of someone doing something they shouldn't."

Like maybe Mark, I couldn't help thinking.

Erica stuck her head into the kitchen. "You have to see these," she said, holding her computer. "Zane really came through—broke the password on the flash drive."

I was painting gold cocoa butter on my milk chocolate coins with a racing horse imprint for the upcoming Preakness.

"Five minutes," I said.

"Hurry." Her face was deadly serious. "It's important."

I put down my brush. "Show me."

She turned the computer around. Two enlarged photos of Larry carrying a computer monitor and then a bulging bag out of a house at night filled the screen.

"Is that who I think it is?"

"Yep," Erica said. "And look at this." She clicked over to another page that reported crimes in the area. A burglary in one of the new developments was highlighted. "Zane matched the photo geotags to that house."

"What's a geotag?"

"It's info that can be automatically attached to a digital photo," she explained. "Denise recorded a lot of technical data with her photos. Photographers like to do that so they can evaluate how the photo came out based on how they set it up. She also recorded time, date, latitude and longitude. Zane matched it to that house at the same date and time that it was broken into."

"Holy cow!" I said. "That's why Larry was searching for her computer. She had proof of him stealing stuff from that house."

"And if he knew she had these photos," Erica said, "it might be motive enough to kill her."

14

"Any other photos on that drive?" I asked.

"This one." She clicked on the final photo. It showed Larry about to enter a small, run-down house, the only light coming from a single bulb hanging from a wire above the porch. "And one more that has a different password. Zane's still working on it."

"Maybe that house is where he lives," I said. "What does the geotag say about that?"

"It's in a pretty bad area of Frederick," she said. "Well, as bad as Frederick gets. It's listed as Larry's address, so I'm sure the police are all over it."

"I guess we should hand this over to Bobby," I said.

"Yep," she said. "Zane already made copies."

"We also need to blow up one of those to show Jake at the Ear." I was hesitant to work on Denise's murder investigation. After getting back to the safety of my kitchen I didn't want to leave.

"Done," she said. "I'll have Zane call Bobby and handle the transfer."

I flapped my elbows and clucked like a chicken.

"Just busy," she insisted.

"So, are we both thinking that Denise maybe used these photos to . . . blackmail Larry?" I asked. It seemed ludicrous.

"Based on what we learned from Jake at the Ear and what Henna said about Denise's financial situation suddenly righting itself, that seems to be one logical conclusion," she said. "Maybe we should talk to Yuli about Henna's claim that Denise had trouble paying the rent."

Yuli Gorshkov was our landlord. His family had bought up most of the Main Street buildings after moving over from Russia in the 1940s and he still held on to his accent. Everyone thought he was in his eighties, but he'd looked eighty when I was in grade school.

"Do we have any reason to ask him to come in?" I asked her. "Maybe we can get him talking while he's here to confirm that, and to find out where the money came from." Although I'd never had much luck getting him to talk.

"I could ask him to check out that loose floorboard outside your kitchen," Erica suggested. "I'll tell him you're concerned that someone could trip over it."

"You could add that I almost fell carrying scalding hot chocolate."

Erica looked alarmed. "You did?"

"No, but it's entirely possible," I said. "Even without a loose board."

"I'll call him now," she said.

Everyone knew that he spent as much time as he could in his garden. "It's sunny out," I said. "Not a chance of him answering."

Of course, Yuli didn't answer, but Erica left a message and he surprised the heck out of me by showing up at the store as we were about to clean up. Kona, Kayla and I had finished up the day making chocolate bars. I was exhausted and happy.

Yuli came in the back door with his ancient toolbox in tow. He had white hair that wanted to stick straight up, stooped shoulders and a perpetual grumpy expression for anything that dragged him away from his flower gardens.

I was in the process of running some chocolates to the wine cooler we keep in the front kitchen when I almost ran right into him with a tray full of Dark Passion Fruit Truffles. Only years of experience juggling errant trays kept me from dropping the whole lot . . . and knocking down an old man in his eighties wouldn't have been a good idea either.

"No pets!" he said.

"What?"

He raised a gnarled finger. "One of you is feeding a cat outside. No pets."

"Um," I said. "Okay." I should've cleaned that up before he came over. Next time, I'd be more careful.

He stared down at the floorboard that rose a little at the end. "This one?"

"That's the one," I said in my most friendly voice, hoping

he'd forget about Coco. "We've hammered it down but it keeps popping up."

"Probably dry rot," he said dourly.

"What?" Anything with rot in it sounded bad to me. Dry rot, root rot, foxtrot.

He waved me away. "I handle. I handle," he said. He dropped the toolbox with a clang and struggled to get down on his knees. I felt terrible for making him do that. The first thing he did was pull out a knee pillow and step his knees up onto it. He pulled out a crowbar to lift the edge of the board and peek under.

"Sorry to bother you with this, but my cart catches on it. And I always worry when we bring field trips through here. Can I get you anything?" I asked. "I don't have your favorite Banana Toffees done yet, but the Raspberry Surprise Milks are amazing."

"No." He put his hand to his back and stood up with a struggle. "I'll be back."

He had to know he sounded just like the Terminator when he said that line in his accent.

I was going to protest, but he left his toolbox off to the side, so I knew he really was coming back.

I was scraping chocolate drips off the linoleum floor in the kitchen when I heard Yuli return. I handed the scraper to Kayla and found Yuli lowering himself back down to the floor with a Duncan Hardware bag beside him.

"Can you fix it?" I put down a plate of raspberry chocolates and a cup of coffee within reach.

He grunted his thanks, and took a bite of one and a loud slurp of coffee.

"Yes," he said. "It is, how you say?" He held his hand out straight and then bent it.

"Warped?"

"Yes."

"So how's the landlord business?" I asked, leaning on the wall.

He glared up at me from the floor, his bushy eyebrows coming together in suspicion. "Not lowering rent," he said loudly.

"Oh no!" I said. Although now that he brought it up . . . I mentally shook myself and focused on my mission.

He lifted the edge of the board and squirted yellow glue underneath it.

"Have your other tenants asked for a reduction in rent?"

"No." He pulled out a nail and hit it with a hammer several times.

When he stopped to check that it was smooth with the wood surface, I jumped in. "I heard that Denise was having trouble with finances, before, you know."

He glared at me. "You pay rent on time?"

"Of course."

"Okay." He pulled out another nail and hammered a few more times.

I guess that meant I should mind my own business. I turned to get Erica before our prey escaped and ran right into Bean.

"What are you up to?" he asked, amused. His hand stayed on my arm, sending a delicious shiver down my spine.

"Trying to find out if Denise was having money troubles before she died," I whispered defensively.

"Let me try." He walked past me to Yuli and spoke rapidly in what sounded like Russian.

Yuli's face lit up and he returned the greeting, standing up and grabbing Bean by the shoulders to hug him.

How did Bean do that? I'd never, ever seen Yuli smile. Maybe I needed to learn Russian. They launched into a fast-paced conversation. At some point, Yuli gestured to me and asked dubiously, "Podruga?"

Bean smiled at me and said something back that made Yuli laugh.

"Back in a minute," Bean said and they moved to the back door. Yuli held the door while Bean picked up a cement block Yuli must have left there.

"You got a towel you don't care about?" Bean asked and I pulled the one off my shoulder.

"Put it over the board," he said, and then placed the block on it.

Yuli moved it to exactly where he wanted it. "Don't move for two days," he told me in a stern voice, and then switched to more delighted Russian with Bean.

He better have coughed up the info for Bean, I thought, just as Erica joined us and spoke in Russian as well.

"Of course you speak Russian," I said to her.

"Just a few words," she admitted. "Bean is the expert."

"What does something like pa-droo-ga mean?" I said.

"Girlfriend," she said absently, focusing on a new conversation Bean was having.

Girlfriend? Right. Bean had dated freakin' models before spending so much time in Africa. And not just models. Models who had half a brain.

I gave up trying to be part of the group and went to find our *Be Careful. Wet Floor* sign to put over the cement block. The solution was going to be more of an issue than the problem over the next two days.

We hovered in the area until Yuli packed up. Bean carried the toolbox outside to Yuli's pickup truck.

"What did he say?" I asked as soon as Bean came back in, trying to ignore how cute he was with his hair all windswept.

He waved us both into the back hallway, away from the kitchen. "Denise was more than three months behind in her rent," he said quietly.

I gasped. "She could've been evicted for that."

"Did Yuli tell the police?" Erica asked.

"No," Bean said. "He doesn't want his other tenants to know and try to get away with being late. Then about two weeks ago, she paid it all in full." He paused. "In cash."

"Holy cow," I said. "That's a lot of cash."

"Did Yuli ask where she got it?" Erica asked.

"Yes," Bean said. "He asked if she'd robbed a bank and she said no, that an old friend owed her money and finally paid up."

I was restocking chocolate bars on Erica's cashier stand. "An old friend who owed her? It had to be Larry the Loser."

"It certainly gives our blackmail theory credence," Erica said.

"You should ask Colleen what she knows," I said. "They were best friends."

"Ask Colleen what?" I heard behind me.

"Speak of the devil," Erica said.

"You know I hate that expression," Colleen said in her cranky voice. Of course, she must be grieving the loss of her friend. And her husband's affair. And his being a suspect. Worse, she had one of the twins in full snotty-nose mode on her hip. He laid his head on her shoulder and sucked his thumb, obviously sick. She certainly wasn't here to help in the store.

I took a step back. "We heard that Denise was behind on rent. Did you know why?"

Her already tired face drooped even further as she nodded. "She didn't want anyone to know. She thought it would hurt her business even more."

"Was the studio having problems?" Erica asked.

"She was doing okay, until that scummy ex-boyfriend stole five thousand dollars from her," she said.

"Five thousand?" I couldn't keep the shock out of my voice.

"Yep." Colleen shifted her son to her other hip. "He drained her savings and took off."

I had a flash of anger at both of them. What did she expect messing with a criminal? "But two weeks ago she paid off her rent in cash."

Colleen looked surprised. "She didn't tell me that, but then, she hadn't talked to me much lately." Her face grew sad for a moment, and then she turned to Erica. "Can you babysit tonight?"

Say no, I thought. Erica couldn't afford to get whatever sickness germ-boy was carrying.

"I'm pretty busy getting ready to reopen," Erica said. "What about Bean?"

Colleen gave her a "yeah right" look and waited.

"Okay," Erica said.

Noooo!

Colleen thanked her and said she'd drop the kids off later, her fatigue undeniable.

"Makes you wonder if it's all worth it." I watched as she turned the corner and went out the back.

"What?" Erica set the latest Michael Connelly bestseller on a display stand.

"The whole kid thing."

Erica looked at me like I was crazy. "Of course it is. Those kids are adorable."

Adorable?

Just then Zane came rushing out. "I got it!" He opened his laptop on the tiny bit of counter not covered with books.

"You have the last photo?" Erica asked.

"Yeah," he said and then paused, turning his laptop away. "It's a little R-rated."

"No problem," I said and then wished I hadn't. A photo of Larry asleep on his stomach, naked, appeared on the screen. "No!" I covered my eyes with my hands. "Now I can never un-see that!"

"Sorry," Zane said.

Erica reached over to touch the keypad. With a few clicks, she zoomed in on Larry's butt.

"What are you doing?" I demanded. "My eyes are already bleeding!"

"I want to see his tattoo," she said, as if she wasn't staring at a photo of a naked man. "It says 'No Regrets' but it's spelled 'Regerts.' " She couldn't help but laugh.

"I'll bet he *regerts* that," I said. "So you want to print that photo out to show Jake?"

"That guy looks nekked," Bean said from behind us.

I jumped. "We have to start locking that door."

"You just missed Colleen," Erica said, trying to change the subject. "She wants you to babysit."

"I heard," he said, moving closer, "which is why I'm avoiding her."

"So you can handle African warlords, but you can't handle two-year-olds?" I asked.

"Damn right." Then he paused. "So you read my book?"

"Of course I read it." Did he think I couldn't read?

He smiled and then pointed to the photo. "Who's that?"

Erica rolled her eyes at his big-brother attitude. "Larry," she said. He already knew our theory about Larry from the project plan and she filled him in on the photos Zane had found on the flash drive of Larry burglarizing a house. "We always thought he was the one who broke into her studio. Colleen said he took money from her. Maybe Denise used these to force him into paying her back."

I added, "Jake Hale said Denise had a fight with a guy at the Ear over some photographs. We're going to take a photo—not *that* one—to see if that guy was Larry."

Bean looked thoughtful. "Do you think she was capable of blackmail?"

"I think we're all capable of many things when our back is to the wall," Erica said.

A tingle of unease tickled the back of my neck.

Bean pointed to something colorful in the corner of the photograph. "Can you blow that up and see what it is?"

"Sure," Zane said. With a few clicks, a part of a neon sign appeared. Blurry, but obviously from the sleazy motel with a reputation for bedbugs in Normal, the next town over from West Riverdale.

Bean got an intrigued expression on his face. "Maybe I should take a trip over there tonight."

"Why?" Erica said. "Don't you have a phone interview with *The Guardian*?"

"This publicity stuff is boring as hell." He stared at the photo, but this time he had the look of a predator hunting his prey. "Do me a favor and wait until tomorrow to give Bobby the flash drive. I just want to see if I can talk to Larry before Bobby does."

I found myself holding my breath for Erica's response.

"Why?" Erica asked.

"Maybe I can get a story out of it," he said.

She didn't back down. "You don't do local stories."

"All news is local news," he said. "Besides, I need something to do while I'm in town."

"No way," she said.

I let out my breath with a soft *whew*.

"Not without me," she said, surprising the heck out of me.

"What?" I said, even though it made me feel like a wuss. What was she thinking? Bean was used to dealing with dangerous situations, not Erica. "I'm going too." I felt a nervous quiver in my stomach.

Bean said to Erica, "You're babysitting." And to me, "Be ready at eight."

I could feel my face freeze, which of course Erica noticed. "You don't have to go."

Bean grinned at me and it felt like a dare. "Come on. It'll be fun."

"I'll be there," I said. *What was I thinking?*

His energy level had jumped a few levels as he walked out, totally expecting me to join him.

"Are you sure?" Erica asked, knowing I didn't go in for adventure.

"It's our store," I said. "And our fudge cook-off." I took a deep breath. "And our friend." Besides, even Larry wouldn't be stupid enough to go back to the same motel.

15

let Erica lock up and I drove over to the hardware store to get a new air filter for spray-painting my chocolates. I had put off making several of my truffles until the next day, knowing my display case would be more appealing with a multicolored mix. I had limited molds and distinguished between different flavors by using different colors. It also made it easier for us to memorize what was inside, and for our customers to be reminded of their favorites.

Just as I was about to go in, I heard a familiar gruff voice say, "Hand it over," from the side parking lot.

I snuck over and peeked around the corner. I saw Howard pull a thick, folded-up envelope from his red Duncan Hardware apron pocket and hand it to the building inspector, a man I disliked with every fiber of my being. He'd made our renovation as painful as he could. I swore he was a sociopath who delighted in the misfortune of others and had the perfect job to make that misfortune happen.

It was the guilty expression on Howard's face that made me slam my body up against the wall so they couldn't see me. I peeked around the corner again and saw the building inspector reach into the envelope and pull out a wad of cash.

What?

He fanned it as if counting it by touch and then shoved it back into the envelope.

Beatrice slammed open the store's side screen door and yelled, "Howard! You need to get a ladder down!" in the you're-an-idiot tone of the long married.

"A minute!" he yelled back.

"Customer waiting!" she responded.

The building inspector snorted and got back into his car, muttering something about wearing the pants in the family. Howard went back into the store.

I waited, breathing hard, as the inspector drove away.

If I hadn't needed that air filter so bad, I would've run back right away and told Erica what I'd seen. Instead, I calmed myself down and went in the front door. "Hi, Beatrice!" I spoke too loudly but she was busy checking out a customer and didn't seem to notice. "I'm just here to get a new filter."

"Okay," she said over the beeps of her machine. "You guys must be busy in there today."

"Yep," I said. "Right back." I went down the aisle and picked up two filters. I glanced toward the back and saw Howard putting the ladder away on a rack. I guess the customer hadn't wanted it after all.

"Any news from that Hillary lady?" she asked when I returned to the front.

"No," I said. "Right now we're just focused on the opening. And Denise's funeral."

She tsk-tsked. "Such a shame." She put my filters in a bag. "I'll be there, but I'm so sad that I won't be able to buy much chocolate." She glanced back at Howard. "Money's tight these days."

When I got back to the shop, Erica was still there, and she didn't take the news well. Everyone loved Howard Duncan. Could he be paying off the building inspector to get approvals for something he shouldn't? I guess my attempts to get on the inspector's good side with chocolates wasn't what worked on someone like him.

Had Denise found out about it? I knew I was reaching, but did Denise have more than one blackmail victim?

Before I risked my life tracking down the criminally minded Larry, I wanted to make sure we were going after the right person, so Erica and I decided to catch dinner at the Ear in order to show Jake a photo of Larry. We hoped to hit a double and talk to Opal as well. She hadn't returned my call yet. I still didn't know what we'd ask her. "Did you kill Denise?" probably wouldn't work.

Jake gave us a warm wave when we walked in. The bar was pretty empty, so we sat there. We ordered appetizers for dinner, my idea of culinary heaven. The only food I was snobby about was chocolate. Opal was nowhere in sight, but maybe it was too early for her.

When Jake delivered our beers, Erica pulled out the photo with Larry's face enlarged to see it better. "So, Jake," she said, trying to be casual. "Is this the guy who had an argument with Denise?"

He checked it out. "That's him." He set our glasses on napkins and then he realized what we were doing. "Wait. Where'd you get that?"

"It was just in a file . . . " I tried.

"What are you doing? Playing Nancy Drew?" He took out a small bowl, poured in a spicy nut mixture, and placed it in front of us.

"What do you mean?"

"I heard you guys were asking people questions." He looked amused. "Just leave it to the cops."

"Of course," Erica said. "We're just gathering information for them and we wanted to confirm a theory."

"What theory?" he asked with some sarcasm.

"We'll let you know when we prove it," she said. "So Opal is one of your very good customers, is she not?"

Is she not? I sent Erica an are-you-kidding look.

Jake smiled. "If you say so. She's here sometimes."

"Was she here Sunday night?"

His smile disappeared. "Look, I kinda have a Vegas thing going in here with the regulars. What happens at the Ear stays at the Ear."

"That's commendable," Erica said. "But I'm sure it doesn't hurt anyone to answer the question. It could actually help her. So how late was she here?"

"Late," he admitted. "We're supposed to close up early on Sundays but we started these pool tournaments and sometimes they go after closing. The blue law says we have until midnight, but that doesn't sit too well with our neighbors if the customers get a little loud. So I lock the door at ten except for the regulars."

"Who was here?" I asked.

"Why you gotta know that?" he complained.

"If they were here, they weren't killing Denise," I said which sounded way more shocking out loud than in my head.

Jake winced and Erica took over. "It'll eliminate them as suspects," she said in a reasonable tone.

"Why are you getting involved in all this suspect stuff?" But it was more of a grumble than a real question.

"We heard that Opal's been ranting about Denise," I said. "Was she talking about her on Sunday?"

"Yeah," he said. "She was on a tear."

"What did she say?" Erica asked, her pen poised over her notebook.

He shrugged. "Some crap about Denise sleeping with someone to get that school gig so fast."

"Did anyone pay attention to her?" I asked.

"Not really," he said. "She was just outta control. Peter got her calmed down."

"Peter who?" I asked.

"Palladine," he said.

"The principal?" I wasn't exactly shocked. It just seemed weird that he had a real social life.

"Yeah," he said. "He comes here sometimes when his wife is doing overnights at her clinic."

"What did he say to calm her down?" Erica asked.

"I didn't pay that much attention," he said. "I have a job to do, you know."

"Did you hear any of it?" I asked.

"Yeah," he said. "Peter told her he'd look into it for her."

"And that worked?"

"Eventually," Jake said. "Except then she said maybe he was the one who slept with Denise, but some others told her that was bull and to shut her mouth. She's always a pain in the ass when she drinks Scotch."

"When did Opal leave?" Erica asked.

"A little after ten," he answered without looking at us.

"She was okay to drive?" I asked.

"No way," Jake said. "I asked someone to drive her home."

"So she was incapacitated," Erica said.

"Oh yeah," he said. "She was hitting it that night. Hard."

"Who took her home?"

"What does that matter?" he said. "Her car was still here in the morning so she must have passed out at home. No way she was able to do anything in that condition."

"So you're sure she didn't have the wherewithal to . . ."

"No she didn't have the 'wherewithal' to kill Denise," he finished for her. He moved to the other end of the bar, totally sulking.

Well, that cleared suspect number two.

Somehow I couldn't imagine Principal Palladine sitting at the end of the bar nursing a beer. Did he wear his sports jacket with the suede elbow patches?

Jake slapped down our plump crab cakes and baked potato skins, dripping with cheese.

"Can you let us know the next time Opal comes in?" Erica asked him, and he nodded.

I couldn't resist one last question. "So what does everyone think about Peter being here?" It was hard not to call him

Principal Palladine. "Don't they worry he'll write them up for detention?"

Jake smiled. "They didn't like it at first, but they got used to it. Come to think of it, they behave better. Until he leaves, and then they revert to their normal revolting behavior." He said it with such affection, I knew he was kidding.

It was eight on the dot and Bean was still on the phone in the living room, where he had escaped to once Colleen had arrived with the twins. Ten minutes before, he'd started pacing, so I assumed he was growing impatient to get going.

Erica had the boys upstairs while Colleen and Mark met with his lawyer. They were driving into his office in DC; given the traffic, they'd probably get back to pick up the kids the next day. Or maybe the day after that.

I was happy to delay our attempt to track down Larry, and busied myself updating the project plan. Erica and I had discussed our latest suspect with relish: Wayne Chauncey, building inspector and general pain in the butt. Erica was sure he wasn't a sociopath out to cause as much damage as he could. At the very least, he was the complete definition of "crotchety old man." He knew every contractor trick in the book, and he didn't trust my newfangled machinery, as he called it about a hundred times.

Anyone who required three visits to approve my state-of-the-art dehumidifier, a complete necessity to a chocolatier in the humidity of Maryland, was clearly unsuited to his job. I'd even enlisted members of the town council, showing them how awesome it was so that they'd encourage Chauncey to approve it.

But I couldn't imagine that mild-mannered, generally henpecked Howard Duncan was capable of murder. He'd been the town handyman ever since he was a young man and was well known for being painstakingly honest. If a job ended up being harder or taking longer than he expected, he still stuck to the original quote. He and Beatrice had just won Lifetime Community Service awards from the West Riverdale Rotary Club, honors that were rarely bestowed. If anyone could be called a pillar of society in West Riverdale, it was Howard Duncan.

As soon as Erica could free herself from the little monsters, she was going to research what jobs Howard was working on that Wayne Chauncey had inspected. But we had no idea if it had anything to do with Denise's murder. We just didn't want to leave anything out.

Bean knocked on my door, looking energized. "Ready?"

"I guess." I was dressed all in black. "Do I need anything?"

He looked me up and down and smiled. "Cell phone?" At my nod, he said, "That's it. Let's go."

Bean had rented a car for his visit, a dark blue Ford Focus that seemed tiny inside compared to my minivan. His arm brushed my shoulder when he put his seatbelt on. I didn't know if it was the excitement of the adventure or the spicy scent of him so close that had me breathing a little fast.

He patted my knee, which didn't help. "Relax. He probably won't even be there," he said. "We'll stake it out for a while."

He asked about our day in the shop and I told him about all the chocolate we'd made. It took me a while to realize he was distracting me on purpose.

I turned it back on him. "So why do you do this? The adventure of it all?"

He shook his head, but then admitted, "Partly."

"What else?" I asked.

He thought for a minute. "It's hard to talk about it without sounding like a pompous ass, but if you can expose injustice, bring it out into the daylight, sometimes you can destroy it. I like to bring the bad guys to justice. There's that moment when you know you have them, you found that one piece of information that makes everything come together." He paused as if reliving it. "And it all clicks into place and now all you have to do is get the story written and out."

He laughed. "Sometimes getting it out is the hardest part. But it's worth it."

"So if you expose injustice, you destroy it?" I asked.

"Not always," he said.

"Not a pompous ass," I said. "More like a card-carrying member of Erica's Super Hero Geek Team." Although his shoulders were a lot bigger than any of those comic book club members.

He laughed. "Yeah, like that."

I didn't want him to think I was discounting his commitment. "It's kinda cool."

"Cool?" His voice was teasing.

"Impressive."

He smiled.

"Admirable," I said. "Maybe even a little commendable."

"Enough."

"Whew," I said. "I just exhausted my thesaurus."

We drove through the town center of Normal to get to the motel we'd seen in the photo of Larry. It looked like a smaller version of West Riverdale's town center, with much less upkeep. Bean drove past the motel and parked around the corner. My heart started pounding. Why oh why had I tagged along?

Bean opened his door and gave me a look that was clearly a challenge. "Coming?"

"Yes," I said, sounding put-upon, and stepped out. The dark pressed in against the only flickering streetlight. Wind whistled through trees hanging over the dilapidated building, making me shiver even though the air was warm.

We approached the motel office and Bean indicated I should stay off to the side. A loud buzzer sounded when he opened the door to the office and went in. I was dying to peek in, sure that such a dilapidated place would hold a clerk with the stringy long hair of a straight-to-video zombie movie actor.

Not that I was an expert, but the motel seemed designed for fast getaways, with open hallways leading through the building to the back parking lot and lots of stairways up to the second floor.

Bean came out, excited. "My new best friend Chris thinks he's in 116 around the back."

"How much did that new best friend cost?" My voice was a little shrill with nerves. "Twenty dollars?"

"Don't be cynical," he said, but didn't answer.

I followed him through the tunnel-like hall to the back parking lot, which was a lot darker without the pinkish light from the neon motel sign. My heart was pounding and I moved closer to Bean. An ancient rusted Ford Fiesta was parked in front of 116. The curtains were drawn but a weak light leaked out around it. Bean was about to knock when we both noticed the door was open a tiny bit. He put his finger to his lips. The adrenaline must have been pumping through my veins because for a second I thought that was really sexy.

Then he pushed open the door with his elbow and walked in. I debated a long moment before he grabbed my arm and yanked me in, closing the door with his sleeve pulled over his hand.

We were in a tiny room made up mostly of a bed with a stained, mud-colored bedspread and beige-painted walls showing the black scars of careless suitcases and at least one fist through the wall. The chipped sink was outside the bathroom, and humidity from a recent shower hung like a sheer curtain looping across the top of the warped mirror that distorted our reflections. I was afraid to inspect the carpet.

The room looked like it had been hurriedly searched, with the suitcase emptied on the floor, drawers hanging open and the mattress listing off to the side.

The scent of something familiar mixed with an unmistakable aroma of Irish Spring soap.

"Larry?" Bean called out, scaring the crap out of me.

I gave him the universal what-the-heck-are-you-doing look and he grinned. He was totally enjoying this. He moved to the bathroom, turned the knob with his sleeve and the door swung open.

Larry's naked body slid to the floor, his tattoo showing in all its glory. His head had been bashed in.

16

Bean moved back to me, as if to make sure I didn't faint. I had to admit, I saw a few stars before shaking my head and breathing deep. "I'm okay."

"You're sure?" he asked.

"Yes. Let's get out of here."

"Not just yet," he said. "Nothing's going to help our buddy here. I need one minute."

He pulled out his camera and took a ton of photos, totally focused, even stepping over the body to document everything in the bathroom. "Do you want to wait outside?" he asked without looking at me.

"No," I said, meaning "yes." But I gathered the guts to pull the sleeves over my hands and open the drawer of the nightstand, the only one unopened in the room. Nothing.

But I noticed a piece of paper peeking out from under the bed and grabbed it.

"Uh-oh." I showed it to Bean.

"What is it?" He walked over to take a picture. "Oh."

It was a piece of our project plan. It looked like Larry had been our vandalizing visitor after all.

"What the hell?" I gestured a little wildly with my hands. "Larry was our number one suspect. How did he end up here? Dead?"

Bean interrupted my little rant by handing me his keys. "Michelle," he talked softly. "Take the car and go home. I have to call Lockett."

"What? No!"

He shook his head, impatient. "I can say I got an anonymous tip and came here," he said. "But I don't want to involve you."

Come to think of it, I was only too happy to leave.

I sat at my kitchen table, staring at the damn project plan. I couldn't get the sight of a dead Larry out of my mind. Erica was still upstairs, although all was quiet, so the twins were either gone or asleep.

Larry's death changed everything. Who could have killed him? And why? The questions kept spinning in my brain like they were in a demented clothes dryer.

A car stopped in front of the house, and I rushed to the window to see Bean get out of Bobby's police car. I met him at the door. "You okay?" he asked.

I blinked at him a moment. "I don't know."

He came in, and I led the way back to the kitchen. "I've been staring at this monstrosity and now it doesn't make any sense." I pointed to the Larry column. "He was the best suspect and now he's dead."

"Are you okay?" Bean repeated a little more insistently, and touched my arm.

I shrugged it off. "I'm fine." The image of Larry's crushed skull flashed into my head and I shivered. I didn't know why I was reacting more strongly to Larry than to Denise. I didn't even know him. But it was my first time seeing a head bashed in. And hopefully, my last.

"It's okay." Bean pushed me down into a chair and sat beside me. "Seeing someone dead is always traumatic."

My hands started shaking and he grabbed both of them. "Just breathe deep." His voice was kind.

My shoulders shuddered with the effort to hold back tears as I tried to fill my lungs. It took several tries.

"Breathe," he repeated and demonstrated, his chest moving in an exaggerated motion that actually kind of helped.

"How many dead bodies have you seen before?" I tried to sound sarcastic but it was a pretty weak attempt.

"Ah, getting back to normal." He smiled and I was glad he hadn't answered me.

His hand moved up to rub the back of my neck and this time I had to tamp down a different kind of shudder that was building. I bent my head so he couldn't see my expression.

His reporter antenna must have been working overtime because his impersonal neck rub slowed, turning into something more suggestive.

I dared a peek up at him and his eyes held a hint of humor, and something else, especially when he glanced at my mouth.

"Did Lockett want to know where you got the photo?" I asked.

"Yes, but I told him I never reveal a source." His hand moved down to rub my tense shoulder.

I smiled. "So I'm a source?"

"Yes." His eyes closed a little, making him even more sexy. "A source of many things."

"Aggravation?" I fished.

"Provocation."

"Really?"

"Vexation."

I laughed and it came out a little breathless. "That's still a word?"

"Yes." He drew out the word.

"Irritation?" I asked, not able to look away.

"Fascination."

He leaned toward me.

"No." I surprised myself. Where did that come from?

"No?"

Now I had to go with it. "Bad idea."

"What is?" he teased.

No way was I letting him off the hook. "Kissing me."

"I'm thinking it may be a very good idea," he said slowly, as if seriously considering, and liking, the idea.

"Really?" For some reason, I held my breath.

"Well," he admitted, "at least not a bad idea."

"No?" I asked, staring at his mouth.

"Not a horrible idea at all," he said, and leaned toward me.

Our lips met. A wild rush went through me. *Whoa.* I moved closer and then heard a knock on the door. "Michelle?" Erica asked.

I nearly tumbled backward in reaction, and only Bean's hand on my arm kept me from pushing my chair over with me in it.

"Relax," he said. I was a little gratified that he seemed annoyed by the interruption. "Well, this is better than spin-the-bottle."

He did remember! "Come on in," I said to Erica, my voice squeaky.

She walked in, looking exhausted. "They're finally asleep." Only the twins made her that tired. Then her face changed as she noticed Bean holding my hand. "What's wrong?"

Another night tossing and turning, with images of Larry interspersed with weirdly hot dreams of Bean. I was still up early enough to run and get the cobwebs from my brain, and meet Kona at eight for another marathon day of chocolate making.

Erica, Bean and I had talked through the death of Larry and all of its implications until midnight. Our theory that Larry had killed Denise was a dead end, so to speak, and we realized that the same person may have killed both of them.

We had examined our plan in detail, but I was beginning to think that project plans might not be suited to murder investigations.

Erica would have none of that. "This system will work."

"It's not a system," I gestured toward the wall. "It's a gypsy carnival game."

"Ooh," Erica said. "We should get one of those for the festival." She made a note and then stared again at the wall. "Let's go over every variable again."

"We need to figure out who knew our security codes," I said. "Because not only did someone get into Denise's studio, they also put poison in my kitchen, so they knew the codes to just about everything."

Once Erica delivered the twins back to Colleen, it was her job to talk to the security company while I got to work on making chocolates. Kona and I had moved on to Mocha Supremes—coffee-flavored ganache in delicious, dark chocolate, spray-painted light blue and white—and Pistachio Surprises, with their hint of orange zest and crunch of organic pistachio crumbles.

I was sitting at my customer counter packing an assortment of truffles into their cute little boxes and trying not to worry about Coco. She hadn't eaten any of the food I'd left out. Then Detective Lockett opened the door and walked in. I instantly felt on full alert—whoop whoop—like on *Star Trek*.

"Why's the door unlocked?" he asked.

"Nice to see you too," I said. "Would you like to try the yummiest thing you've ever eaten?"

"Sure," he said, leaving a seat in between us. The better to question me I guessed.

I got up to pour him some coffee and give him a small plate, staying on the other side of the counter. "Here, try my caramels." No one could resist their buttery caramel sweetness.

He took a bite, and a little bit of caramel dripped onto his chin. "Oh my Gawd," he said. "That is the best thing I ever ate."

"Not the yummiest?"

"I've never used that word before, but maybe I'll start today." He took another bite and finished it, his eyes closing for a moment.

"Wait until you try the Spicy Passion," I said, and then realized what that sounded like. "It, uh, has passion fruit in the ganache," I stumbled slightly over the words, "and the Japanese salt on top has chili flakes."

"Hence, 'Spicy Passion,'" he said, with a hint of a smile.

I handed him a napkin and pointed to his lip. "So what can I help you with? I'm assuming you didn't come here to get chocolate."

He wiped his mouth and put the napkin down. "I'm sure you heard about Larry Stapleton."

"Yes." I had to clear my throat. "Bean told us."

He nodded. "During our canvassing, a long-term motel resident said a red-haired woman entered the room with Mr. Russell."

I gripped the counter to keep my hands from shaking. "Well that leaves me out."

Of course he noticed my hands and raised his eyes to meet mine. "Howzat?"

"I'm strawberry blond," I said oh so casually.

"Leaving the scene of a crime like that was pretty suspicious," he said. "So I asked around."

I tried to change the subject. "How long did it take you to get rid of 'axed'? My roommate said it all the time."

"Ten years away from Pittsburgh to lose that," he said,

but wouldn't be distracted. "Anyway, it seems that in addition to Mr. Benjamin Russell's discovery, you and Ms. Erica Russell have been nosing around about your buddy's murder."

"Why would we do that?" I asked, trepidation edging up my spine.

"You tell me," he said.

"Hypothetically?" I asked and he nodded. "If you were one of us, wouldn't it be in your best interests to find out what you can? We need our shop to get over this crisis. It's our livelihood. And the whole town needs Memorial Day weekend to be a success."

He stood up and even though he didn't move closer, it felt like he was in my face. "Hypothetically? If I was you, I'd be letting the police handle it. Because whoever killed Denise probably just killed again."

His words seemed to hang there in the air, sounding a lot worse than the theoretical way Erica and I had discussed them last night. Then Kona stuck her head out and yelled, "Where's the lavender?"

It took me a moment to answer. "I'll find it." I stepped back. "Sorry, Detective. We'll stay out of your way from now on."

That was probably a lie.

Erica was holed up in her office sending out a press release about our opening, and I was back to stuffing chocolates in boxes when someone tried to open the front door, followed by a brisk knock. I'd locked up after the detective left to keep out more interruptions from the real world. Why couldn't I just make my chocolates in peace?

"Erica? Michelle?" Mayor Gwen tried to peek through the tiny space left between the wooden blinds and the door frame.

I sighed and unlocked the door. "Hi, Gwen."

"Oh, it smells delicious in here." She bustled in. "That chocolate scent just swooshed by when you opened the door. It does my heart good to see you getting ready for the big opening."

"Thanks," I said. "Can I help you with anything?"

She turned around to peek out the door. "It's gone," she said. "The cutest cat followed me here. Bristol at the hair salon said its name was Phantom."

"No," I insisted. "Its name is Coco."

Gwen blinked at my weird insistence and changed the subject. "We're planning a press conference for tomorrow and I wanted to include an update on our amazing Memorial Day weekend," she said. "Is Erica here?"

My shoulders suddenly felt heavy with responsibility. "Yes, I'll get her." I pointed to the chocolates I'd been packaging. "Help yourself. There are some caramels and a few Black Forest Milks."

"Ooh, my favorite," she said.

Erica was combing through an online book auction site when I walked into her office. She grabbed her huge Fudge Cook-off binder when I told her what Gwen wanted, and we joined her at the counter.

"A press conference?" Erica asked after their greeting.

"Reporters are clamoring for information about the unfortunate death of Mr. Stapleton," Gwen said. She picked up a napkin to wipe at her mouth. "And even though it happened in another town, because of his connection with

Denise, we've been pulled into it." She sounded affronted that Larry had the gall to be killed so soon after Denise. "Of course I'll let them know that the death of a criminal like Mr. Stapleton, while unfortunate, will result in an even safer Memorial Day weekend."

"What do you mean?" Erica asked.

Gwen raised her eyebrows, as if objecting to being questioned. "He was most likely the victim of one of his criminally minded friends, as well as a person of interest in Denise's murder." She pulled down on her jacket and smoothed it over her hips. "It seems to me like the world executed its own rough justice."

Erica's eyes widened. "Are you saying that you think Larry murdered Denise and then was killed by a criminal friend?"

"I know the police will investigate both deaths *thoroughly*, but that would be the best outcome. A chance for all of us to put this behind us." She spoke in such a reasonable tone that for a moment I believed her.

Then my natural suspicion kicked in. "That's a little convenient, don't you think?"

"Of course," she said, "and I'm only saying what I hope the police find." She turned to Erica. "We're still on track for the cook-off and arts festival, right?"

"So far, so good," Erica said, but I could tell half of her brain was on the theory Gwen was pushing.

"Great!" She clapped her hands together. "And the book signing?"

Erica nodded. "Everything's going according to schedule."

"We are so lucky to have such a talented citizen in your

brother. And so willing to come back and help out our Boys and Girls Club," she said. "Just so you know, the press conference will be right before you open tomorrow, and then I'm going to lead everyone over to your store."

A store full of reporters? "Is that a good idea?"

"I think it's a fabulous idea," she said. "They'll see that everything is back to normal here in West Riverdale."

With one last bite and a wave, she left.

Something about Gwen made me breathe a sigh of relief when she was gone. "What did our WestRiv Security guy say?"

"He wouldn't tell me anything," Erica said, sounding annoyed.

"What?" I asked. "Don't they work for us?"

"Bobby told them they weren't allowed to tell us anything while there's an active investigation," she said.

"That's bull. We deserve to know how someone broke in. For our own safety." I was beginning to sound as sanctimonious as Gwen. "You know, I have Johnny's cell number from the time he fixed the camera in the back hallway." I pulled out my phone and swiped down to "S" for "Security." "I think it's time we had little Johnny take a look at our broken camera."

"What broken camera?" Erica asked.

"The one I'm going to break," I said.

17

Johnny Horton was the son of the security company's owner, and had started working with the company as soon as he could hook wires together—way below the legal age requirements. No one minded because he was a nice kid. Not the brightest bulb in the pack, but hardworking and good-natured.

He timidly knocked on the door to my kitchen. I'd wanted to leave it open so I could catch him as he came through but the humidity was increasing and I couldn't risk my chocolates. Soon we'd be hitting the summer swampland levels we were used to.

Denise had usually been our go-to girl to handle any workmen we needed. She'd raised flirting for discounts to an art form, but I'd never been able to fake anything in my life.

Johnny wiped his nose with the back of his hand and hiked up his falling-down pants. I wanted to buy him some suspenders. I bet if I could find Halo ones, he'd wear them.

I pointed. "The light for this camera isn't on."

He evaluated the height. "I'll need the ladder."

"I have one in my storeroom." The same one I'd used to pull out the wire.

"What do you think about the Orioles chances this year?" I tried on the way to the storage room.

He shrugged. "They need to beef up their bull pen."

"*And* their fielding."

Johnny nodded, took the ladder from me and put it on his bony shoulder. I didn't know how it even fit.

I tried to think of something else to fill the awkward silence back to the camera. "So, you graduating this year?"

"Yep." He set the ladder up and climbed it like a monkey. "Here's your problem. The wire came loose."

"That's weird," I said. "How could it just fall out?"

"I don't know," he said. "Maybe something long caught on it."

"Yeah," I said. "We're just a little nervous with everything that's happened here."

He nodded as if remembering.

"I mean," I said as if trying to figure it out, "how could someone turn off both the alarms and the cameras? He'd have to be a security genius."

"Not really." Johnny took a pair of pliers out of his toolbox that he'd placed on the top rung of the ladder.

I really wanted to ask him how someone could break in, but I backed off instead of stampeding him like Erica said I did. "So how many are at your company?"

"Just the six of us." He twisted something. "But we have plans to expand to more towns."

"It must be hard to find qualified people." I squinted up as if trying to see what he was doing. "You have to know so much technical stuff."

He shrugged, not really paying attention.

"I mean, it's not like you can Google how to get around security systems." I chuckled.

He smiled like he knew something I didn't.

"What? You can?" I laughed as if that was scandalous. "But you still have to know the codes, right?" When he nodded, I tried again. "I bet you can break into any building in the county," which was my feeble attempt at Denise-type flirting.

"Nah." He blushed.

"What if you knew the codes?"

"Well, smart customers change their codes all the time." He climbed down from the ladder and folded it up.

I didn't want to admit that the only time we changed ours was when Denise's studio had been broken into. "But how could someone figure it out?"

Johnny perched the ladder on his shoulder. "He just needs to know the backdoor code."

"Oh," I said. "What's a backdoor code?"

He looked at me like he'd made a terrible mistake. "Uh, nothing."

"Johnny," I said in a serious tone. "You can't leave me hanging like that."

He looked around as if making sure no one could hear us. "Sometimes the owner wants to use the same code to get into all of their stores or apartments or something."

"So Yuli has his own code for getting in?" I asked as if it was interesting and not kinda creepy.

"Yes," he admitted. "But he never uses it. He just wants it for an emergency."

"That's so smart," I said. "And everyone who works for your dad knows that code?"

He shrugged. "It's in the files."

"Hey, is it easy to find out if that's the code someone used to get in Sunday night?" I pushed.

Some kind of self-preservation must have finally kicked in because he went into his dumb teen lingo. "I dunno."

"Really?" I asked. "You don't know or you won't tell me?"

"I don't know," he said, but he looked worried.

"Let's make a deal," I said in a friendly-but-I-mean-it voice. "You find out if the special code was how he got in, and I won't tell anyone who told me."

I found Erica in her office surrounded by books of all shapes and sizes. She was going through a publisher's catalog of books to be released next quarter. "I'm not surprised Yuli has his own code," Erica said a little absentmindedly. "He has to be able to enter in case of an emergency."

I should've known she'd think of that. "But in the files where anyone can see it?"

"That's not very secure," she agreed.

"Denise would agree." *Did I say that out loud?* Erica didn't respond to my morbid humor.

I changed the subject. "How's Colleen holding up?"

She put the catalog down. "Actually, she's doing better than I thought she would."

"I haven't seen her at the store." Did that come across as judgmental?

"She's trying to figure out what she wants to do with . . . everything." Erica seemed troubled. "And discover how she got to this point."

"What point? Do you mean with Mark or the store?"

"Mostly family issues," she said. "As far as I can tell."

It had to be difficult growing up as the more normal sister to the hotshot boy and genius girl. Erica's expression turned thoughtful, maybe wondering how she got to this point as well. She had been on some kind of academia fast track and then decided it wasn't for her and came home. Now she seemed totally happy managing a bookstore and used book business, and helping the academia types with their research. But maybe having more brains and energy than any one person should have had drawbacks I couldn't see.

It is weird that all three of us ended up here from completely different paths.

She shook herself as if coming out of her introspection. "I want to go back to the beginning and add to the project plan. We need to include everyone with a connection to Denise, no matter how small," she said. "No matter how much we know and love them."

"Does that mean you and me?"

She laughed. "Except for us."

Her cell phone rang and she sighed heavily before answering it. I listened to her side of the conversation, which included "It's on schedule" and "Of course" and "No problem" over and over. And then she sounded irritated. "You do understand that we're volunteers, right?"

"What was that about?" I asked when she hung up.

"The president of Get Me Some Solar." She tossed the phone onto her desk. "He wanted to ensure that everything we had contractually agreed to was on schedule." She actually gave a little huff. He must have pissed her off.

"What was that last bit about?"

"He kept referring to Gwen like she was our boss," she said, "and that he'd be reporting to her about our performance. Give me a break."

Kona had banned me from the back kitchen while she slaved away at tortes and other pastries, so it was the perfect time for Erica and me to work up a quick list of what had changed in Denise's life soon before her death.

First, her mother died. Second, her ex-boyfriend stole her money. Third, she may have blackmailed him to get the money back and he broke into the store, perhaps to find the photos. More recently, she was named senior-class portrait photographer and was invited, and then disinvited, to show her work to the gallery owner in DC.

"What about the stuff we don't know about?" Erica asked.

"You're right," I realized. "We all assume we know everything about everyone's lives, but we didn't know about Mark. Or that Larry stole money from Denise."

"And I didn't know you made X-rated chocolate." Erica smirked.

I groaned and changed the subject. "Maybe we could get Colleen to fill in the blanks?"

"She said she'd stop in later to talk about the opening and the funeral," Erica said.

"She'll be here tomorrow for the opening?" So far, Colleen hadn't been around much, which was totally understandable.

"Of course," she said.

"So how far back in Denise's life should we go?" I asked.

Erica put her thinking expression on. "First, two weeks ago. Then month-by-month until, say, six months ago."

"I'll check her Facebook page and maybe you can see what Zane can dig up," I suggested.

Colleen rushed in, this time holding a folder for West Riverdale's only funeral home instead of a snotty kid.

Erica spoke to her. "We're at a standstill on this investigation, and I was hoping you could help." When Colleen nodded, she went on. "What was new in Denise's life in the past few months?"

"Other than her finding out that my husband was cheating on me?" Colleen's tone was bitter, but she answered. "She was happy that her photography career seemed ready to take off. Especially when that DC guy finally agreed to see her stuff." She pushed aside a small stack of the latest teen vampire bestsellers and sat down on the edge of the desk.

"But that jerk of an ex really did a number on her," she said, disgusted. "Just like a man. He pretended he was trying to turn his life around. Some sob story that he was in therapy now and dealing with his issues of being kicked out of the house when he was fourteen."

She continued. "Not that he should've died or anything,

but it was awful the way he constantly criticized her, but made it seem like he was complimenting her. Like saying it was amazing that she had so many clients when anyone can take photos with their phones now. And then he stole her money and left."

"What did she say about that?" Erica asked.

"She was upset," Colleen admitted. "She knew she'd been stupid, but she said she was definitely getting her money back."

Erica was working with Zane, so after looking around for Coco, who was probably warm and cozy in her own home, I drove out to the highway to pick up a sausage and pepperoni pizza from Zelini's and headed home. It wasn't until I parked and saw my dark house that I admitted to myself that I'd been hoping to see Bean again. I was worried about the opening on a bunch of different levels, and I didn't want to be alone.

While I was debating the merits of eating in the car, a huge SUV parked in front of Henna's house, its Lexus LX insignia right in my face. Someone was compensating for something. A man with slicked-back hair jumped out and adjusted the Bluetooth hooked on his ear. "I'm here."

I recognized him from our fudge cook-off meeting—that solar company president. What was he doing here?

He pulled out a *Get Me Some Solar* magnetic sign with its happy sun logo and placed it carefully on the passenger door. "Yeah, I know." His voice was impatient. "The old-lady pitch. I got it. And you can tell Williams that if he isn't here in ten minutes, he's fired."

He made a monkeylike grin to check his teeth in the side

mirror before picking up his briefcase and walking toward Henna's door.

I mentally debated ignoring all that so I could eat my delicious pizza, but curiosity got the best of me and I decided to barge in on what looked like a sales call. Some of that was concern for Henna; she was getting up in years and I didn't want anyone to take advantage of her. But I was also curious why so many people in town were getting solar panels on their roofs.

"Hi!" I called out and walked toward him. "Are you the solar guy?"

He pulled the Bluetooth off of his ear and sent me a winning smile. "Yes, I am."

I pointed to my house. "I live next door to Henna. Can I listen to your little pitch too?"

His smile dimmed. "I could schedule—"

I got close enough to touch his arm. "Don't tell Henna, but her son has asked me to look out for her. She's starting to have memory 'issues.'" I pointed to my head and grimaced. "So really, it'd be better for both of you if I was here."

Henna would kill me if she heard that. I rang the doorbell, not giving him a choice, and Henna opened the door as if she'd been waiting close by.

"Henna!" I hugged her, totally getting in the way of his handshake. "Your solar guy said it would be okay if I joined you for your meeting." I walked in, and her bewildered expression totally fed into my claim about her memory.

"Terrence Jaffe," the president said, introducing himself.

"Welcome," she said, sounding delighted. "My best friend, Sadie, signed up for your service so I'd like to learn more."

The butterfly motif had spread from the chicken coop and

taken up discreet residence in Henna's house. Compared to her artwork, these butterflies were tiny, and they were scattered across the house, like little fairies in a fantasy painting.

"This is delightful," I said, pointing to a rainbow-colored one perched on a fern in the corner.

That seemed to placate her. "Let me get the tea," she said, heading to the kitchen. "And another cup." That last bit was a little huffy.

"Thank you!" I called after her, and then turned to Terrence. "I've heard that solar is a good investment."

"Are you the home owner?" he asked, and then he punched in a few numbers on his phone.

"Um, no," I said, in the event that he was looking up my info as we spoke. "I've been talking to my landlord, Yuli, about buying it from him." I was getting good at this thinking-on-my-feet thing.

"You have?" Henna asked from the doorway. "But he told me he was never selling your house."

Shoot! "We're just talking so far." I sat in one of Henna's overstuffed chairs and it smushed around me like a hug. "I *love* this chair," I told her and then turned to Terrence. "So how does this whole solar thing work?"

Mr. Jaffe was only too happy to launch into his pitch as Henna served us both tea. "I'd like to show you how you can save twenty-five percent or more off your electricity costs." He talked about the evils of the electric company, the glorious benefits of using the sun to create our energy and how Get Me Some Solar was the best option for us.

Henna was starting to look annoyed that he was directing many of his comments toward me. Between my hard work all day, lack of sleep and the weirdly comforting feeling of sitting in that chair, I was having a hard time focusing on his words.

He pulled out a laminated chart showing how much we'd save at different levels of energy usage.

"I have a lot of trees," I said. "Does that still work?"

"Good question," he said. "The installers will choose the best location, usually facing as directly south as possible, and will recommend trimming trees that are in the way."

I looked at the chart, which included a column for savings from state and federal rebates and tax credits, including one for West Riverdale. "Our town offers a rebate?"

"Yes it does," he said. "Five hundred dollars, as soon as you fill out the paperwork. Very generous for a town your size, which shows how committed your town council is to green energy."

"Can I keep this?" I asked.

His face didn't change, but I felt a tightness come from him. "All of this information is easily available on our website." He reached for the chart but I pulled it back as if examining it. No wonder everyone was buying solar. This made it look like a no-brainer.

I turned it over. "What's this 'We'll Buy It' program?"

"I was just getting to that." He became even more enthusiastic. "For those customers who would like to join the ranks of those enjoying the benefits of solar energy, but aren't ready to make the financial commitment necessary, we offer the We'll Buy It program. Get Me Some Solar will install the equipment at our own cost and you lease it from us. Our company applies for the incentives and shares the electricity savings with you."

My BS meter went into the red zone. "Wow," I said. "That sounds so easy."

"That's what we do," he said. "We make it easy to join the future. The future of clean energy in a safer world."

I nodded. "So how many of my neighbors are installing solar?"

"A lot." He pulled a stack of papers out of his leather binder and riffled through them. "It's a simple decision for anyone with a significant energy bill."

"This calls for some more tea," I said. "I'll get it." I picked up the teapot, which wasn't close to empty, and went into the kitchen, clutching the laminated chart.

"I'm sorry, Henna," I called out. "I can't find the lemon."

"Excuse me," she told him, managing to sound both annoyed and bewildered.

"Don't sign anything," I told her in a low voice when she joined me in the kitchen. "I'm going to have Erica look into this and see if it's legit."

She scowled at me. "I'm not a little old lady who can be conned, you know."

"I know," I said. "You're a successful business owner. I didn't want to say anything in front of Mr. Jaffe, but I'm pretty sure he won't tell you that those solar panels use wireless technology. I know you don't like that."

Her eyes widened and then drew together in frustration. She knew I'd found her weak spot. "By the way, Opal is totally mad at you for telling the police about her," she said.

"What? But I didn't."

She crossed her arms and smiled.

Henna lied to Opal to get back at me? No wonder Opal never returned my phone call about photographing Hillary Punkin. "Just tell Terrence I had an emergency," I said. "I'm going home this way."

I went out the back door and waited in the dark by the chicken coop. A minute later, the president left, looking back in confusion, probably wondering where he'd gone wrong. He stared at my house for a minute and then put on his Bluetooth, got in his car and drove away.

A solar guy driving a gas-guzzling car. How did he explain that?

18

I woke up the next morning way before my alarm, worry running through my head like a live electrical wire hopping around on the ground. The minutes dragged and then suddenly rushed by so fast that I skipped my morning run.

I worried incessantly on my drive to the store. Would anyone show up to buy my chocolate? Would people even take my free samples? Would I ever hear back from my hotel again? Would I have a heart attack before the store opened?

Kona was leaning on her car, sipping coffee by the back entrance of the shop, and I sniffled a little. I loved that girl. She opened her car door as I pulled up beside her, grabbed another huge travel mug and slammed the door shut with her hip. "Ready for the big day?"

"Have I told you lately how freakin' awesome you are?" I took a mug from her so she could lock her door, and the

smell of her special mocha with a touch of cayenne pepper
wafted into my nose. I took a sip and immediately felt calm,
as if the caffeine in the drink was fighting my nerves and
using up all the negative energy.

"Not since yesterday," she said.

"You didn't have to come in so early," I said, "but I'm
really glad you're here." The sound of gravel shifting under
our feet seemed loud in the morning quiet.

Coco sauntered up from around the corner. "Oh look,"
Kona said. "Minotaur is back."

"Minotaur?" I asked. "That's Coco." The cat took turns
winding around our ankles.

Kona gave me a pretend scowl. "Minotaur hangs around
the library sometimes. The college kids feed her."

That cat gets around.

I welcomed the reassuring feeling of every step of opening the store. Bringing an assortment of chocolates from the
back wine cooler storage unit to the display case, turning
the chocolate warmer on to dip strawberries and pineapples,
making coffee and filling the cream dispensers.

Erica arrived a little later. "Are we ready to rumble?" she
yelled with the delivery of a pro wrestling announcer. She
held up both hands, showing crossed fingers, and then
started her own opening process. Colleen joined her, looking
exhausted.

We weren't planning to make any more chocolate until
we saw what happened with sales, so I focused on everything else—turning on the register and documenting the
money we'd left there Sunday night, rearranging the chocolates on display and worrying about what to do if no one
showed.

We were ready early, so I distracted myself by telling Erica about Henna's solar guy. "Maybe you can research that company," I added. "It sounded fishy to me."

"From what I understand," she said, "the great majority of solar companies aren't doing anything illegal. But they don't always explain to customers that the best benefit to them is to pay for the system up front and then enjoy more of the savings themselves."

"That's not illegal?" I asked. "What about someone who doesn't understand all the complexities like you do?"

"Again, it's all legal." She shrugged. "But I'll check them out."

As the last half hour before opening sped by, I started panicking. Why had we made so much chocolate?

I couldn't stand the suspense. "Kona," I said, waving to the front door a few minutes before opening time. "Would you like to do the honors?"

She smiled and headed to the door, pausing as if she heard something. She clicked open the lock and turned the knob tentatively. When the door opened, I could hear what had made her pause. A crowd had formed outside the door. A crowd of my neighbors and friends who had lined up to buy my chocolate.

I stood by the counter and stared before dropping my tray of free samples on the closest table and rushing over to give everyone a hug as they filed in, fighting back tears the whole time. I was a big sloppy mess.

Thank goodness Principal Palladine gave me his handkerchief. I was sure seeing the person who was about to serve them chocolate wiping her snot on her sleeve would make them turn around and say, "Never mind."

I couldn't help but stick my head outside to see how many people had lined up. Leo and Bean brought up the rear, a good thirty people back. "Hey, Berry," Leo said. "How about getting to work?"

"Did you do this?" I asked him after I made my way down the line, thanking everyone along the way.

"Nah," he said. "Erica called a few folks who passed the info along that you needed some help."

Bean gave me a crooked smile, and I melted a little. Leo squinted at me, as if wondering what was going on.

I rushed back to help Kona, who was happily ringing up a small plate of truffles and a coffee for Beatrice. I handed her a gift box of three chocolate bars. "That's for being first in line."

"Oh, thank you, sweetheart," she said. "But I was just as anxious as you to get back here. I don't know how I survived this week without your delicious Raspberry Surprises."

"Ten percent off?" Kona asked quietly.

"Fifty," I said, perhaps a little delirious in my happiness.

She smiled and shook her head. "Ten is plenty."

We sped people through the line. Some took their orders to go, but about half sat down in our dining area or headed over to the bookstore side to pick up the latest bestsellers.

Finally it was Leo's and Bean's turn. They stood a little awkwardly, as if something was going on between them.

"You guys okay?" I asked.

Bean had his poker face on but Leo's eyes narrowed. "Not now."

"Really?" I asked.

Leo shook his head and answered with a short, "No."

I didn't push. I was in my happy place, where all was right with the world. Even seeing some of our customers looking around, obviously wondering where "it" had happened couldn't dim my joy.

Abby Brenton, who had been the town's deputy mayor for the last fifteen of her sixtysomething years, came in after the early rush, wearing a bedazzled rose gingham shirt over a jean skirt and white flat shoes that could only be described as "sensible."

"Abby!" I said. "So nice to see you. I thought you didn't like chocolate." I held out the sample tray, half empty.

"I'm allergic," she said.

I pulled the tray back. "Really? What happens when you eat it?"

"Relax," she said. "I just break out." She chuckled. "In fat."

I made an exaggerated "whew" gesture across my forehead. She ordered a large assortment from Kona and then spoke to some older ladies at the counter before heading on out.

One of my customers who always hid her tiny dog in her huge purse stopped in. I'd given up on telling her it was against the health code. She'd always hold him up and say, "Who could kick out this lil' face?"

I had just finished serving a pack of women in yoga clothes, glowing from their workout, when Mayor Gwen Ficks arrived. A few reporter types followed, taking photos. She seemed pleased at the crowd. "I was all set to buy a big box of chocolate and eat it all over town," she said. "Obviously, I don't need to."

I felt a rush of gratitude. "Well, we don't have the *whole*

town in here, so maybe that'll work on those on the fence."
I couldn't stop smiling. "Black Forest Milks?"

"Absolutely," Gwen said. "And throw in some caramels
for Abby. I've been out of town so much lately that she's
been going above and beyond. Not that she doesn't
always."

I watched the mayor walk outside, ostentatiously taking
a bite out of her truffle. She probably was even saying,
"Yummy," as she walked to her office in the courthouse. I
couldn't thank her enough for doing her part.

Then I noticed Reese taking photos. What was she up
to now?

The rest of the morning passed in a blur of neighbors
stopping in to support us, as if we were the last known
survivors of a major disaster, coupled with a pent-up demand
for my chocolate and Erica's and Colleen's books. I guess
absence really does make the heart grow fonder. Or maybe
people didn't like it if they couldn't get something they used
to have access to. At noon, we were out of Preakness coins,
as people prepared for their race parties later in the day. We
closed up and posted a *Closed for Funeral* sign.

Colleen changed into a black dress and headed over to
the funeral home. Erica, Kona and I had agreed to go home
to change into our own somber outfits and meet there. My
morning bliss faded away, disappearing completely by the
time we arrived.

From the street, the West Riverdale Funeral Home looked
like the dignified redbrick building of historical record that
it was. But over the decades, owners had added on various

wings pointing out in different directions, giving the side and back views a ramshackle appearance.

The parking lot was more than half full, indicating that they had other services going on as well.

"I've read hundreds of murder mysteries," Erica said, "and the funeral is often a great place to get clues."

I smiled. "I'll keep my eyes open."

The very atmosphere of the funeral home seemed to ooze grief, as if past mourners had left some of their emotion behind to gather in corners and attach itself to the tasteful yet subdued wallpaper. I couldn't help but remember my parents' service, in this very building.

The enormity of Denise's death hit me. Denise was gone. Forever.

Tears pressed against my eyes and I escaped to the ladies' room, luckily empty. I holed up in the end stall to get control.

Two young women in clicking heels walked in and went straight to the mirror. One of them groaned. "When can we leave?" They must've been attending another service.

"My mom said we can't be the first ones outta here," the other said. "He's our boss. And he's grieving. Blah, blah."

"Then how long can we stay in here?" Her groan was more of a whine this time.

"As long as we can."

"Did you hear back from Rusty about his party?"

I heard fumbling and assumed the other woman was rummaging through her purse for her phone. Should I come out now? I didn't recognize the voices, so what did it matter if they saw me splashing water on my face and repairing my makeup?

"He says it's on," she said. "He said I should bring these chocolates."

"What chocolates?"

"From this video that Reese woman has on her blog," she said, laughing. "Here, check out my phone."

I heard the screechy sound of Reese, trying to sound like a television reporter. "Today I'm embarrassed to call myself a citizen of West Riverdale. How is it possible that the mayor of our town endangers the very people who voted her into office? Why is she sacrificing public safety to support one store? I can't imagine how anyone would risk their life just to eat chocolate. Perhaps they ordered these."

And then the unmistakable sound of me yelling "Nooo!" Reese had obviously posted that damn video again.

The girls laughed.

Screw it, I decided. I'm not hiding from some idiot kids because of crazy Reese. I deliberately flushed the toilet and stepped out. "Hello."

I walked to the sink while they stared at me, open-mouthed, obviously recognizing me, and then looked back at the phone.

"Uh," one of them said. "Hello." They left, stumbling over each other in their hurry.

I dug for my phone and brought up Reese's blog. There it was, the headline reading, *Reopening: Under Same Old, Same Old*, with a photo of me serving Mayor Gwen, right over a link featuring me about to toss the X-rated chocolates in the air.

I didn't bother with the video and just read. Reese was really going at the mayor, the police and, of course, me. Me, for serving poisoned chocolate; the mayor for a variety of things, including supporting our store, pushing through the special sales tax and helping to sell more of the now-empty homes in her development. And the police, for not arresting me.

My resentment of Reese certainly pulled me out of my pity party, and I met Erica on the way back.

"You okay?" she asked.

"Does this place have a banned guest list?" I shoved the phone at her.

"I'm sure it does." She read Reese's blog, her face showing her growing anger. "I'll take care of it."

The only clue we discovered was that Jake Hale had a big mouth. And we watched it in action before the funeral even started.

I had the first inklings of a problem when I saw Jake talking to Henna while everyone gathered in the parlor before the service, and they both turned toward us. He must've told her about our conversation in the bar. Then Henna raced off to talk to a group of older women. When they all turned to look at us with the same expression of surprise on their faces, I knew we were doomed. "Did you see that?" I asked Erica.

"Yes." She frowned. "An interesting case study in small-town dynamics."

"So you're not as freaked out as I am that the whole town is finding out we're investigating Denise's murder?" I said out of the corner of my mouth.

The group dispersed and soon parts of the whole room

were staring at us. "Well, that cat is out of the bag." I wondered what kind of trouble this would cause us.

Erica shrugged. "Maybe it'll help us somehow."

It was back to avoiding speculative glances sent our way as we moved into the room for the service, and the funeral proceeded. Denise's pastor gave a heartfelt sermon and there wasn't a dry eye in the house when he discussed Denise joining her mother in heaven. Colleen was able to put her other problems aside and give a moving eulogy of the great friend Denise had been, the loving daughter who handled her mother's illness with grace and the successful businessperson who contributed so much to West Riverdale.

Since I found it nearly impossible to do public speaking even when I wasn't emotionally involved, I'd convinced Erica to speak for both of us. She did a wonderful job, talking about Denise's problem customers, from the woman who wanted her to use Photoshop to make her dog's teeth straight to the man who insisted on a nude photo to post to his online dating account. And of course, she highlighted how much fun it was to work so closely with Denise.

Next Principal Palladine told the funny story of Denise deciding to skip school and then her car breaking down, causing a traffic jam on Main Street. So many people called to tattle to her mom that she never played hooky again.

Finally, Gwen spoke of Denise's dedication to the town's Memorial Day weekend. "So, let's fulfill Denise's wish to make this weekend truly special for everyone."

When some of the audience murmured their approval, I met Erica's eyes, just to make sure I wasn't imagining that the mayor had highjacked Denise's funeral for her own efforts. Erica's face looked as what-the-hell? as I felt.

I hoped Gwen wasn't losing her small-town mayor touch and turning into a politician with a capital P.

Principal Palladine must have had the same thought, and he was never shy about telling people to do the right thing. He peeled her off for a private talk during the short walk outside to the reception hall. She didn't look very happy with what looked like a lecture, but she seemed to listen.

The thought of a Preakness party with a restaurant filled with people yelling for their horse to win was too much for me after the funeral and small reception that followed. I escaped to my own home, closing the door to let Erica know I'd rather be alone in case she also skipped the festivities. I suspected some of the parties would be way more subdued than usual, even for people who didn't know Denise personally.

Unable to settle in any of my favorite spots for more than a few minutes, I got ready to take the run I'd missed in the morning, hoping to dispel the restlessness that had settled around me.

Heat from the afternoon sun was still hanging on, but a light breeze hinted at the promise of a cool evening as I struggled through my first mile. Cicadas buzzed, birds swooped to catch low-flying bugs and dogs barked in the distance.

My neighborhood was normally quiet, but with practically everyone at Preakness parties, I didn't even hear children playing outside at my neighbors' houses like usual.

My parents had always had a big party for the Preakness, inviting tons of friends. When I was thirteen, I'd won the betting pool, accurately predicting the trifecta, the top three horses in order. That was enough to convince myself that I must be psychic. Leo had played along, reinforcing my new-found talent by saying I kept reading his mind, until my mom forced him to confess that he'd been messing with me. Of course, he'd have kicked the butt of anyone else who dared to make fun of me that way.

I filled my lungs, feeling like it was the first time I could breathe deeply since I'd discovered Denise's body. Having the support of the town had gone a long way toward believing that the shop would be okay. We had a heck of a lot of work to do for the fudge cook-off, and too many people in the town were counting on Memorial Day weekend, but knowing Erica, it would all come together.

A few cars passed as I hit my two-mile marker and I focused on holding my pace steady. Summer league softball started soon and even though it was more about hanging out with friends than winning, I didn't want to let my team down. We were like a weird little family that laughed and teased, fought and made up, and partied after games together.

I don't know what clued me in that the car coming up behind me was a problem. It slowed down as it rounded the corner, like drivers always did when surprised by a runner in the road.

But then I heard the driver gun the engine. That determined acceleration made me turn my head. A black pickup truck was aiming right for me.

19

leapt to the side of the road at the last second, low, like I was diving into home plate.

Time slowed and every sensation was amplified. My hair whipped around as I pivoted to see where I'd fall. The rubber of my shoes squeaked as I pushed off the warm asphalt. Air whistled past my ears. My left arm instinctively pushed out as if to stop the assault and was knocked aside in midair, the pain shooting up through my shoulder. The thigh-high weeds scratched at the bare skin on my face, arms and legs, and the firm seedlings dug into me as I fell heavily into the ditch lining the road.

The fall stunned me for a painful moment, and then I realized the driver had slowed as if to evaluate his handiwork. A tiny sob caught in the back of my throat. Would he come back to finish the job?

I tried to still the swaying weeds, watching until the truck drove around the corner, and then I scrambled desperately up the slight rise into the trees, which seemed far too sparse to hide me.

My breathing was now frantic and I held my arm, hurting so much I was convinced it was broken, against my body. The nearest house was across the road, a wild, dangerous space I couldn't face. Instead I began lurching home, angling through the trees until they broke into farmland. Still, I stayed in the shadows of the trees until I saw my house.

Relief rushed through me as Erica pulled up and parked in front, and I hobbled out into the open.

Erica drove me straight to urgent care. The waiting room was empty except for us, and the Preakness was being replayed on the TV hanging on the wall in the corner.

Nurse Tonya got me in right away to see a doctor, who looked like he was twelve. After an exam and an X-ray he told me my arm wasn't broken, but bruised badly. It needed to stay in the sling until it stopped hurting.

Tonya brought Leo back. He limped in all worried, until he saw me sitting up with my legs over the side of the exam table. I was banged up but managed a smile for him.

He cleared his throat. "Worst day?"

Tears came to my eyes but I shook my head. "Not yet."

He sat beside me and gave me a gentle hug. "I woulda been here sooner, but I was up fishing." I leaned my head on his shoulder, grateful that he wasn't asking questions.

Erica drove me home, my left arm in a sling, with Leo following on his motorcycle. "Where's Bean?" I asked, as if I hadn't been thinking it the whole time.

"In DC for a dinner with his publisher," she said, her eyes on the road. "I texted him and he said to tell you he was looking forward to writing something obscene on your cast."

I hid my smile.

"I told him you'd be sorry not to have one." She had avoided asking any questions other than about how I felt. "So do you think someone hit you on purpose?"

I nodded. "Whoever it was slowed down and then aimed for me."

She bit her lip. "I think we should listen to everyone and make sure we're not alone until this is over."

I nodded and we stayed quiet until we made it home, where Bobby and Detective Lockett waited for us, both of them leaning on the patrol car with their arms crossed.

I groaned when I got out of the car and added a little more to my limp, hoping they'd back off. Bobby looked distressed to see me that way, but the detective's determined face never changed.

In the living room, I took the most comfortable chair and cushioned my arm on top of a pillow. Leo brought a chair close to me and held on to my other hand.

Lockett took the lead. "What can you tell us about the vehicle that hit you?"

I'd been thinking about that damn truck the whole time I was at the hospital, and still couldn't come up with anything except that it was one of the larger models and black. Our town had about fifty of those; add in neighboring towns and the number grew astronomically.

"Could you see lettering on the back?" Bobby asked. "Did it have two tires in the back or four?"

When I shook my head, he suggested, "Close your eyes and try to remember."

I did what I was told, and made a tiny gasp. "The back door was missing." I opened my eyes. "Four tires."

"Could you see the license plate?" Lockett asked. "Any of the numbers or letters?"

I shook my head.

A wave of exhaustion swept over me, making me sway in my seat. Even Lockett couldn't ignore that and he allowed Erica to lead them outside, where they had a brief conversation. Leo stayed long enough for Erica to assure him that she'd take good care of me.

She helped me put on my favorite ripped Orioles shirt and shorts. Before I fell asleep, I asked, "What was that about outside?"

She grimaced. "They want us to stop looking into Denise's death."

At the moment, I couldn't disagree. I fell asleep immediately, but woke up at one in the morning, my shoulder throbbing. My whole body joined in on the complaining when I got out of bed, aching from my leap into the ditch.

I made my way to the kitchen, turning the cow-painted teakettle on and pulling the painkillers out of my purse, all one-handed. A gentle knock sounded on my door, and Bean stuck his head in. "You okay?"

Great. I probably looked like hell. I nodded, giving up the idea of looking even remotely human, let alone normal. "Tea?"

"You sit," he said. "I'll make it." He took a couple of muffins out of the plastic container in the refrigerator and popped them into the toaster oven. "You should eat something when you take those."

My brain was still cloudy and I stayed quiet while he served my tea and a muffin and sat across from me with his own. "Thanks."

"In case you're nervous, or if you need anything," he said, "I'm sleeping on the couch in the living room for a few nights."

I blinked at him. "Do you think he'll come here?"

"I doubt it, but you shouldn't be alone until they find out who did this."

I was having a hard time figuring out what I was feeling, like a strong emotion was being held down, wrapped in a big fuzzy blanket.

"Here." He upended the prescription bottle and handed me a pill.

"Do you agree with the police that we should stop investigating?"

He smiled. "They don't know you very well, do they?"

I must've looked confused, because he explained. "You're an adventurer."

His words struck a deep core inside me. No one thought of me that way, not even me.

"How?" I stopped to clear my throat. "What makes you say that?"

"I could say because you started this investigation. Or because you came with me to find Larry, even though you were scared, but it's not just that. You started your own business from scratch. You wanted stability for Leo, but if that was all, you'd have picked any job. Instead, you took a huge risk and opened your shop. It took a lot of courage."

I bit my lip, shaking my head and he reached out to grab my hand, his face filled with understanding. "It's not soldier kind of courage, but it counts. It's brave. You're brave."

I stared into his eyes, and then his other hand gently circled the scratches on my cheek. "These are going to be colorful tomorrow. A badge of courage." He dropped his hand and got to his feet. "Now back to bed before those drugs knock you out."

"Is Leo still mad at you?" I asked, as he guided me to my bed with one hand on my arm and the other on my lower back.

"Nah," he said. "It was just a misunderstanding."

"I'm not going to stop." My mouth felt like it couldn't cooperate with my brain.

He nodded, knowing I was talking about the investigation. "Never doubted it." I crawled into the bed on my hands and knees like a child and he helped me with the tangled covers. I closed my eyes against the cotton-filled air around me. When I opened them for a moment, he was still standing there with a tender expression that made me smile.

Bean must have silenced my cell phone while I was dead to the world, because I didn't wake up until ten the next morning. Erica had coffee and bagels waiting for me in my kitchen, and had left a note that Kona and Kayla were handling the normal late Sunday opening at eleven.

I'd missed a slew of messages, most of them asking how I was, and Kona's. "I don't know why I'm wasting my breath, but you don't need to come in. We have enough chocolate to get through the day. Kayla and I will make the caramel after we close so it can cool for tomorrow. Stay home and rest!"

Of course, I didn't listen.

The only person I called back was Leo, to reassure him that I was fine and going to work. He told me to call him if

I needed anything and I insisted he go back to fishing so he didn't waste his cabin rental. He protested, but I put my foot down. He'd missed out on enough.

I decided against the painkillers, opting for ibuprofen instead. My regular morning routine took a lot longer than usual with only one arm and my body all stiff and sore. But I made it to the shop soon after opening.

Coco was waiting for me, meowing louder than ever when she saw me, as if she knew I was hurt. I spent a long time cuddling with her on the back porch and even came back out to watch her eat from one of the cans of gourmet food I'd bought. She rubbed along my leg as if saying thanks and then hopped off the porch and went on her way.

By early afternoon, I was already tired of everyone asking *how are you feeling*, and *who could have done it*, and *you should be more careful*. Like it was somehow my fault that a truck tried to hit me.

Bruised and limping, I was wiping down tables after the Moms on a Mission group left. They were raising money for an orphanage in Haiti, and unfortunately had toddlers. I always had to wipe down every single surface of the tables and chairs after they left. One time I'd found caramels smashed into the back of a couch, in the shape of a smiley face. How could the moms not have realized so many of my delicious caramels were missing?

If I ignored my pain and the way people looked at me out of the corners of their eyes, the shop seemed almost back to normal. But I couldn't help thinking about who could have tried to kill me. Our number one suspect, Larry, was dead. Our number two suspect, Opal, had an alibi, as long as being too drunk to kill anyone qualified. Had someone moved up to the top of the list and we didn't know it? Was someone else out there we weren't even aware of?

As I picked up newspapers and returned them to the rack at the front of the dining area, I noticed a tall, thin man in oversized sunglasses cupping his hands around his eyes and peering into Denise's studio. He had a sports jacket on over jeans, and a black T-shirt with a blue scarf artfully thrown around his neck.

I was just about to run out and ask him what the heck he was doing when he pushed his sunglasses to the top of his head and came into our shop.

"Can I help you?"

He seemed a little taken aback, either by my beat-up appearance or the suspicion that had sneaked into my usually customer-friendly tone. "I'd like to inquire into the . . . property of your next-door neighbor."

"Denise?" I asked

"Yes." He looked a little uncomfortable.

"I'm sorry," I said, giving him the benefit of the doubt. "She died recently."

"Yes, I know. I'm Emberton Dansby," he said, drawing out the last name in a nasally tone that annoyed me. He paused as if I should know who he was.

I waited.

"Denise was scheduled to meet me on the day she died," he said.

"Oh, you're the gallery guy." I held out my hand. "I'm Michelle."

"Yes." His eyebrows drew together as he shook my hand. "Do you know who will be handling her estate, her artwork in particular?"

"No," I said. "Why? I thought you weren't interested in her work."

"That's not true," he said. "I was looking forward to meeting with her and learning about her artistry, but she cancelled our appointment."

I was sure my surprise showed on my face. "She did?"

"Well, I thought she did," he said. "Someone claiming to be her assistant called and said she needed to reschedule. I thought it was rather unprofessional, but what could I do? Then a few days later the police told me she didn't have an assistant. It's all a big mystery."

"Uh," I said, suddenly feeling in way over my head. "Hold on."

I winced as I hurried to find Erica, trying to figure out what this meant. Someone had cancelled Denise's appointment without her knowledge. Did that someone want to keep her photographs from being seen?

Erica was having an argument with one of the comic book teens about the advantages of holding onto something called "covenant weapons" in a video game, but I had no idea what she was talking about. "You need to come with me." My voice was urgent.

She apologized to the boy, who ran up the stairs two at a time to join his posse on the second floor. "What's going on?"

"Denise's gallery owner is here. He wants to talk to whoever will be handling her 'effects.'" I resisted using finger quotation marks, mostly so I didn't have to lift my arm. "And he said Denise's assistant cancelled their meeting."

Erica eyes widened in shock. "That could have something to do with her death!"

"I know!" I said. "Let's figure out how we can use this guy."

Erica introduced herself to Mr. Dansby.

He dove right in, sounding impatient. "I'd like to purchase the rights to Ms. Coburn's photos. Who do I need to talk to?"

"Unfortunately," Erica said, "that will take a while, since no one has been able to find a will."

"That's terrible!" He looked aghast. "I advise all of my artists to leave instructions behind about how their work is to be handled upon their passing."

"It's too bad she wasn't yet one of your clients," she said. "Why don't you sit down and have some chocolate while we discuss what you'd like to do?"

He stared with disgust mixed with longing at my display case. "I don't eat processed sugar."

"Of course not," she said. "Just coffee then?"

"Espresso?" he asked hopefully as if that would help soothe him.

"So how did you find out about Denise?" Erica asked, oozing concern, as I made his espresso.

"The police came to see me," he said. "I was shocked at the news." He clasped his hands and pressed his thumbs together in a weird nervous gesture that was a little hypnotizing. Press. Thumbs turned red. Release. Color went back to white. "I'm assuming the circumstances were suspicious because those police officers asked quite a lot of questions about why I cancelled the appointment. Even after I told them she'd been the one to cancel on me." Press. Red. Release. White.

I willed my machine to hurry so I could join them.

"That must have been disconcerting, to say the least," she said, leading him on.

"I'll say," he said, as if remembering the affront. "I actually thought I might be under suspicion for a little bit."

"I'm sure they were satisfied with your alibi," she said.

Finally! The last bit of espresso dripped out and I delivered it to Eggbert, I mean, Emberton.

"They had to be," he said. "I was working with my assistant on our next show, a wonderful new artist who uses paper tapestry. The colors! You would not believe the gorgeous landscapes she produces. It's as if she simplifies nature to its very essence and weaves it for us to experience."

He and Erica must have taken the same how-to-talk-snooty class.

"So Denise called you directly to tell you she couldn't be there?" Erica probed. "I find that very surprising since she sat right there telling us she couldn't wait to show you her work."

"I already told Michelle that a man pretending to be her assistant called." He looked where Erica had pointed. Press. Release. "The police told me she didn't have one. But how could I have known that when he called?"

"Did the police take your phone?"

"Of course not." He was adamant. "They requested it, but I told them they must produce a warrant first. My whole life is on this phone."

"Did you tell them the phone number the assistant called from?"

"Yes, of course," he said.

"What do you want to do with her photos?" I asked. I could tell that Erica really wanted to get a hold of that phone.

He sighed dramatically. "I envision her glorious artwork filling my gallery space with her spirit, the soul of a true artist, interspersed with news articles on her untimely death.

It's a story of a promising young artist whose life was cut short by tragedy."

I couldn't help but imagine that scene and then I realized it may have been exactly what the killer was trying to avoid. "Erica, can I talk to you a second?" I grabbed her arm and pulled her out of earshot of our theatrical visitor. "Someone did not want him to see Denise's photos. What if we hosted a show of Denise's work? It might flush out whoever wanted to keep her work hidden." I felt a growing excitement that we could be moving in the right direction.

Erica was intrigued. "That could work. We'd have to obtain her photos from the police. But how would we figure out which she intended to show Emberton?"

"It doesn't matter," I said. "We just *tell* everyone it was the work she was going to show him."

"We'll have to actually set up a show," she said. "Maybe Emberton can help."

We walked back to the counter, where he was taking a final sip of the espresso.

Erica sat down facing him. "I think you are the perfect person to handle her work, so I'll offer you a deal. I will put all of my considerable resources into getting you the rights to her photos in exchange for two things: you hold a memorial show here in West Riverdale first and you also let me borrow your phone for, let's say, twenty minutes to let my tech guy have a go at it."

"Why would you want to do that?" he asked.

Erica smiled. "Let's say we have a vested interest in helping the police solve this thing."

He looked at me, seeming to reevaluate my injuries. "Oh. A plot twist," he said. "Amateur sleuths at the ready."

20

Emberton angled his head as if framing pictures of us in his mind. "I'll agree to your plan only if I get to include photos of you two and your story in my exhibit as well."

"No," Erica said. "It wouldn't be . . . prudent."

"Ah." He held out his phone and then pulled it back. "Twenty minutes with the phone. But he has to stay away from everything else on my phone not having to do with that call."

"Of course," Erica said.

"Let me see my availability." Emberton used his phone to review his schedule and then handed it to Erica. "If the show here can be Friday night, it's a deal."

We left Egghead tsk-tsking over the small art section of the bookstore while we tracked down Zane.

"What do you think Zane can do with a phone number?" I asked.

"I don't know," she said. "But I'd like to find out."

Both of us descended on his office. The walls were floor-to-ceiling metal shelves, most of them stuffed with books. Erica had installed her own climate control system to create the best atmosphere for preserving books.

Zane pushed his bleach-tipped hair out of his eyes and looked at us warily. Maybe our arrival was a little too breathless.

"Hi, Zane." Erica held out Emberton's cell. "Someone called this phone on Sunday and we'd like to learn whatever we can from it."

"Okay," he said. "Like what?"

"We're hoping to learn more than the phone number. Who they are? Maybe where they called from?"

"I don't know anything about phones," he said.

"Can you find out from one of your hacker buddies?" I asked.

He frowned, affronted. "I'm not a hacker, and I don't have 'hacker buddies.'"

Erica sent me a shut-the-heck-up look. I impatiently turned away and pretended to examine a shelf of ancient books.

"Don't touch those," Zane said. He was about to stand up to keep me away from them.

I backed away, raising up my one good hand as if he were holding a gun. "Okay, calm down."

He relaxed back into his seat, but kept a wary eye on me.

Erica brought his attention back to the phone. "Do you know anyone that can get information off of a cell phone?"

"I can ask my professor," he said, his eyes on me.

I fought back the urge to reach out and poke a random book.

He continued. "She's always warning us about how easy it is to break into phones, computers and stuff."

"Can you do it in ten minutes?" I asked. "The guy who owns it is out in the store and wants it back."

He reached for his phone. "I'll try."

We left him alone and stood in the hall. It certainly wouldn't help our efforts to hover.

"Someone went to a lot of trouble to keep Emberton from seeing those photos," I said. Suddenly the excitement of finding a new avenue to investigate seeped away, and I was left with worry and sadness. Was it really possible that something in those photos led to Denise's murder? And could whoever didn't want that photo seen be the one who tried to run me down?

Zane joined us in the hall. "She can track where the phone is right now. Do you want her to do that?"

"Yes!" we said at the same time.

"Okay," Erica said. "Michelle, can you check on our friend and tell him that we'll just be a few more minutes?"

"Sure," I said. "But, Zane, one more thing. Do you know where Denise stored her photos?"

"Yeah," he said. "On two computers and an external drive, and she also had a cloud service."

Erica asked, excitement in her voice, "Do you know how to get into her cloud service?"

"Maybe," he said. "Depends on the passwords."

"Wait," Erica said. "Will someone—the cloud service or police—be able to trace it to you?"

He frowned. "I'll ask my professor. I'll bet she can get in and out without anyone knowing."

"Okay, try," Erica said. "But we don't want you to get into trouble, okay?"

"He couldn't get in *that* much trouble for just one peek," I said.

Erica glared at me. "We are not risking Zane's future over our fishing expedition."

But what if we caught a big, fat murderer on the hook? I thought, but kept it to myself.

Emberton was over the moon about the possibility of hosting a memorial show for Denise in such a "quant little town," as he put it, and even more excited to move the show to his studio afterward. But first we had to get the police to agree.

I called Bobby, who answered with a terse, "I'm on vacation."

"Really?" My shock was clear even over the phone. I was hit by a truck and he was on vacation?

"Lockett ordered me to take the day off. If you need anything, contact him." He hung up.

I called him back and it went straight to voice mail. I stared at Erica for a moment, stunned, until I remembered that I'd told Leo he should go back to fishing.

"I know where he is," I said. "Leo always rents the same cabin near Cunningham Falls." I had a little flashback to when my whole family would spend a week up there. My mom had liked to complain about the lack of a real kitchen, but we all knew she loved hanging out around the fire pit. I sent Leo a text asking if he was having a good time at Cunningham Falls.

Just got back from fishing, he texted back. *Caught a bunch of panfish.*

"Let's go." I showed her the text. "They're probably cooking them now."

We gave Emberton his phone back, said our good-byes and left Kona and Colleen in charge of the store. It took thirty minutes to drive up into the hills, twenty if I'd been driving, and we found Bobby's car right away. Zane texted us that the phone was turned off and couldn't be located until it was turned back on.

I was lucky it wasn't a far walk from the parking lot to their site. Getting hit by a car had taken a lot out of me, and I was huffing and puffing the last few steps.

Leo and Bobby were both enjoying the sunshine and the quiet, leaning back in the most comfortable camping chairs I'd ever seen. They even had extending footrests. The remains of their lunch were scattered around them. Bobby had a baseball cap propped over the top of his face and Leo had removed his prosthetic leg and was rubbing his thigh. He smiled and waved when he saw us.

Bobby must have heard us approach because he stood up and cursed. "I'm not telling you anything," he said.

I couldn't see behind his sunglasses. I was pretty sure that Erica was looking at his chest where it was exposed by his open shirt.

"What are you talking about?" I said. "I'm here to see my brother."

Bobby scowled at Leo. "Why did you tell 'em we were here? This is a no-work zone."

"Sorry," Leo said, enjoying Bobby's discomfort.

"You've been holding out on us," I accused Bobby.

"On so many things." He sat down in the chair and deliberately put his hat back.

"Guess who showed up today?" I didn't wait for him to answer. "Emberton Dansby." I drew out the pronunciation.

He scowled and moved his hat up. "Playing the vulture?"

"Yep," I said. "He wants to display Denise's work and thinks he can make a buck off the tragedy."

Bobby shook his head.

"The thing is," I said, "having a show in a real gallery is what Denise really wanted."

He snorted. "You're leaving out the part about her wanting to be alive for it. And get the money herself. Now it doesn't benefit anyone but the egghead."

I smiled. "I called him the same thing! So we were thinking that maybe we should do some kind of show, and the money raised from selling the photos would go to a charity or something. Like for cancer, in honor of her mom."

He saw right through me. "What are you guys up to?"

"What could be wrong with a show? It could be a wonderful tribute for Denise." My tone rose higher.

He just stared at me with his head tilted in a do-not-lie-to-me way. "Why don't you just tell me what's going on?"

Erica stepped beside me and pushed her sunglasses to the top of her head. "It's obvious that whoever cancelled the appointment with Mr. Dansby didn't want Denise's photos to be seen. A public show may be the best way to flush them out."

Bobby's jaw tightened. "What the hell are you talking about? Listen, as much as I understand that you're frustrated, whoever did this is dangerous and you need to stay away from them."

I rolled my eyes and he appealed to my brother. "This is

your sister, Leo. The one who was almost killed last night. Do you want this to turn into a triple murder? That'll qualify him for serial killer status."

Inside I quaked at his words, but I scowled to show him how tough I was. Unfortunately, the scowling hurt my face.

Leo got that maybe-I-should-pretend-to-parent squint that had usually preceded some idiotic attempt at grounding me as a teen, and then he relaxed.

It was almost as if I could read his mind. "You're thinking that the fastest way to get me to do something is to forbid it, right?" I said.

He turned to Bobby. "You're on your own on this one. Good luck."

Bobby took some convincing. It helped that we started on the same page; we all believed that finding out who had called Emberton could be the key to unmasking Denise's killer. And much as he didn't want to admit it, we were all involved in the investigation, and all targets. The sooner the mystery was solved, the better.

"Lockett will never agree to it," he warned.

I disagreed. "He cares more about solving the case than he does about us."

Bobby didn't argue that point, which made Leo frown.

I changed the subject. "What is Lockett doing with the photos?"

Bobby hesitated but then relented. "He has someone analyzing them to figure out if any of them are incriminating."

"Aren't there thousands of photos?" Erica asked, and he nodded.

I tensed. "Don't you think our idea is better?"

He looked right at Erica. "Unfortunately, yes."

Finally, he told us more about what the police had learned. Denise's computer, external hard drive and big leather portfolio had been taken when the chocolate was left in her studio. The second computer that was hidden in her apartment was badly damaged, but they had been able to discover that she used a cloud service. With a warrant, they'd gained access but hadn't been able to figure out how, or if, her photos were connected.

He agreed to talk to Lockett about the show and let us know as soon as he could.

"Can you answer just one last question?" I asked Bobby. "Then we'll leave you two alone in your bromance."

He scowled and I backtracked fast. "We'd just like to know what time they broke in."

"No," he said.

"It's just a time, Bobby," Erica said.

Bobby stared at her a moment until she looked away. I was sure he wasn't going to tell us anything and then he said, "Someone broke into the studio at eleven that night and turned off the security alarms and cameras. Ten minutes later, the cameras came back on and the chocolates were sitting on Denise's counter."

Erica met his eyes again and the tension grew even more.

Leo shifted in his chair and the creak broke the mood.

Maybe we should retreat to fight another day. "Thanks. You won't regret it."

He leaned back in his chair. "I already do."

21

Zane met us at the back door. "I got the photos from Denise's account." He held up a flash drive, looking triumphant.

"All of them?" Erica asked.

"Ye-up." He seemed very pleased with himself.

"How many are we talking about?" I asked.

"We put her portraits on a different drive, and there are still thousands."

"Thousands?" I asked. How could we search through those? "Are they labeled or something?"

He nodded. "Same as before. Geotags and other stuff. And she titled them."

"Was there a file labeled for the Dansby Gallery?" I asked.

"Let's see."

We followed him to his tiny office and he plugged the flash drive into his computer. With a few keystrokes, the screen filled with thumbnail photos. Pages and pages of them. And one of the folders was called Dansby.

"Awesome," Erica said.

Zane beamed.

We were having a show whether the police approved or not.

"That's interesting," Zane said as he clicked on several photos. "The geotags have all been stripped from this folder."

As we were cleaning up after closing, the shop phone rang. Something told me not to answer it, but I didn't listen. "Hey, Fireplug," Jake the bartender said.

Great. I had a new nickname that made fun of my hair and my size. "Hi," I said cautiously.

"That jewel you wanted has made an appearance." His voice was muffled as if trying to keep someone from overhearing.

Did he really think anyone wouldn't decipher his ingenious code?

I sighed heavily. "Be right there. And thanks."

I walked back to Erica's office and found her with her librarian glasses on, deep into a book the size of Nebraska.

"What is that?" I asked.

"I'm pretty sure it's a one-hundred-and-fifty-year-old *Mitchell's New General Atlas*." She gave a sigh as if she'd just finished meditating, or had a massage, or hugged a puppy.

"Jake called." I gestured out the door before she launched into any more info about her old book. "Opal's there. Let's go."

"Cool!" Erica jumped to her feet.

She drove, since my shoulder was aching like crazy, and I warned her that Henna had told Opal we gave her up as a suspect to the police. "So how do you want to play this?"

"Let's just apologize as if we did tell them," she said. "That should diffuse the situation." She looked at my arm. "You're getting soda."

We arrived at the Ear, the parking lot more than half full. "Ready?" I asked, and Erica nodded. The scent of the bar seemed reassuring, always the same mix of beer and sweat.

Jake waved when he saw us. "Michelle and Erica," he said. "Fancy meeting you here."

Opal's bleary eyes latched onto us as we walked by her leaning on the bar. "Well if it isn't Sherlock Shit-for-brains and her sidekick, Wiseass Watson." Several of her somewhat less drunk friends laughed loudly.

I guess everything's funnier with alcohol. Wait. Was I Sherlock or Watson?

I was sure that Opal had already been questioned, but we weren't bound by any police ethics, like not questioning her when she was drunk. I sure hoped sloppy Opal was very different from professional Opal. Tonight she was bleary-eyed, with mascara smudged in the corner of her eyes—one of the reasons I never wore mascara.

We retreated to a booth out of sight of her and her bevy of drunken buddies, and one of Jake's multitudes of young cousins came over to take our order.

Jake brought over my soda and Erica's wine, waiting impatiently as a group of heavily made-up girls in their young twenties sloshed by with their appletinis. "Sorry," he said. "Had to wait for the train of trollops to get out of the way."

"Lovely alliteration," Erica said.

"I could've sworn you said, 'Mine!' about that last one," I added.

Jake smiled. "Nope. Happily married man here. You must have heard that from Tiny." He pointed to the middle-aged man wearing a cowboy hat at the bar. "Just so you know, Opal arrived pretty much in that condition. She thinks she's drinking gin and tonics right now, but there's barely a drop of gin in there." He headed back to the bar, just as Opal decided to lurch her way over to us and stand swaying at the edge of our table.

"I'm truly sorry we inadvertently caused you trouble, Opal," Erica said. "We didn't mean any harm."

Opal didn't look mollified. "I should sue you for libel."

"You mean slander," Erica offered.

"Don't help her," I hissed. I could tell Erica was about to launch into a long-winded legal explanation of why it was slander and not libel, so I dove in. "You could do that. But think of all that media attention you'd get about what you were doing that night."

Her glassy eyes seemed unsure.

I continued. "You know those reporters. Just think what a hundred Reeses could uncover." I couldn't believe I'd found a use for Reese.

"Opal," one of her drinking buddies yelled. "Your round!"

She turned unsteadily to gesture to Jake, who nodded back to her, and then she stumbled onto the bench beside Erica. "Why do you even care?" she said. "The guy who did it is dead."

"We have reason to suspect that Larry wasn't the killer," Erica said. "Which means there's a murderer running around West Riverdale."

"Not me!" Opal said.

"We never thought it was you," Erica said. "We just mentioned that you could lose a lot of money with Denise becoming an approved senior-class photographer."

Opal waved her hand around listlessly. "That was all BS."

"What do you mean?"

"Peter tol' me. He was jus' giving her a trial run," Opal said. "She still had to get approved by the school board and that takes for freakin' ever, believe me."

Really? Denise had seemed so sure she had it.

"Maybe you can help us piece together what happened that night," Erica said. "Who was hanging out here? Did anyone leave right before eleven?"

"I dunno. I was gone by ten," Opal said. "I'm told."

"Who took you home?"

She glanced around as if making sure no one could hear her. "Peter."

"Oh," I said. "Okay."

She gave a suggestive shrug and gave us what she thought was a sexy look over her shoulder. "Seems like we both have an alibi."

"Oh," I said, trying not to appear shocked. Erica had less luck.

"Stop acting all innocent Mrs. High and Mighty," Opal said to Erica. "People have sex all the time. Like you and that Lieutenant Bobby."

"We're not—" she started to respond, and then stopped.

"So you and Peter," it took all my focus not to call him Principal Palladine, "slept together that night?" I asked, trying to sound totally nonjudgmental.

"Hmm. I'd say we didn't get much sleep," she said with a ginny leer.

My face must have betrayed some emotion because she brayed like a cynical donkey.

"You kids think you know everything. And the world's full of unicorns and rainbows." She smirked. "People cheat. Even principals cheat. It happens. Get over it."

"So he stayed with you?" Erica asked.

"He was with me all night long." She dragged out the last three words. "I have the best alibi."

"So we haven't heard this because Principal Palladine was too honorable to tell anyone what happened," I said.

"Honorable?" She laughed so hard tears started leaking out of her eyes. "You're such a child." She lurched to her feet. "Later, losers," she said, and rejoined her group.

I sat blinking at Erica until Jake came over with two more drinks, even though we'd barely started the first. "I told you. Sometimes it's better not to know."

"I guess when you own a bar, you see a lot more than the average person," I said.

Erica interjected. "So exactly how intoxicated was Opal?"

"Are you still on that?" I asked, exasperated.

"Totally blitzo," Jake answered. "Bad. Worse even than tonight."

"Bad enough to totally lose track of time?"

Jake looked wary. "Sure, I guess."

He started to walk away, but Erica called him back. "Is that the first time Peter has ever taken someone home?"

He shrugged. "As far as I know."

I stared at her when Jake was out of earshot. "Really? You think Principal Palladine was so diabolical that he could plan ahead to pick up Opal and spend the night with her in order to have an alibi for when he killed Denise?"

She was in her thinking place, and didn't realize how upset I was. It just couldn't be the principal.

Because of our pact to never be alone until the killer was found, Erica followed me into the shop Monday morning. We locked ourselves in and went our separate ways. Coco was nowhere to be found; she was probably hanging out at the hair salon or the library, the tramp.

I tried to figure out why I was so troubled about Principal Palladine. Part of it had to be the father figure role he'd played right after my parents died. But also how he'd taken my side when Leo had tried to stop me from dropping out of college.

My arm was much better, so I followed the doctor's orders to keep it in the sling, but was able to use it to stir and lift everything but my largest bowls. I stayed busy making Rosewater Caramels, until I heard raised voices. Imagining the worst, I ran to open the door, but it was just Colleen with the stressed voice, and Erica trying to calm her down.

I heard something about a therapy appointment for Prudence and an unavailable babysitter, and quickly closed the door again. Erica was stuck with the twins again.

A little while later, Erica knocked and peeked her head in. "Zane called! The phone has been turned on and they located it."

I put down my dried organic rose petals and wiped my hands on the towel tucked into my pocket. "Where?"

"Behind the inconvenience store," she said.

That was the nickname for the West Riverdale

Convenience Store. While they were the only store in town open all night, they never had what anyone needed, unless it was condoms, cold beer, tiny sewing kits or stale Cheetos. It's where teens gathered to smoke; if our town had a wrong side of the tracks, this store was in it.

"Bean's on his way here to pick me up," she continued. "You have to watch the twins."

"I can't watch the twins!" I screeched.

"You have to," Erica said, and opened the door. "You're already hurt and we don't know who's using that phone."

I came out into the hallway and saw that she had brought the double stroller right outside my kitchen door.

Two blond heads simultaneously turned to stare at me.

"But I don't know what to do with them." I tried a high happy voice that I'd often heard parents use but it didn't come out right with my teeth clenched.

Their heads moved back to see what Erica would say, like they were watching a tennis match.

Erica tried to reassure me. "Just let them sit right here for ten minutes, until Kona comes. She's always here by nine. Even you can manage them for ten minutes."

The boys frowned matching frowns, as if they couldn't believe it either.

"No, I can't," I said. "What if, if . . . something happens?"

"Nothing will happen," she said, edging toward the door. "Boys. Be good." And then she was gone.

The twins watched her leave with wide eyes and then turned to stare at me with no expression, so simultaneously that it seemed like a crazy CGI special effect. For a horror movie. Then they searched for something more interesting. I swore their little demon heads turned completely around on their necks before they both reached for the seatbelts holding them in their stroller and started wriggling their butts in an odd synchronized dance.

In seconds, they escaped. In different directions.

"Gabe! Graham!" I yelled, which caused them to giggle uncontrollably. I'm not sure which was scarier, their silence or their maniacal laughs.

It didn't help that they were wearing Dr. Seuss Thing 1 and Thing 2 T-shirts.

Thing 1 headed for a couch in the dining area, throwing one leg up to climb on it, and Thing 2 took off right for the wooden stairs leading to the second floor of the bookstore. I had a vision of him attempting to skydive from the railing and decided he was most urgent. Just as he reached the stairs, he swerved away, laughing over his shoulder at me and running between the aisles of books.

The whole thing reminded me of the velociraptors in *Jurassic Park*.

I ran after him and picked him up with one arm, like a shortstop catching a grounder speeding toward the outfield. He wriggled like an oversized ferret, and I allowed myself a moment of triumph before carrying him back to the café.

It was then that I realized I'd been played. Thing 1 had dragged a chair over to the counter and was shoving an Acai and Blueberry chocolate bar in his face like he was competing in a food-eating contest.

Thing 2 struggled mightily to join his brother and with only one good arm, I was forced to let him go.

They started talking in twin gobbledy-speak and Thing 1 handed the rest of the chocolate bar to his brother. They both looked at me as if they'd found heaven.

....

When Kona arrived, both twins were sitting in my lap, their faces and hands covered with chocolate. They'd insisted on sharing with me, which made my heart melt along with my chocolate, so my face was a mess too.

She looked shocked and then laughed. "What happened?"

"Erica had to run out and I was elected game warden." The affection in my voice surprised both of us.

One of the twins pointed to the sling on my shoulder. "Boo-boo." He made a sad face.

"Will wonders never cease," she said. "Do you want me to take over?"

I thought about my cell phone back in the kitchen and what Erica and Bean were doing. But there was something about holding those two that made me all squishy inside. Then Thing 1 bounced a little on my leg and I felt something else squishy. "They're all yours."

They went to Kona happily, Thing 2 giving me a sticky kiss on the cheek before grabbing her hand.

I'd missed one call from Erica, so I called her back, anxious to find out what happened with the phone. Had they caught the guy who called Emberton?

"The police are here," she said. "I'll call you later." She hung up.

22

Erica and Bean arrived at the store five minutes before we opened at ten. Bean filled me in while Erica finished getting the store ready. A teen had dropped his last cigarette in the tall grass behind the inconvenience store. When he moved the grass aside, he found a cell phone and turned it on, and it pinged off the closest tower. The poor kid was fooling around with the phone and enjoying his smoke when Detective Lockett and Lieutenant Bobby drove up and scared the crap out of him.

The police had decided that the phone most likely had been thrown from the highway soon after the call to the gallery owner was made. It was a prepaid "burner" phone, commonly used by criminals like Larry.

They were not happy to see Erica and Bean show up, but neither one admitted how they knew where to find the phone.

Bean took Colleen's usual place at the store, working the cash register. As the morning wore on, I realized I had some kind of radar for him, constantly feeling the tug to see if he was still there. And he was often looking back with a warm smile.

He was probably smiling because of my ridiculous scratched face and my arm in a sling. His presence certainly added to my tension—as if I didn't have enough to worry about.

At noon, Erica brought over small flyers for the Denise Coburn Memorial Photography Exhibit. She'd worked fast; the flyer used a photo of the beautiful oak tree that had grown beside the town church for decades and noted that the event would be held Friday evening in the community center.

"It's beautiful," I said. "Is that one of Denise's?" Erica nodded. "She was so talented."

I stared at the photo, realizing that the shadows on the bottom were gravestones from the old cemetery. I couldn't help feeling like we were on a runaway train that might not stop in time.

As Friday approached, Emberton threw himself into the show, calling us constantly to inform us of his progress in printing the photos over and over until they were perfect.

Erica had asked him why Denise had stripped the geotags from the photos for his gallery.

"That's not so uncommon," he said. "Especially for nature photographers. They don't want another artist to go shoot the same scene." He sniffed. "Although it would be nearly impossible for another photographer to capture the same photograph."

We never told him our secret motive for the exhibit; he was so entranced by Denise's art that he'd be totally heartbroken if he found out. He used his considerable public relations reach to promote the show and we were getting calls from all over northern Maryland and as far east as DC and Baltimore. We encouraged each contact to stay for the rest of our weekend events.

Kona, Kayla and I ramped up our chocolate production for the arts festival, still unsure what to expect. We held daily meetings with the Great Fudge Cook-off committee to keep everything going according to schedule and attend to last-minute details. Hotel reservations had dropped off even further after Larry's murder, and no amount of press releases by Erica or new slogans by Gwen were bringing people back in.

We still hadn't heard anything concrete from Hillary's people, so we assumed the worst and asked Nurse Tonya, our YouTube star, to fill in as our celebrity judge if we needed her.

Colleen made herself scarce most of the week, and Bean was taking up the slack, so I had a lot of unnerving moments seeing him across the store. Kona noticed. "Someone's got a boyfriend," she teased.

"Nah," I said. "That would really be a bad idea. He's leaving right after the book signing."

"But just think how much fun you could have before he goes." She laughed at my intrigued expression.

It didn't help that word had spread that the great

Benjamin Russell was helping out in his family bookstore. Fan girls started arriving from all over, even as far away as Baltimore. The one who showed up right before closing wearing a halter top and almost illegal shorts caused me some worry, but Bean sent her on her way.

Other than a few flirty looks, he didn't try anything with me either, no matter how many times I left the door open to my kitchen. I could not figure him out.

The arts festival stuffing party took over the dining area on Wednesday night, with the drama club and math team coming together to help us out. Though from the sullen expressions some of the kids had, they may have been there to fulfill volunteer hours.

Steve and Jolene herded them all with humor and genuine fondness. "Okay, we're setting up an assembly line here," Steve explained. "Put these tables together, sit down, take your pile of junk that's depleting our environmental resources, I mean valuable advertising that everyone will want to read, and put it neatly, and I mean neatly, into the bag."

Johnny Horton, our security kid, had tagged along with an adorable teen with *Nerd Girl* on her T-shirt and huge manga girl eyes that reminded me of the stuffed animals Erica sometimes sold. He sighed as he saw me and came over, while she stared longingly after him, as if she couldn't bear to be away from him for one freakin' minute.

I felt like sighing too. I'd forgotten about Denise for a little bit with the place full of young, bubbly energy.

"Hey, Johnny," I said, while I finished wiping down the counters. My arm was doing much better but still twinged if I overdid it. "Any news for me?"

He nodded. "Wanted to let you know that it was the back-door code that guy used to get in here."

"Thanks," I said. "Any way to figure out who all knows that code?"

"I can't," he said with a that's-all-I-can-do jerk of his shoulder, and then he shuffled back to Nerd Girl.

I finished cleaning up while the group continued stuffing flyers into the plastic Get Me Some Solar bags, which reminded me that with all the other stuff going on, Erica hadn't researched that company.

Just as the students were about to finish, Principal Palladine stopped in. "I heard some of my juvenile delinquents were here trashing the place." He smiled affectionately as they greeted him, some with more enthusiasm than others. Johnny gave the principal a high five as he stood behind the chairs, and his girlfriend beamed.

School sure had changed if it was actually cool to know the principal.

•

Colleen was waiting for me outside the store on Thursday morning. Even though she was sitting down, petting Coco, I knew something was up. "What's wrong?" I asked.

"Nothing," she said. "Well, not really. I need to ask you . . ." She seemed to run out of steam and then blurted out, "What do you think of me handing over management of the store to Erica and going back to school full time?"

What? I needed more coffee for this. Coco left Colleen and started winding herself around my ankles. "What does it matter what I think?"

She scowled. "Do you think Erica would be okay with

it? I mean, I'm sure she'd be able to handle it, but do you think she'd feel trapped?"

"That's a good question," I said. "I know she liked being away, but she seems really happy being home. Did you feel trapped?"

She got a faraway look. "I'm figuring that out, with my therapist. I do. But she's helped me realize that I always trapped myself."

I thought carefully about what I would say. "Everything I know about Erica is that if she felt trapped, she'd find a way out. But I think she feels that she's got it made now. She gets to be around her family, especially your adorable kids." Hey! I was able to say that without a grimace now. "She loves working with books. She does research whenever she feels like it. She—"

Colleen interrupted me. "But Bean's been helping her and he's going to leave soon."

I felt a pang at her certainty that Bean would be gone. Of course he was leaving. I was an idiot to hope he wouldn't. "Then Erica will hire and train someone. They won't be as good as you, but they'll be good enough. Look at Kona and Kayla—they could run the place without me."

Well, they couldn't *really*, but Colleen didn't have to know that. She left, appearing to feel better. I hoped she planned to tell Erica soon. This was one secret it'd be hard to keep.

Later that afternoon, Emberton and his assistant drove up from DC with a van full of Denise's mounted photos in various sizes, stands and lighting, and we started setting up for Denise's memorial photo exhibit.

Plenty of people tried the door handle and then knocked to offer their assistance, but we firmly but politely told them we were handling it. The show would open early Friday evening with a simple wine and cheese spread, donated by Emberton himself.

Detective Lockett had approved Bean using his own "photog," as he called him—a leathery-faced man in a cowboy hat who silently went about setting up hidden cameras around the community-center-turned-gallery. Bean said he'd worked with him on some undercover story, but I didn't want to ask too many questions.

Every once in a while, I'd position a photograph and my hands would tremble until I got control again. It felt like I was holding something sacred—the work of someone who had just died. Denise had worked on her craft as hard as I worked on making chocolate, and she didn't even get to eat the result.

If this worked like we hoped, we'd catch a killer, which had to be good. Someone would try to get a photo out, or hide it, and we'd know the bad guy. Just like on TV.

I should have been more excited, but instead I was scared that we were causing something monumental to happen, something that would affect the whole town.

Erica was quiet, perhaps feeling the same trepidation I did. "I looked into Maryland inheritance law," she said. "Since Denise had no relatives, not even distant ones, her estate goes to the local school district."

"That's kinda nice." I looked around at the carefully placed photos. Then worry got to me. "What if no one shows up?"

She knew I meant the killer, not our neighbors. "Then we'll think of something else," Erica said.

....

Bean and his photog, appropriately nicknamed Cowboy, set up a pseudo command center in the back hallway after we closed up the store. We'd gone into stealth mode, shutting the blinds and turning off the lights. We'd stocked up on pizza and caffeinated soda, determined to keep watch on the community center all night.

The desk lamps competed with the glare from multiple computer screens set up on the tables we'd dragged in from the dining area. Zane and Cowboy hit it off right away, talking tech stuff as they watched the various camera views.

Bobby, Bean, Erica and I took turns paying attention to the view from the outside cameras. Bobby wasn't all that sure he should be there. While Lockett had supported our little sting operation, Chief Noonan had protested the use of "civilians," as he described us.

"Remember when Lucky got sprayed by a skunk and we chased him through the house?" Bean seemed to be trying to put everyone at ease.

Erica met Bobby's eyes when they laughed, and then she looked away.

Bobby cleared his throat before adding, "I don't know who your mom wanted to kill first—us or the dog."

By midnight, we decided that Bobby and I should take a break and nap on the couches in the dining area until our shift at two. Zane and Cowboy exchanged a sneer that said, "*Wimps.*"

"This is weird, right?" I murmured as we dozed in the dark in couches across from each other.

●

He yawned. "Definitely weird."

At one, Erica said, "There he is!"

Bobby and I jumped up and dashed to the hallway, pushing our desk chairs back to the table.

An outside camera showed a man letting himself in the back door of the community center. We all scrambled to crowd around Zane and Cowboy's table, craning for an inside camera view. The man walked between the photos with a small flashlight, scrutinizing each one. It was impossible to see his features, but something about the way he held himself seemed familiar.

Bobby called Detective Lockett to bring him up to speed.

I squinted at the screen. "Who is it?" I was surprised by the urgency in my voice. "I swear I know him."

No one responded, each of us trying to figure it out. The man stopped in front of one of the larger photos and picked it up from its easel. He stared at it for a long time. Then in one angry gesture, he ripped off the cardboard backing, folded the photo and shoved it in his jacket pocket. He lifted a tablecloth and hid the cardboard underneath.

As he replaced the photo with one from the wall, the flashlight fell against his face and I recognized him.

I ran for the back door, ignoring Bobby's yell to stop and took off for the community center two blocks away. He caught up with me just as Principal Palladine came out the back door and two police cars drove up behind us, lights flashing. Peter looked around wildly, realizing he had nowhere to go. Then he met my eyes.

I sidestepped Bobby's grab for my arm and parked myself in front of the principal. "How could you?" I yelled, sounding more like a betrayed child than an angry adult. I pushed him hard in the chest and he took a step back.

Bobby grabbed me then and didn't let go. Bean skidded to a halt next to a police car with Erica right behind him.

"You killed Denise? With my chocolate?" The outrage I felt made my voice shake. "You tried to kill me?"

The principal shook his head. "I didn't . . ." he said, but his voice was so full of sorrow that it sounded like a confession.

The chief himself walked up to read the principal his Miranda rights, taking the photo out of his pocket and clicking on the handcuffs.

Erica wrapped her arm around my shoulder and tried to lead me away, but I stopped when Peter's eyes watched me over the roof of the police car before he was helped inside. It seemed like an apology.

"Why?" I asked as he was driven away.

No one answered. We were shuttled away by the police and went back to the store.

"Did you see the photo?" I asked Bean.

He nodded. "An old car moving past a barn," he said. "Seems like it was taken early in the morning using some kind of trick photography that elongated the exposure."

"How do we *know* he killed her because of it?"

That brought Bean up short. "Actually, we don't." He thought for a minute. "Unless we can figure out something from the photo and get him to talk."

"Wait," I said. "What kind of car was in the photo?"

"A classic Corvette," he said. "Light blue. Maybe sixty-seven?"

My heart sank. That was the principal's car.

. . . .

How did people live on so little sleep? I thought as I poured my third cup of coffee in my kitchen the next morning. This mystery-solving stuff was exhausting. And unsatisfying. I wanted to march into that jail and shake the principal until he told me what the hell was going on.

Erica knocked on the door and stuck her head in.

"Morning," I said in my grouchy voice.

She was carrying her laptop, looking way too awake for how long she'd slept. "I've been checking out these photos, but I don't know why he would steal this one."

"Did you check all the geo-stuff?"

"Zane taught me how, but like the others, the geotags are missing," she explained. "He'll help me when he gets out of class."

"That barn's familiar," I said. "Isn't that the Grubakers'?"

"Yes," she said. "It's the only barn around here that doesn't have some kind of sign on it." She brought up Google maps and zoomed in. "That's close to Peter's house. He could have been coming from anywhere."

"Then why is the photo worth stealing?" I asked. "And maybe," I felt a hitch in my throat, "killing over."

"What do men try to hide?" she asked.

All I could think about was Colleen's husband, Mark. "An affair?"

"But to kill to hide it?" she asked.

Some people will do anything to save their reputation, I thought, except for not having an affair in the first place. "Why wouldn't he just get divorced?"

"Peter's wife has a great deal of money from her family," Erica said. "Maybe he didn't want to change his lifestyle."

"Let's try to put some pieces together," I said, "and see if any of it makes sense. After Denise successfully blackmails Larry, she tries her hand at blackmailing the principal with the photo. He makes her senior-class photographer and maybe that's not enough for her. So he feels like he has to get rid of her."

"But why kill Larry?"

I thought for a minute.

"Maybe Denise and Larry were working together?" I ended with a question mark because it seemed so ridiculous. Denise couldn't stand Larry.

Chief Noonan held the press conference announcing the principal's arrest in the murder of Denise Coburn. I felt that I had to be there, but the event didn't help my dissatisfaction that I didn't know the whole story.

The chief thanked the fine police work of Detective Lockett and the Maryland State Police but seemed to be more in charge than at the other public meetings. When he was asked by a reporter if the principal had also killed Larry, he said, "He's a person of interest in that crime as well, and we are investigating."

Not many of my neighbors were there. Maybe everyone in town was press-conferenced out, as well as dumbfounded that someone we all trusted for so many years was an alleged killer.

We had very few customers that day. We often had a lull on Thursdays, but never on Fridays. I'd assumed that chocolate was part of every weekend, and now I wondered if our customers were mad at us.

No one would have even known our role in the principal's arrest if it wasn't for stupid Reese. I discovered when I woke up that she had posted on her blog breathless details about how Erica and I had tricked the principal, and fellow towns-folk, in order to lure him into a trap.

Even with the press conference, not everyone believed the principal had done it, as we overheard from our few customers. The Larry theory—that Larry had killed Denise and then been killed by one of his criminal buddies—was still winning, but unless Peter came up with a great explan-ation for stealing a photo by Denise, I expected more people to change their opinions.

Bean came by to let us know that the principal's wife had come home long enough to bail him out and head back down to DC, and now Peter was holed up in his house refusing to see anyone, not even a lawyer.

I spent the rest of the morning on the phone answering questions from the ten people who were entered in the Great Fudge Cook-off and taking it far too seriously. They all started with comments about the principal, but soon segued into what they were really calling about, how to make sure their fudge would win.

Kona had supplied each of them with a numbered plastic container and would be the one to place the entries on the trays. After the grief people had given us when we narrowed down the entries from forty to ten, I was grateful that I wouldn't be judging the final round.

The fudge would be judged on flavor, consistency and appearance. If I had a nickel for every time one of the cooks had asked which of these categories would be given more weight, or how important color was, or if their prize could be in cash instead of a gift certificate to our store, I'd be rich.

Since it was such a slow day customer-wise, I did a quick online search for Get Me Some Solar but the only iffy thing I could find was a bankruptcy in Florida by the owner. He'd been a pool contractor but started the solar company years before.

Mayor Gwen stopped by our last official Great Fudge Cook-off meeting, which we held during Jolene and Steve's lunch break. For the first time ever, Gwen's hair was disheveled and she wasn't wearing her mandatory Ralph Lauren scarf. No wonder. We had a crazy crime spree right before the town's big weekend and the longtime high school principal was allegedly the killer of one of her citizens, and a possible killer of someone else.

The only other customer in our store was a man in his fifties in a sports jacket who brought a sandwich in to eat with his dessert. Before he took a bite, he always inspected the area where he was about to bite from. It was oddly fascinating to watch. Peek, bite, chew, swallow. Repeat.

I tore my eyes away. "How are you holding up?" I asked Gwen. "You look like you could use a hug." Not that I was offering.

She shook her head. "I'm fine. Thank God the nightmare is over and we can continue with our normal safe lives here in West Riverdale." It sounded like something she'd been forced to say more than a few times.

"I still can't believe it," Erica said. "I've known him forever."

The mayor's face tightened. "Let's try to move past this tragedy and make sure this weekend is a success." She pulled out her phone. "I noted a few more ideas." Grim determination had replaced her normal cheerleader enthusiasm.

As the day wore on and our customers only dribbled in, I convinced Erica that we might want to distance ourselves from Denise's show and ask Emberton to run it alone. Reese's article was beginning to make me think people were blaming us for the principal's arrest.

I wasn't totally convinced of his guilt myself. "So you really think he bashed Larry's head in too?" I argued with her in the back hallway while I was taking a break from making Cardamom and Orange Caramels for my more adventurous customers.

Zane stuck his head out from his office. "He couldn't have."

"What?"

"I checked his schedule. The principal was at a school board meeting when Larry was killed," he said. "He couldn't have killed Larry."

Oh. My. God.

23

Erica convinced me to be the one to contact Detective Lockett. "I think he secretly wants you," she said.

"You're dreaming," I told her but made the call.

He picked up right away and I told him what Zane had figured out, that the principal was at the meeting and didn't kill Larry.

"We know." He spoke with exaggerated patience.

"So who killed Larry?" Anxiety laced my words.

I could feel his exasperation through the phone. "Thank you very much for the info. When we figure that out, you'll be the first person I call."

"Was that sarcasm?" I asked.

"Whatta ya think?" He hung up.

"He didn't tell me anything," I said to Erica. "I told you he doesn't want me."

"Who doesn't want you?" Bean asked.

I jumped. "Will you stop sneaking up on us? I'm beginning to think you get all of your stories by eavesdropping."

"Only the best ones," he said. "Who doesn't want you?"

Was he jealous? That thought pleased me a little too much.

Erica seemed delighted to tell him. "Detective Lockett."

"Interesting," he said. "What were you trying to get out of him?"

I filled him in on what Zane had figured out. "I wanted to find out if he still thought that Larry killed Denise."

"I don't think he ever believed that," Bean said.

"Then why did he let the chief imply that at the press conference?"

He shrugged. "Could be anything. Maybe trying to put the real killer at ease."

Kona rushed back and pointed an accusing finger at Bean. "You didn't tell her!"

"Oh yeah," he said. "That pumpkin lady is here."

"You mean Hillary Punkin? Here? Now?" I followed the frantic Kona back to the front, worried what my hair, face, everything looked like. Erica followed behind.

Kona took charge. "I'll get a box for her to sample. You be, um, gracious or something." Her desperate tone made me realize that she was as invested in the store as I was.

A group of very fashionable people dressed only in black were outside staring at our store, surrounding Hillary Punkin.

I couldn't miss her. She was tinier than me and had flaming orange-red hair sticking up in a modified mohawk. She looked like a lit matchstick.

I swear I could see her psychotic little pupils from here, even through her sunglasses.

How should I handle her? Fawning deference? Snottiness that she'd respect? Definitely not what I felt like doing, which was throwing up.

Why hadn't I figured this out ahead of time?

"They never told us she was coming!" I hissed.

Erica gave me a little push. "Go out there and invite her in!"

Hillary must have deemed our store good enough to enter, because one of her entourage opened the door for her. I was speechless. On TV, Hillary was tiny, but in person she was doll-like.

She walked in wearing a yellow dress, looking like the sun with her entourage circling around her in a galaxy of yes-men planets. They all clutched matching orange plaid–covered notebook computers with her logo on them.

I was jealous. Where was my entourage?

Erica moved around me. "Ms. Punkin. Welcome," she said, not sounding worried that the devil herself may have arrived.

"Oh this shop is delightful!" Hillary said, clasping her hands together. One of her assistants typed that one-handed into his notebook. I wanted to record it and put it on our website. *Hillary Punkin said our store is delightful.* Just to get it out there before she went all random on me.

Erica gave my arm a little yank, luckily on my good arm. "This is Michelle Serrano, the amazing chocolatier I told you about."

"Nice to meet you," I started, but then Hillary walked right up to me and stood on her toes to give me a hug. She wore tiny ballet shoes, making her seem even more pixie-like, and I had to bend over to reach her, not a normal occurrence for me.

"I feel like I've known you forever," she said. "My folks have been following your town's news blog and told me that you helped solve the murder of your very good friend. I knew I had to meet you in person." She turned both hands up like a politician gesturing during a debate. "A crime-fighting chocolatier. Why didn't I think of that?"

She followed Reese's blog? We were doomed. "I could have my own comic book," I joked. Erica stepped back as one of Hillary's assistants took a bunch of photos. I tried to lose the weird, stressed-out smile that must be on my face. "I'm kidding. It was just a onetime thing."

"Of course." She patted my arm. "Do you have a minute to show me around?"

"I'd love to." Uh-oh. Our dining area was practically empty. "Um, it seems like our townspeople don't know how to take the whole principal thing and are staying home today." That was my story and I was sticking to it.

"So you sacrificed greatly to right a terrible injustice," she said, and then mouthed, *Write that down,* to another assistant.

"Well," I said, "I'm sure they'll be back another day."

"So where did you find your friend?" She peered around the dining area with ghoulish delight.

"Excuse me?"

"Your friend," Hillary said. "The poor victim."

I met the eyes of the assistant taking notes, who gave me the tiniest nod. Did that mean "answer the question" or "yes, she's nuts?"

"Well, we rearranged everything and that furniture has been taken away," I said carefully.

Hillary gave a little pout. "Oh, pooh."

Pooh?

"I heard she had chocolate in her mouth," she said. "Did you see it?" She gave a morbid little shudder. "Was it, like, dripping out?"

I turned to Erica, my eyes opened wide.

"We're still too traumatized to talk about that," Erica said in a smooth but firm tone. "Would you like to see the kitchen where all of Michelle's magic happens?" She held her arm out indicating the direction to the kitchen with all the composure of a game show spokesperson.

"I'm sure it's not what you're used to," I said, and then inwardly cursed myself for appearing so ridiculously self-conscious. My kitchen was perfect for me.

Hillary sighed as if suffering a major disappointment, which made me want to make her feel better. She had one of those faces that you just wanted to see happy. I controlled myself and led her to the kitchen with her entourage trailing behind her. She walked in, her ballet shoes practically silent on my linoleum floor.

"It's darling." She clasped her hands together. "And what are you making here? Do I smell cardamom?"

"Yes," I said. "It's a new recipe. Would you like to try it?"

She stopped still, stunned. Oh man. I blew it. Hillary had strict rules for tasting chocolate. I had glanced at her long list of requirements the week before, but hadn't expected her to actually show. I tried to remember what they were: spring water from Europe, not the United States, at room temperature; chocolates representing the best we had to offer, placed in a box and given to her assistant; absolutely no hazelnut anything; and some others that hopefully didn't apply to me.

Kona saved the day. "I've included one of those in this box for later." She handed a box to a relieved assistant.

"Would you like to see the bookstore?" Erica broke in. "We have your latest cookbook on display."

Hillary perked up at that, and I stayed at the back of the pack with Kona as they moved out. "Did I blow it?" I asked quietly.

"No, not at all." She tried to reassure me but her voice was tight with worry.

It was very early Saturday morning and I yawned along with the other volunteers in the West Riverdale Community Park. Tents, tables and chairs were being unloaded, and Erica directed like the gentle tyrant she was, ruthlessly keeping us all on schedule.

I was grateful she'd taken over the tour with Hillary and her entourage the afternoon before, including avoiding answering any more inappropriate questions from the twisted Hillary, and delivering our guest to the only bed-and-breakfast in West Riverdale. Her staff had arranged to stay in a motel near the highway. They asked when Hillary was to be at the park, but were quick to say there was no guarantee she'd show up. She was one loony lady.

Beatrice had helped Emberton at Denise's photography exhibit the night before. She had called to say that the crowd was somber but sales had been pretty good. Emberton had not figured out the exhibit's dual role. He appeared to just be happy with the additional publicity caused by the principal's arrest.

This morning, Beatrice was pushing her fist into her lower back before unloading more tools from the Duncan Hardware panel truck. "I'm too old for this."

Erica was happy to report that she'd received emails from a few of the local hotels, saying that some of their cancelled reservations were calling again to rebook. The news about the principal's arrest was spreading. Maybe tourists were feeling that West Riverdale was safe again.

I couldn't help my mixed emotions about that. Guarded happiness that our Memorial Day events might actually be successful after so much work. But sadness that Denise had died and that someone I admired might be guilty of a horrible crime. And maybe the worry that whoever killed Larry was still around, regardless of the theory that one of his criminal buddies was responsible. I tried hard to get that out of my mind.

Erica jogged over to where I was trying to push the magical button on my tent leg that would allow it to go higher. Jolene, Steve and a drama kid with streaks of purple in his hair waited patiently by the other three legs, which had gone up without a problem. "You're not going to believe this!" she said.

"What?" I grunted as it finally moved. I held up the leg with my fingertips, trying to get the pin to pop back out through the hole so it would stay up. Right about now, I'd believe anything. "Did Zane find something?"

She frowned at me. "We are not thinking about that this weekend, remember?" She held up her phone and I saw the headline, *Hillary Punkin Supports Crime-Solving Chocolatier.*

"What is that?" I was flabbergasted.

"It was posted early this morning on the Grand Chef Network's website! It's about her visit to the store, and our role in the principal's arrest."

"I checked her site ten times!"

Erica reached out to jiggle my tent leg, and of course, the pin dropped into place. I grabbed her phone and read the short release announcing that Hillary would be judging our fudge contest. Then it went into some detail about how Erica and I had been the masterminds behind the photography exhibit trick that had uncovered the alleged killer of promising photographer, Denise Coburn, in a town besieged by a crime spree. "Did you read the whole thing?" I asked. "Crime spree?"

"Yes," she said. "That part's a bit much, but what great publicity!"

I wasn't convinced. It was bad enough having Reese's ridiculous blog spouting her ideas on our involvement in the principal's arrest. But I felt distinctly uneasy about having thousands of Hillary's followers believing this version.

Erica's balloon arch arrived, weaving back and forth until it was anchored to the ground, and soon red, white and blue tablecloths were being clipped to tables.

I took a breather. The park looked awesome. The sun came through the trees, highlighting individual leaves in a glorious display of nature. The way the park gazebo was lit reminded me very much of the barn in Denise's photo.

"Hey, Erica," I said. "Can you come here for a second?"

"Not really. I have to check on the coolers—" She focused on me and worry shot across her face. "What now?"

"Over here," I said, to get her alone. "Look up through those trees."

She sighed. "Okay. Trees."

"In Denise's photograph, the sun was coming through just like this and hitting the barn just like that. It had less light, more stark, so it was probably taken even earlier in the morning."

"And?"

"So to catch the light that way, the side of the barn with the sliding door has to face southeast," I said. "The Grubakers' barn faces west."

She frowned. "We have the wrong barn." She brushed her bangs aside with one hand, trying to figure out how to do more even though she was stretched to the limit. "Okay, we have to prioritize. We'll figure out which barns face southeast later. Tomorrow. When the cook-off is a huge success, our artists sell the pants off of their work and the book-signing makes beaucoup bucks for the Boys and Girls Club."

"It's a deal," I said, but couldn't help feeling that another shoe was waiting to drop for our town.

I shook it off and went back to decorating. An hour later, the park was festooned with the red and blue banners, contrasting nicely with the white pop-up tents. Like a patriotic circus.

"It's beautiful," I told Erica, who smiled widely. "Anything still to do?"

"Not at this moment." She sounded a little surprised.

"I'm heading over to meet Kona and Kayla at the shop," I said. "We'll be back to set up for the fudge contest and our booth."

She turned to answer a question from one of the electricians, and I hopped into my minivan.

While Erica was in charge of just about everything else, the Great Fudge Cook-off was definitely my responsibility. Kona and Kayla had given each of the ten finalists their own marked plastic container, and all of the fudge entries were to be delivered by nine, well before the opening ceremonies at ten and the blind taste test immediately after.

We had an interesting assortment of fudge finalists. Everything from the standard Old-fashioned Chocolate, Cookies and Cream, and Peanut Butter fudge, to Piña Colada, Mint, and Velveeta Cheese fudge.

Kona and Kayla had outvoted me on that one.

"Love the hat," I told Kona, who wore a huge beach hat with a scarf woven through it. She'd painted some kind of animated squirrel on the parts of the scarf showing through, so when she whipped her head around, it looked like the creature was chasing an acorn.

We loaded the minivan with two smaller wine coolers to take to our booth at the park, plugged them in and then headed back again for our chocolates, already packed in boxes of four, nine and sixteen. We'd decided to sell only preset boxes, but we could always change gears later in the day if we felt like we were losing sales.

I opened the drawer by the cash register, searching for the Square cell phone attachment that let us take credit cards outside the store, when I noticed Kona's handwritten cheat sheet listing our top customers' favorites. She kept it tucked under the cash register, and I'd seen her surreptitiously peek at it a thousand times as people entered.

I hadn't realized what a wealth of information it contained. Most of our customers liked it when we remembered their favorites, but it was hard to keep them all straight and to stay up-to-date when they changed. Sometimes the new flavors I introduced became favorites and sometimes they didn't work at all.

I saw the principal listed toward the top and again felt the combination of anger and sadness. Kona had crossed out his old favorite flavors for new ones several times over the last few months. His newest favorite was Black Forest Milks, a popular choice.

"Ready to go?" Kona asked, and I put the paper away.

Early birds were entering the park, some volunteering to help with last-minute odds and ends and some putting down their camping chairs and blankets to reserve space in front of the small stage at the end of one of the rows of booths.

We set up our table for judging, which would be to the right of the stage, in full view of anyone who wanted to watch. I couldn't imagine that it would be very exciting. Our ten contestants excitedly handed over their entries to Kona, who arranged them on trays with their assigned numbers in front of them. One of the contestants held up a hand. "Can mine be the third entry?" but the others shushed her, telling her that she couldn't mess around with the order.

Kona was very gracious, saying that the three judges would start at different corners of the table, so there was no advantage in going first, last or third. Then she turned firm. "If the coordinators of the event observe any of you trying to communicate or influence the judges in any way, your entry will be disqualified."

That caused a little bit of good-natured grumbling. "Guess I better cancel that skywriter," one of them joked.

My two chef judges arrived together, a married couple who owned rival top restaurants in Frederick. They were rumored to be competing against each other on the newest Grand Chef Network show called *4 Star Chef Showdown*.

I welcomed them and explained the process, and then I heard my cell phone buzz with a notice from my website. Excusing myself, I clicked on the phone and saw I'd received a large order from my hotel. My best customer was back!

A wave of relief made me laugh out loud. My chocolates had survived being a freakin' murder weapon. They were that good. Maybe even good enough to survive a bad review from Hillary.

Five minutes before ten, a Hummer stretch limo emblazoned with photos of Hillary and logos of her show arrived. It narrowly missed one of the generators before stopping right behind the stage.

I held my breath until the driver placed stairs by the back door and Hillary got out, her thigh-high red leather boots with four-inch-heels leading the way. Her flag-inspired dress was more subdued than yesterday's, and her assistants also wore some combination of red, white and blue. I wondered if they color coordinated their outfits every day.

Right at ten o'clock, Mayor Gwen and some other members of the town council walked onto the small covered stage. Gwen was back to full professional mode, with her trademark scarf and everything.

"Welcome to the First Annual West Riverdale Great Fudge Cook-off and Arts Festival!"

First annual? How about first and last? At least that involved me.

The crowd gave her a smattering of applause and she smiled.

"This contest is a wonderful kickoff to an amazing weekend of the best family-friendly fun that West Riverdale has to offer. I can't wait to taste the delicious fudge recipes.

A little birdy told me that one of them is actually made with Velveeta cheese! Isn't that fun?"

She pulled a notecard out of her pocket and glanced at it while the crowd groaned at the mention of the unusual flavor. "I encourage all of you to take advantage of this opportunity to buy artwork from our local artists, eat the delicious cuisine by our food vendors and enjoy our beautiful Maryland sunshine." She gestured around as if she'd provided the beautiful weather herself.

"I'd like to thank our Titanium Sponsor for all they have done to help get this event off the ground. We all know who it is—Get Me Some Solar. Isn't that the cutest name?" She led the audience in applause. "Please welcome their president, Terrence Jaffe."

I stood behind Kona when he ran onto the stage, hoping he didn't want his laminated info sheet back.

"Thank you so much, Ms. Mayor. We are delighted to work with such a forward-thinking town like West Riverdale. You guys have a great mayor, don't you?" He applauded and the crowd joined him. "She knows how important green energy is to the future of your town, your country and your world. And we're happy to help. We hope you all will check out our website and learn how you can make a difference too."

Reese appeared as if by magic from behind a tent, and cornered him as he jogged down the three steps to the ground. I was dying to know what she was asking him, but then Gwen said into the microphone, "I'd like to welcome Erica Russell and Michelle Serrano to the stage to begin the Great Fudge Cook-off!"

24

Erica seemed happy to go up on stage after the mayor's introduction, but I just waved from the ground.

"Oh no, you don't," Gwen yelled into her microphone. "Come on up here."

Breaking into my stressed smile, I walked up the steps, tripping just a bit as if my feet knew I didn't want to be on-stage. A dull roaring started in my ears, which always happened during any kind of public speaking.

Out of the corner of my eye, I saw Reese still talking to poor Terrence Jaffe, throwing her arms around him as if she was in a Fellini movie. It was hard not to stare. Even Gwen couldn't keep her eyes off of them.

"Why don't you let everyone know how the judging will work?" Gwen shoved the microphone at me, and I'm sure panic showed on my face.

I handed it off to Erica, who went over our simple rules and introduced our judges. The quickly growing crowd applauded politely for the two restaurant chefs, but cheered wildly for Hillary. All three judges waved from their spot behind the judging table, while Gwen introduced the high school jazz club. They clambered onto the stage and Gwen rescued Terrence from Reese's clutches. I thought I could hear Reese gnashing her teeth from the other side of the stage.

Kona waved at me to join her behind the table. Each judge was given score sheets on clipboards. Hillary directed one of her assistants over; he took the sheets off the simple brown clipboard and put it on an orange plaid–covered one, which seemed to delight Hillary.

She and the other judges took their time walking around the table while the jazz band played, tasting each fudge entry and making notes. Hillary took just the tiniest bite of each one. As she passed my position at one corner of the table, she whispered to me, "I hate fudge."

I laughed. "Me too!"

The contestants huddled together, waiting for the verdict. Hillary and the two chefs compared their score sheets, and then Hillary started arguing with them in a loud whisper.

Kona was closest and seemed about to burst into laughter. Then all three judges turned around. Hillary was smiling but the others seemed grim.

"Can I announce the winner?" Hillary asked with child-like enthusiasm.

"We'd be honored," Erica said with a little bow as Hillary danced up the stairs and grabbed the microphone. Hillary started reading from her own score sheet. Had she convinced the others to only use her results? "In third place, Chocolate Raspberry Hedonism!"

Everyone clapped and the contestant ran up on stage to get her gift certificate to Chocolates and Chapters. "In second place, Coconuts in Paradise!"

A disappointed elderly lady didn't bother with the stairs. She waved from in front of the stage and held her hand up for her gift certificate.

"In first place," Hillary said slowly, drawing out the suspense, "the winner of the first ever West Riverdale Great Fudge Cook-off is . . ."

The audience groaned at her delay.

"Mint Espresso!" Tonya the nurse's mom dashed to the stage, hugged Hillary and did a little happy dance before taking her gift certificate from Erica. The audience clapped and the jazz band started up again.

thanked all of the judges, and Kona remembered to give them their gift baskets filled with chocolates and the latest best-selling books. I invited them all to enjoy the festival, but they had other places to be.

Hillary gave me one last hug and pointed to her assistant, who handed me her card. The whole group piled into the Hummer and left. I felt a wave of relief. Whatever she decided, my chocolates, and I, would be okay.

The First Annual Great Fudge Cook-off was over. I looked over the crowded festival and grinned at Erica. We had done it.

Kona and I joined Kayla at our booth in the food area. Granny's Funnel Cakes was doing a brisk business along with Dublin Roasters Coffee, but we weren't selling much. I understood my regulars not buying, since so many had been in the shop this week, but I needed to drum up business with the tourists. Time to pull out the gateway drug. No one could eat just one.

Kayla placed a bunch of the tiny caramels on a chilled silver tray and I dove into the crowd, inviting attendees to take a chocolate along with a business card with our booth number on the back. I was quickly relieved of my chocolate. It was so much fun seeing people enjoying their bite of heaven, especially when many of them headed over to our tent. I walked around the back of Sweeney's Weenies' tent and noticed Reese arguing with the mayor. They were too far away for me to hear much except something about Boys and Girls Club funding.

Since the proceeds from Bean's book launch and silent auction was a fundraiser for the Boys and Girls Club, it got my attention. I inched closer to listen, but then Gwen said loudly, "Can I borrow your pen? Thanks!" and pulled the pen that we all knew was a camera out of Reese's pocket and walked away.

Reese looked stunned, and I couldn't resist a smile. She caught me and marched over. "Did you put the mayor up to that?" The way she loomed over me, glaring like a cranky vulture, made me giggle.

"Up to what?" I said. "So she took your pen. Big deal. She'll return it."

"You are not that stupid," she said. "She took my camera so I couldn't catch her doing something illegal. There is a crapload of corruption going on in this town and everyone goes on their merry way as if this really was Mayberry."

"What corruption?"

"Where do you think our illustrious mayor is getting her money to run for Congress? Her major donor is Get Me Some Solar. Guess who's making a bloody fortune off of every installation? And what town in America can afford to offer a five hundred dollar grant to everyone who gets solar?"

"So you think she's encouraging everyone to install solar, so the company will donate to her campaign?" I started my question with sarcasm but ended it with uncertainty in my voice.

"It's obvious, isn't it? Connect the dots."

"Do you have any evidence?"

"Not yet, but I will," she said. "There's always a weak link and I'm going to find it."

I saw the mayor shopping at the Peaceful Heart Glass booth. She'd worked so hard for West Riverdale for many years. Would she really sell her soul to make it to Congress?

"You might want to think about why we suddenly need fundraisers for the Boys and Girls Club," Reese continued. "Maybe because the town council secretly cut their funding in order to pay the stupid rebates." She stomped off, probably to get another pen camera.

Was that why the mayor had talked us into a fundraiser? I remembered my now-warm silver tray, empty of chocolates, and headed back to the booth.

. . . .

The afternoon sped by as Erica dealt with small emergencies and I sold chocolate and helped when I could. Leo showed up for the last hour and introduced me to a lovely woman named Star.

"What a beautiful name," I said, as I shook her hand enthusiastically.

Leo sent me a "watch it" look and I backed off. But that didn't stop me from stalking them to a couple of booths as I tried to figure out if he was on a date. As far as I knew, he hadn't dated since he came home. He touched her back and guided her to the next artist. This was great!

Suddenly it was six p.m. and the First Annual West Riverdale Arts Festival was officially closed.

Kona, Kayla and I were exhausted, and I was a little sunburnt from not putting on my sunscreen early enough in the day.

Bean was on cleanup duty and stopped by in between taking down tents. "Cute," he said, touching a finger to my nose. "More freckles."

Wonderful.

"How'd you do today?" he asked.

"Good," I told him, feeling sweaty and dog tired. "Really, I'm just happy it's over."

He smiled. "I'll have the beer waiting at home."

Home? Was he thinking of it that way? It gave me a warm feeling.

The mayor was making the rounds of all of the booths, thanking people for their participation. "Michelle, I can't tell you how much I appreciate all of the hard work you and the rest of the committee put into this event. It was truly extraordinary."

"Thanks, Gwen." I was almost too tired to form words. "I can't believe it's over."

"You'll have just enough time to rest before the book launch tomorrow," she said ruefully. "We really piled it on for you all, didn't we?"

Was that a royal 'we'? "That'll be easy compared to this," I said, happy that she finally seemed to realize she'd asked too much. "Hey, while I have you. I had a question about that solar company. I saw this article—"

Anger flared in her eyes and I stopped talking.

"Have you been listening to that crazy Reese?" Her voice was more exasperated than angry, which reassured me.

She patted my arm. "I know how much you and Erica contributed to uncovering Denise's killer, but you can't let that go to your head. People are going to think you're a conspiracy theorist like Reese. I think it's time to get back to your usual spectacular job of making your delicious chocolate. Or would you rather put out your own private investigator shingle?" she said with a laugh.

I forced a smile. "It'll be great when everything gets back to normal."

A cold breeze swept through the park, always an indicator for an incoming storm, and everyone rushed to finish packing up before the showers hit.

We got a little wet unloading everything into our store, but it seemed to energize the bunch of us.

"Let's get some beer and have everyone meet at our house," I suggested, and Erica agreed.

I texted invites to a few people, and decided to see what trouble I could cause by including Bobby as well.

Soon our kitchen at home was filled with an impromptu party. To my delight, Leo brought Star and I was able to question, I mean, get to know her. "So where did you meet?" I asked her in my most obnoxious nosy-parker voice.

She looked up at Leo, and he said, "It's okay."

"A PTSD support group meeting," she said simply. "At the West Riverdale Veterans Club."

I bit my lip. I'd researched services for vets when Leo came home but he'd always rejected them. Finally, he was ready to do what he needed to do to get better. Maybe not all the way back to normal, but further along the path in his new life.

My pride must have shone in my face, because he said, "I'm trying, Berry." His voice was rough. I resisted hugging him tight, but I may have made Star a little uncomfortable by fawning over her way too much.

Jolene and Steve had brought some of their teen volunteers, along with a cooler full of soda to make sure they stayed away from the beer. Most of them didn't seem the partying type, but what did I know? They spent the night in the living room playing some game that involved wizards and planeswalkers, spells and lands. It also seemed to involve a lot of arguing and yelling about rules.

Beatrice and Howard stopped by with Sammy, who went straight for the beer. Beatrice started in on him immediately. "We had a great day, Sammy, but now you have to follow up with all those people I took notes on."

I was pretty sure he rolled his eyes.

When Howard went to stare outside at the rain, his basset-hound eyes seeming even more sad, I joined him at the window. He gave me a brief smile. "Nasty out there, ain't it?"

"Howard, I have a difficult problem that I need your help with," I started. "If you were me, and you saw, entirely by accident of course, someone give a lot of money to, um, let's say someone in authority, what would you do?"

His face turned wary. "It depends who the person is, doesn't it?"

"Or the person in authority, like, maybe the building inspector."

His eyes widened and he looked over his shoulder at Beatrice. "Please don't tell Bea," he said. "I'm done with that poker game anyway. I told 'em I was out. For good."

"So that was gambling money?"

"I got a problem, you see?" he said. "Bea made me quit a long time ago. I thought I could handle it now, but that jerk made me keep bidding higher . . ." He shook his head. "It was good that it happened, really. Now I'm truly done."

The whole thing made me hate that Wayne Chauncey more than ever, but I was relieved that Howard was in the clear.

Bobby stopped by, and I was sure Erica noticed how cute he was with his hair all disheveled from the windy rain. He thanked me for the beer I handed him, and even though he didn't look at her at all, his attention was on Erica.

I saw Bean watching him and our eyes met. I was the first to turn away.

At midnight, Erica kicked everyone out. Bean went upstairs, sending me an enigmatic smile on his way. What was he doing? Inviting me up? Asking me to invite him down? I was too confused to decide anything.

After diving into my pajamas, I heard a male voice. Peeking out the kitchen window, I saw Erica and Bobby talking on the porch. Like, actually talking. I was dying to find out what that was about but once I hit my bed, I fell asleep instantly.

The much more relaxed fudge cook-off committee spent the morning collecting silent auction items and setting up the community center for Bean's book signing. Kona made Erica's stupid softball cupcakes, which even I had to admit were very cute.

Kayla was in charge of the store while Kona and I helped Erica with chairs and tables.

Erica was very subdued but wouldn't respond to my "Are you okay?" questions with anything but, "I'm fine."

"So what did you and Bobby talk about?" I asked when we were setting baskets on the silent auction table.

She looked surprised that I'd seen them. "Just working through a few . . . issues."

"Did you apologize for being a butthead all those years ago?" I didn't really think she was a butthead, but I knew it would get her to talk.

She smiled, seeing right through me. "I did, although I didn't express it so succinctly."

"And then what happened?"

"Nothing," she said.

"He didn't kiss you?" I asked, astounded.

She laughed. "No. I think he wanted to, but he has, I don't know, to think about things." Her face grew serious. "Like if he can forgive me."

"You should have kissed him," I suggested, thinking that maybe I'd take a chance and use my own advice.

And just like the perfect timing that only happened in the movies, the delivery boy from Eugene's Flower Shop walked in with a huge bouquet of flowers and called out, "Erica?"

Her eyes widened and her mouth made a little O as she signed for them.

"They're beautiful," I said. "Read the card."

She smiled a little coyly and opened the tiny envelope. Her smile faded. "They're a thank-you from Emberton."

Those damn romantic comedies.

Reese waylaid me as I left the community center to change before the book signing. Maybe she had a GPS tracker on me or something.

"Michelle," she said, falling into step beside me. "I know this is going to sound crazy . . ."

I had to take nearly two steps to her one. "If the shoe fits."

"I need to tell you something." She looked over her shoulder. "I don't think you poisoned Denise."

"Of course you don't," I said, regretting that I'd driven over with Erica and had to walk back to the shop to get my minivan. "No one does. You were just making it up to get back at me for taking your place on the basketball team a hundred years ago in high school."

"And also for taking Guy Finestone away from me," she said as if that made any sense at all.

"Who?"

"You don't even remember. You played basketball with

him near my house every Saturday," she said, resentment in every word.

"Oh yeah, Guy," I said. He was part of a group of boys who didn't mind playing basketball with a girl who could hold her own on the court. "Didn't he move away in high school? And how could I take him away from you when I never even went out with him?"

"He wanted to date you."

"How could you know that when *I* didn't even know that?" I remembered a time when he kept fouling me like crazy. Was this all in Reese's head or was I really that clueless?

"I asked him to the Sadie Hawkins dance in ninth grade, and he told me he was waiting for you to ask him."

This girl was crazier than I thought. "Okay, is this real?"

She ignored my question. "I was fine until my divorce and everything." She paused. "And then all this old stuff came up in my therapy. And I got mad again. But my therapist told me that I have to apologize to you and let it all go."

"I accept your apology." *You lunatic.*

"And I think we should work together on this investigation."

I actually choked on nothing when she said that. Like that would ever happen. "Why would I want to do that?"

"Because I have evidence that could help." She waved her folder at me like she thought it would tantalize me. "I found the weak link."

Now that was tempting. Except it was coming from Reese. "Why don't you give it to Detective Lockett or the chief?"

"They won't listen to me anymore. But if we go together, they'll have to. And I can make a deal with you that you'll give me an exclusive on the behind-the-scenes story."

"How about this," I said. By now we had made it to the front of my store. "I'll think about it and let you know."

She squinted at me, wondering if I was just blowing her off. She must finally be developing some kind of reporter instincts. "Okay, but don't take long. This is time critical."

Right. Critical for her blog deadline. I closed the door in her face, the twinkling bell sounding like sarcasm.

The community center was packed. I didn't know where all of these people came from, but one group of yuppie-looking folks were talking about the traffic in DC. I'd helped set up all the chairs, but I hadn't expected them all to be filled.

There was a mixture of people in the crowd. Definitely a lot of locals who probably couldn't believe the scrappy kid with the too-long hair was now a world-class journalist, but also sunburnt tourists, and another chunk of people dressed to impress with designer clothes, manicured nails and hair. We even had a few hipsters in their vintage clothes and nerd glasses.

Mayor Gwen let Erica run the show, seeming to be content with charming people into bidding more on the silent auction items. I hoped what Reese had said wasn't true—the town council knew how important the Boys and Girls Club was to the community. Many of them had hung out there themselves.

Erica's comic book club members were taking selfies with their phones and giggling in the back row. Jolene had negotiated extra credit for them with the English teacher if they helped.

Bean had been standing near the table packed with silent auction items, graciously talking to whoever had the courage to come up to him. His publisher had paid for the wine and cheese spread, and also for a lot of my chocolates that Kona and I were slowly putting out on the trays, trying to keep the teens from grabbing them all. Zane had figured out our routine and was taking way more than his share. Kona gave him a flirty smile. Maybe he wasn't hanging around just for chocolate.

"Zane," I said. "Did you find out anything about that photo?"

He sent one last look at Kona before focusing on me. "Erica kinda ordered me to drop it this weekend." Then he gave me a crafty smile.

"But you found it?" I was so excited, I couldn't stand it. "You found the barn?"

He pulled out his phone and brought it up on the screen. "Erica told me what you said about the direction it faced, and I used Google maps to find the latitude and longitude and match it to the original photo."

It was hard to see it clearly on his phone, but I recognized the big barn with a huge advertisement for Gable's Heating and Plumbing. "Whose barn is that?" I asked.

"It's the old Durham farm," Zane said. "Denise Photoshopped the ad out and here's what it looks like now." He showed me the modified photo. "Once Denise changed the photo, it lost its geotags."

"Any idea why the principal wouldn't want that photo to be public?" There wasn't much out that direction except the housing development that had gone bankrupt and a two-lane road to the next town. Most people drove more miles and took the highway instead. What could have caused the principal to risk everything to get that picture?

Then I got completely distracted when Bean excused

himself from his latest fan and headed toward me. "Thanks," he said, grabbing my hand.

My fingers curled into his. "You're welcome but—" and then he kissed my cheek and walked to his place in the front of the room to begin his talk.

It wasn't just a kiss on the cheek like you'd give your great aunt. It was a warm face touch, with cheeks turning and meeting before the kiss. More intimate than many kisses I'd had on the lips. I was stunned.

Bean told great stories from his trips researching the impact of global warming on the different communities of Africa. Even though his often heartbreaking anecdotes were about individuals, he also demonstrated how vulnerable Africa was as a continent, and then made connections to areas of the United States, bringing the reality home.

He also kept meeting my eyes, as if he was talking directly to me. What was going on?

Bean finished his talk and the crowd started lining up for the signing. Erica prepped the books.

Kona moved closer to the silent auction table as the bidding started in earnest. Two women in matching pink suits kept outbidding each other for the five day spa trip. One of them had a blunt haircut that seemed to point right at her huge chin. Her hairdresser must hate her.

My cell phone buzzed and I pulled it out of my pocket.

"Uh-oh." It was an emergency text notifying me that my dehumidifier was malfunctioning. Shoot! So much for state of the art.

"What?" Kona asked.

I *so* did not need this. "You know that smart alarm feature on the dehumidifier? It's texting me that the unit is off."

Panic flittered in my chest at the thought of losing the chocolate we'd worked so hard to make over the last few days. Even with all the sales we'd made today, I could not afford another disaster. "I'll just go see if it's something I can fix on my own," I told Kona.

"Want me to go?" she asked, but her eyes drifted to Zane again.

I smiled. "No, I got it. I'll be right back."

The town was quiet as I cut through the alley leading to the back parking lot. Coco greeted me with an urgent "Meow!"

"Right," I said to her. "Like you need any more food. The whole neighborhood is feeding you, you hussy."

I unlocked the door and Coco surprised the heck out of me by running right in. What? Had someone trained it to actually go into a building?

"Coco!" I called when it disappeared down the hall. The door slammed behind me with an echoing bang, and I realized the alarm was turned off. After all we'd been through, I couldn't believe we'd forgotten to turn it on when we'd left.

I could take care of that after I checked my equipment and put Coco back outside. Switching the lights on, I opened the door to my kitchen.

Mayor Gwen was standing by my dehumidifier holding a gun. With a lifeless Reese at her feet.

25

"Gwen?" I said calmly, as if talking to a crazy person. Which I suppose I was. "What's going on?" My voice shook as the gun pointing at me grew huge in my mind, like a cartoon. Too bad it was real and wouldn't push out a little flag that said "bang" instead of a bullet. Had she *shot* Reese? I took a deep breath and looked away from the gun. There was no blood near her.

Gwen tilted her head. "So you don't know."

"Know what?" My heart started racing while I tried to figure out how this could be happening. I couldn't even tell if Reese was alive.

"I saw you talking to Reese and I was sure she'd told you," she said. The gun in her hand started to point away from me while she considered her miscalculation.

I slid one tiny half step back toward the door. "She didn't

tell me anything, so why don't you put that gun down and we'll figure this out?"

The gun zeroed in on me again. "You would have found out eventually," she said. "You just don't quit. I didn't realize you had that in you. Erica maybe. But not you. My mistake."

"Uh, thanks?" I said. "Is she dead?" I tried unsuccessfully to keep the quaver out of my voice and took another step backward as she glanced down at Reese and gave her a little kick.

Reese groaned and I felt relief sweep through me. Maybe Gwen wasn't really going to kill us.

"Not yet," she said. "But you're going to take care of that." She shifted to the left, keeping the metal utility table between us.

"But why do you want to kill her?" I couldn't say the obvious *"Or me?"* out loud.

Her lips tightened. "You two just don't give up. She got to one of my campaign guys—they told me to watch out for the hangers-on with nothing special about them. I knew I had one on the campaign I couldn't trust, and sure enough, he told her about my donors."

"The solar company?" Maybe I could keep her talking long enough for Kona to realize something was wrong.

Her gun hand jerked and I tried something else. "So you pulled out the plug on my equipment? How did you know it would notify me?" I tried to use my peripheral vision to search out anything to use as a weapon, but Kona had thoroughly cleaned, leaving only the heavy pot of caramel on the back burner with a ladle in it and my bottle of gold cocoa butter on the stove.

"You showed it to me when it was installed." She

grimaced. "I have to fake interest in a lot of crap in this town, but that was hard. But like a lot of what I do, it paid off, didn't it?"

"But how do you know the security code to get into the building tonight?"

"That I had help with," she said.

"The principal?" He'd been so friendly with Johnny. Had Johnny let him know our backdoor code?

Why was the mayor doing this? It was so extreme. And then the pieces fell into place. The Durham barn was on the way to the mayor's housing development on the outskirts of town, the one that was practically empty. Then Kona's list of customer favorites flashed into my mind and I saw the connection. The principal's favorites were the same as the mayor's. Oh. My. God. They were having an affair. Denise's photo had caught the principal's car driving by the barn near the mayor's house, not by his own house.

So the principal was driving away from her house at dawn. An affair was enough to kill Denise over? To kill Reese and me as well?

"So you killed Denise because you're having an affair?" I sounded appalled. "You're a widow. Why does that matter to you? Wait—did you try to kill me with that truck?" I imagined her driving that black truck, aiming right for me, and rage mixed with my fear.

"I did not kill Denise," she said. "Peter did that all on his own. The idiot. We wouldn't be in this mess if he had just thought it through."

"So was it you or Peter who tried to kill me?" I had to know.

She laughed. "I'll plead the fifth on that one."

"Why did you kill Larry?" When she just stared at me, I added, "Surely you can tell me that one thing before you kill me."

"That scumbag was blackmailing me. Me! After all I've done for this town. Could still do . . ." She took a deep breath. "It's still going to work out. Now pick up the ladle." She pointed with her gun.

I inched around the table. "So how do you think you're going to get away with this?"

"Obviously, Reese went over the deep end with your little rivalry." She talked as if it made sense. "She surprised you while you were cooking and you were forced to kill Reese by hitting her over the head with the ladle in that pot."

"Really? A ladle?" The irony wasn't lost on me.

She went on undeterred. "Too bad she shot you as she was falling."

"Do you really think anyone will fall for that nonsense after what's recently happened?"

"They'll believe what I tell them," she snapped, and then forced herself to calm down. "There weren't any witnesses to the other murders. But I came with you to check out your kitchen equipment so you wouldn't be alone, and I'll tell everyone the whole tragic story."

"Do you really think Erica or Bean or Leo will give up? They won't believe any of this."

Her face grew even colder and I felt fear for anyone who got in her way. "You better hope they do. For their sakes."

Great. A homicidal maniac was going to be in the United States House of Representatives. It probably wasn't the first time.

"Most of the people in this town are a bunch of sheep that fall in line. But not you. And this idiot."

I moved to the stove. "Okay. Now what? She's all the way over there."

Her eyes narrowed, not trusting me.

I pretended to attempt to lift the ladle with my left hand. "The caramel got too cold. It's stuck."

It took all of my courage to turn my back on her, picking up the bottle of gold cocoa butter in my right hand.

Then I heard a loud hissing sound that scared me to death until I realized it was Coco. She was attacking Gwen's ankles! I turned and fired the bottle at the center of Gwen's forehead, as if I was throwing out a runner at first base. It stunned her enough that I had time to pick up a ladle full of burning hot caramel and whip it across the table at her.

She screamed. The gun went off and she dropped it to put both hands to her face. I ran around the table and, using both hands, hit her with the ladle like I was swinging for the fences.

She fell to the floor with a thud.

I dropped my weapon, fumbled with my phone and dialed 911. "Maxine! Send the chief! Send Bobby!"

Gwen moved and I picked up Coco and ran for the back door, realizing that I sounded incoherent. "This is Michelle at Chocolates and Chapters. I need help now! The mayor just tried to kill me!"

26

Bobby heard the 911 call and was the first to arrive, quickly followed by Leo, Erica, Bean, Kona and just about everyone left at the book signing. I learned later that Zane had been forced to stay back and protect the silent auction items from a few rabid PTA moms who really, *really* wanted to win twelve hours of Saturday night babysitting from one of the town's best sitters.

Even groggy, the mayor tried to bluster her way out of trouble, but she couldn't explain the gun in her hand. The chief himself arrested her and charged her with the murder of Larry Stapleton and the attempted murder of Reese and me. Reese was rushed to the hospital, still unconscious.

Coco had made her escape as soon as the crowd arrived. Once word got out that she'd saved the day, that cat would never go hungry again. Not that she did now.

Leo hovered as I sat in the dining area, watching the action. "Worst day?"

I shook my head, smiling. "Not yet." When he still looked worried, I added, "She didn't hurt me, Leo. Just scared me."

Lockett arrived to take my statement.

"I think I deserve a trip to Kennywood for this," I said after I relayed the whole story.

"Dat's right," he said in his strongest Pittsburgh accent. "I'll take ya back 'air and we'll ride the Thunderbolt."

Bean scowled but I couldn't stop smiling. Two murderers were no longer on the loose.

For the first time in weeks, I woke up with no anxiety. The Great Fudge Cook-off and Arts Festival had been a success. And we'd solved the mystery of Denise's murder and completely cleared the reputation of our store.

I headed to the kitchen, expecting at least a few friends to stop by for all the details before the parade at noon.

Erica was downstairs almost as soon as I had the coffee beans ground. "Feeling better?" she asked, with an affectionate hug before heading to the refrigerator to pull out bacon.

I grinned. "I can't believe it's finally over." The sun was shining, the coffee was ready to brew and I still had a business to run. I pulled ingredients for pancakes out of the pantry just as my phone vibrated with a text message.

"Want me to see who it is?" Erica asked while she poked at the bacon in the pan.

"Sure." I closed the door with my hip.

"Leo." She picked it up and squinted. "He wants to know if we're decent."

"Tell him to come over." Erica had barely pressed "send" and I was still throwing together my dry ingredients when we heard Leo letting himself in.

"Smells great," he said and limped into the kitchen in his full dress uniform.

"Hey, gorgeous," Erica said, while I stared at him with tears gathering in my eyes.

Leo gave Erica a quick smile before focusing on me. "You doing okay, Berry?"

I bit my lip and nodded, too emotional to talk.

"Then let's get this breakfast going," he said. "I have a parade to march in."

The morning passed in a blur of grateful neighbors and friends calling, texting and stopping by. Tonya called to tell me that Reese had a concussion, but was already demanding her laptop and cell phone. Never suspecting that Gwen could be so dangerous, she'd agreed to meet her at my shop, but didn't remember anything after coming in the back door.

I went through pounds of flour and sugar. Bean had filed a story about murder in a small town that was being shared across the country.

"Maybe I'll stick around West Riverdale for a while," he told Erica. Was he looking at me when he said it? I stopped mixing the batter to pay attention.

"Really?" Erica said excitedly.

"There's certainly enough corruption around here to check out," he said.

I ducked my head to hide my smile and let the warm feeling of happiness rush over me. Maybe he was staying for another reason.

Every chance he got, Bobby called us with updates about the case. First, a teen volunteer who was the daughter of our 911 dispatcher confessed to being Reese's informant. Reese had tricked her into revealing one detail and then threatened her with exposure—saying it would go on her *permanent record*—if she didn't cough up more information. It kinda made me wish Gwen had hit her at least one more time.

Even though she'd been right about a few things.

Once Peter learned that Gwen was arrested and wouldn't be applying any political pressure to get him cleared, he started talking. He'd fallen in love with Gwen and was planning to get a divorce once she was elected. But then the blackmail letters started to arrive.

Larry's computer was found in Gwen's attic; she claimed to not know how it got there, but her fingerprints were all over it. It was full of photos of her and the principal having an affair, along with letters demanding money. It also had photos of her and the principal in late-night meetings with the president of the solar company. Maybe Larry had threatened Gwen with exposure of the photos. Maybe he even figured out that the solar company was funneling money into her campaign in exchange for the town council paying five hundred dollar rebates to their customers. Who knew whether the affair or payoffs were worse in Gwen's mind?

All of the photos on Larry's computer were taken after Denise's break-in. We could only speculate, but it seemed like Larry got the idea to blackmail the principal after seeing the original photos when he broke into Denise's studio, after *she* had blackmailed him. Maybe he realized how suspicious it was for the principal to be driving by that barn so early in the morning, and then had followed Peter himself. He probably thought he hit the jackpot when he got photos of Peter having an affair with none other than the mayor.

Denise had pushed Peter to come to her studio to see her work to prove she was capable of becoming a school photographer. He had gone, intending to give her a polite brush-off, but then he saw the photo of his own car driving in front of a barn. She'd told him how she modified the photo to remove the Gable's Heating and Plumbing advertisement to make it look timeless, and he had incorrectly deduced that Denise was his blackmailer. He'd made her a senior-class photographer, but it hadn't stopped the blackmail demands.

When Denise started talking about showing her work in DC, Peter had panicked and killed her before she could meet with the gallery owner. He tried to claim that the whole thing wasn't planned, but he'd not only planned the murder in detail, he'd also planted evidence and slept with Opal to give himself an alibi. Way premeditated.

The poison had been cyanide. Peter had found a bottle in the basement of the high school years before and held on to it. Who knows what other problems he would have solved with that bottle if he'd gotten the chance.

Fitzy the locksmith felt terrible. His palsy was getting bad, but he never wanted anyone to know he could no longer do his job. When Colleen needed him to change the locks, he'd called Peter to do the work, giving him the chance to plant the needles.

The blackmail letters had intensified after Denise's death. Gwen and Peter assumed Denise had an accomplice, and they had to fix that problem too.

Larry had certainly underestimated Gwen. According to Peter, she'd been the one to bash Larry's head in.

It was all anyone would be talking about in West Riverdale for quite a while. We were able to roust everyone from our kitchen when it was time to hurry over to the parade route.

Steve and Jolene had reserved space for us by setting up camping chairs on Main Street in front of the grandstand. Our neighbors let us through the crowd with some friendly kidding about special treatment, but patted us on the back as we moved by.

Erica, Bean and I folded up the chairs and stood cheering as the floats from local businesses and organizations and the high school bands marched by. I recognized a lot of Erica's comic book kids beneath the fuzzy hats of the West Riverdale High School Stars. They tried hard not to smile at her and then became completely focused on their performance when the drum major whistled for the music to start for their grand entrance down Main Street. The music swelled and my heart felt like bursting when they played "Stars and Stripes Forever," even if some of the trumpets had a little trouble keeping up with the fast pace.

Then the West Riverdale Veterans Group approached, their military bearing obvious even with disabilities and age. Leo held a small flag in one hand and grinned at me, and Star walked beside him in her own spiffy uniform. He seemed so happy and hopeful. I bit my lip, but still, joyful tears spilled over.

My cell phone pinged with a message from Hillary Punkin's assistant. I clicked on it and the slide for her "Yay or Nay" segment appeared on my screen:

> Chocolates & Chapters
> West Riverdale, MD
> YAY!

RECIPES

• BY ISABELLA KNACK •

❃ Lavender Truffle

> *12 fresh lavender flower heads*
> *⅓ cup heavy cream*
> *10 ounces bittersweet chocolate, chopped*
> *2 tablespoons unsalted butter*

Place the flower heads and cream in a small pot. Heat on high until cream starts to simmer and melt the butter in the mixture. Take off heat and set aside to steep for 15 minutes.

Divide the chocolate into two equal 5-ounce portions, and set one portion aside.

Heat up the cream mixture again and, using a fine-mesh strainer, strain the cream into the chocolate in a small mixing bowl; discard the flower heads and bits of lavender.

Stir the cream and chocolate together until smooth. Chill in the refrigerator until somewhat firm, but not hard, for about 1 hour. Melt the other half of the chocolate in the microwave in 30-second increments until liquid.

Line a baking sheet with a piece of waxed paper. Roll the lavender mixture into 1-teaspoon-sized balls, and dip into the melted chocolate mixture using a skewer or toothpick. Place onto the prepared baking sheet and chill in the refrigerator for at least 2 hours to harden.

❋ Lemon & Thyme

1 cup heavy whipping cream
1½ teaspoons fresh thyme leaves
9 ounces high quality bittersweet chocolate,
    chopped
3 tablespoons fresh Meyer lemon juice (this will be
    about 1 lemon)
1 teaspoon Meyer lemon peel zest (yellow part only)
Cocoa powder

Bring the cream and thyme to simmer in a heavy small saucepan. Let sit for 15 minutes, then bring back to barely simmering.

Remove from heat and strain the hot cream over the chocolate pieces in a small mixing bowl.

Add the juice and zest and stir until all the chocolate is melted.

Refrigerate for at least 3 hours, until ganache is firm enough to work with.

Use a small ice cream scoop (you can also use a table-spoon or two spoons) and shape little balls of chocolate. Roll the truffles in cocoa powder.

❋ Applewood Bacon Truffle

12 ounces best quality hardwood smoked bacon,
*   such as applewood or hickory*
2–4 tablespoons turbinado cane sugar (raw sugar)
1¼ cups heavy cream
2 pounds semisweet chocolate

Cut bacon into 2-inch pieces and fry until just crispy. Reserve ⅓ cup of bacon fat, taking care to avoid the little fried bits in the fat. Chop bacon into small granular bits until you have ¼ cup for truffle topping. Combine bacon with 2 tablespoons sugar, doubling these amounts if you are rolling the entire truffle into the bacon-sugar mixture. Save remaining bacon for another (non-chocolate) use.

In the top of a double boiler or in a heat-safe bowl over simmering water, combine the cream and bacon fat. After thoroughly combining, add 1 pound of the chopped chocolate. Cook, stirring occasionally, until the chocolate melts. Remove from the heat and stir or whisk until smooth.

Pour into a shallow bowl. Press plastic wrap directly onto the surface of the chocolate and put in fridge overnight.

With a sharp knife, scrape off most of the bacon fat that has accumulated on the top of the hardened chocolate. Using a teaspoon or melon baller, scoop out chocolate and roll with hands to form 1-inch balls. Refrigerate for at least 1 hour.

In the top of a double boiler or in a heat-safe bowl over simmering water, heat remaining pound of chocolate, stirring intermittently. Let the chocolate melt completely.

Using two small spoons, dip the truffles, one at a time, into the chocolate mixture, rolling the truffle into the chocolate to cover completely. Lay chocolate-dipped truffle on a sheet pan covered with wax paper or parchment. Sprinkle the bacon-sugar mixture on the truffle while the chocolate is still warm.

Refrigerate the truffles, covered, for at least 1 hour. Can be refrigerated for up to 1 week or freeze airtight for up to 1 month. Remove from freezer 15 minutes before serving.

FROM *NEW YORK TIMES* BESTSELLING AUTHOR

Jenn McKinlay

Going, Going, Ganache

A Cupcake Bakery Mystery

After a cupcake-flinging fiasco at a photo shoot for a local magazine, Melanie Cooper and Angie DeLaura agree to make amends by hosting a weeklong corporate boot camp at Fairy Tale Cupcakes. The idea is the brainchild of Ian Hannigan, new owner of *Southwest Style*, a lifestyle magazine that chronicles the lives of Scottsdale's rich and famous. He's assigned his staff to a team-building week of making cupcakes for charity.

It's clear that the staff would rather be doing just about anything other than frosting baked goods. But when the magazine's features director is found murdered outside the bakery, Mel and Angie have a new team-building exercise—find the killer before their business goes AWOL.

INCLUDES SCRUMPTIOUS RECIPES

jennmckinlay.com
facebook.com/jennmckinlay
facebook.com/TheCrimeSceneBooks
penguin.com

M1287T0313

Starting over from scratch can be murder...

FROM NATIONAL BESTSELLING AUTHOR
VICTORIA HAMILTON

Bran New Death
A Merry Muffin Mystery

Expert muffin baker Merry Wynter is making a fresh
start in small-town Autumn Vale, New York, establish-
ing a new baking business in the castle she's inherited
from her late uncle, Melvyn. Merry soon finds that quite
a few townsfolk didn't like Uncle Mel, and she has inherited their enmity as well as his home. And when one of
the locals turns up dead in her yard, Merry will need to
prove she's no killer—or watch her career crumble...

PRAISE FOR VICTORIA HAMILTON'S
VINTAGE KITCHEN MYSTERIES

"Smartly written and successfully plotted."
—*Library Journal*

"[A] wonderful cozy mystery series."
—Paige Shelton, national bestselling author

victoriahamiltonmysteries.com
facebook.com/AuthorVictoriaHamilton
facebook.com/TheCrimeSceneBooks
penguin.com

M1433T0214